Praise for Carla Neggers' *New York Times* bestselling Swift River Valley novels

"A potent friends to lovers story."
—*RT Book Reviews* on *The River House*

"A page-turning mystery and clever, slow-building romance featuring two wounded type-A personalities. [Neggers] seduces readers by expertly marrying characters, story lines and scenes, and keeps them up-to-date with series catch-ups. Her family dynamics keep it real, her costars add insight and her stars make it a keeper!"
—*RT Book Reviews* on *Red Clover Inn*

"Masterful attention to detail, conversational dialogue and past-character catch-up expertly draw readers into her potent mix of romance, mystery and small-town drama."
—*RT Book Reviews* on *The Spring at Moss Hill*

"Appealing protagonists, good neighbors, small-town Christmas traditions, and Neggers' own recipes make for a fine romance."
—*Publishers Weekly* on *A Knights Bridge Christmas*

"Neggers does the near impossible: she brings a small-town, family-loving heroine and a footloose hero together in an engaging romance that has its fair share of surprises."
—*Library Journal* on *Echo Lake*

"Her people, places and things are colorfully and expertly rendered in this compelling work of fiction."
—*RT Book Reviews* on *Cider Brook*

"Neggers captures readers' attention with her usual flair and brilliance and gives us a romance, a mystery and a lesson in history."
—*RT Book Reviews* on *Secrets of the Lost Summer*, Top Pick!

Also by Carla Neggers

Look for Carla Neggers' next novel
in the Sharpe & Donovan series
RIVAL'S BREAK
available soon from MIRA Books.

CARLA NEGGERS

STONE BRIDGES

mira

mira

ISBN-13: 978-0-7783-5127-6

Recycling programs
for this product may
not exist in your area.

Stone Bridges

Copyright © 2019 by Carla Neggers

For questions and comments about the quality of this book, please contact us at
CustomerService@Harlequin.com.

www.Harlequin.com

Printed in U.S.A.

To Sally Fairchild Schoeneweiss, with thanks

STONE BRIDGES

Dear Vic,
I just arrived at the Farm at Carriage Hill! I can't believe I'm now an innkeeper. I'm excited but nervous. Wish you could be here but I hope you're having good meetings in DC.
Love,
Adrienne

Dear Adrienne,
Wish I could be there, too. I drafted a "cheat sheet" to help you keep people in Knights Bridge straight. It's a work in progress with upcoming weddings and babies on the way, but it's a start.
Love,
Vic
P.S. I added Loretta Wrentham and Julius Hartley at the last minute even though they don't live in town.

Dear Vic,
Thanks for the "cheat sheet." It's a big help. Do you think Loretta and Julius will return to Knights Bridge?
Love,
Adrienne

Dear Adrienne,
Oh, they'll be back. It's the Knights Bridge effect.
Love,
Vic

KNIGHTS BRIDGE CHEAT SHEET

Olivia Frost McCaffrey:

Graphic designer and owner of the Farm at Carriage Hill. Married to Dylan McCaffrey (see below). Their first child (a girl) is due in November.

Dylan McCaffrey:

Organizer of adventure travel and entrepreneurial boot camps and venture capitalist in Knights Bridge; former NHL player and San Diego businessman.

Jessica Frost Flanagan:

Olivia's younger sister. Works at Frost Millworks and married to Mark Flanagan (see below); they're expecting their first child early next year.

Mark Flanagan:

Architect based at the Mill at Moss Hill.

Randy and Louise Frost:

Olivia and Jess's parents; owners of Frost Custom Millworks.

Audrey Frost, Randy's mother:

Retired Knights Bridge school bookkeeper.

Felicity MacGregor:

Event planner, engaged to Gabe Flanagan (see below).

Gabe Flanagan:

Start-up entrepreneur recently returned to hometown of Knights Bridge.

Elly O'Dunn:

Longtime widow who works for the town and raises goats on her small farm near Echo Lake; four adult daughters.

Phoebe O'Dunn:

Elly's eldest daughter, former town librarian, engaged to billionaire Noah Kendrick (see below).

Noah Kendrick:

Founder of a high-tech entertainment company in San Diego, owner of a Central California winery, expert fencer.

Maggie O'Dunn Sloan:

Elly's second daughter, caterer, partner with Olivia McCaffrey in the Farm at Carriage Hill, married to Brandon Sloan (see below), two young sons, Tyler and Aidan.

Ava and Ruby O'Dunn, twins, Elly's youngest daughters, just completed studies in theater, not presently living in Knights Bridge.

Eric Sloan:

Knights Bridge police officer, single, eldest of six siblings.

Justin Sloan:

Carpenter and volunteer firefighter, second-born of six siblings, married to Samantha Bennett (see below).

Samantha Bennett Sloan:

Pirate expert and granddaughter of famed adventurer Harry Bennett.

Brandon Sloan:

Carpenter and adventure travel guide, third-born of six siblings, married to Maggie O'Dunn (above).

Adam Sloan:

Stonemason, fourth-born of six siblings, single.

Christopher Sloan:

Knights Bridge firefighter, fifth-born of six siblings, single, recently broke up with Ruby O'Dunn.

Heather Sloan Hancock:

Studying interior design in London while husband Brody Hancock (see below) is assigned there, sixth-born of six siblings (and only sister).

Brody Hancock:

Grew up on Echo Lake and now a Diplomatic Security Service agent.

Jack and Cora Sloan:

Parents of Eric, Justin, Brandon, Adam, Christopher and Heather, owners with their offspring of construction business.

Evelyn Sloan:

Retired nursery school teacher and widowed mother of Jack and grandmother of the six Sloan siblings.

Clare Morgan Farrell:

Knights Bridge librarian for the past year, recently married to ER doctor Logan Farrell, mother of Owen by her first husband (widowed).

Charlotte Bennett:

Samantha's cousin, a marine archaeologist due to marry DSS agent Greg Rawlings in Knights Bridge the day after Thanksgiving.

Russ Colton:

Security consultant, recently married to children's book author and illustrator Kylie Shaw/Morwenna Mills.

Grace Webster:

Nonagenarian retired Latin and English teacher, birth mother to Dylan McCaffrey's father, Duncan McCaffrey (deceased).

Loretta Wrentham, Dylan McCaffrey's friend and personal attorney in San Diego, and her husband, private investigator Julius Hartley.

One

For the first time in the five days since she'd started work as a small-town New England innkeeper, Adrienne Portale felt relaxed and comfortable as she took her coffee outside on a beautiful early September morning. She stood on the edge of the stone terrace off the kitchen of the classic center-chimney house built in 1803 on what had been then, and was now, a quiet country road.

She looked out at the inn's extensive herb and flower gardens. "I'm not in over my head," she whispered to herself. "I didn't bite off more than I can chew."

The Farm at Carriage Hill was a unique establishment. It wasn't exactly a farm, and it wasn't a traditional inn, either. It wasn't open to drop-ins. Adrienne's first guests wouldn't arrive until next weekend. The inn was booked through the popular foliage season with the type of small events for which it was ideally suited—showers, weddings, birthdays, lunches, seminars, reunions. The antique house-turned-inn was off the beaten track, part of its appeal. It was situated amid rolling fields and woods two miles from the center of Knights Bridge, a classic New England village west of Boston.

Adrienne sat at a round table and listened to birds twittering in the trees, herbs and flowers. She didn't know what kind of birds. She could learn. *Wanted* to learn. She recognized some of the herbs—parsley, oregano, thyme, basil, cilantro, at least three kinds of mint—and could tell a maple tree from an oak or a white pine. She wasn't bad with flowers. Not great, but not bad. She'd trimmed a bed of coreopsis yesterday. The property needed a regular gardener. That was right at the top of the list of changes she planned to recommend.

She leaned back, cupping her mug with both hands. The garden had bark-mulched paths and was bordered by an old stone wall. Carriage Hill, for which the inn was named, loomed across fields dotted with wildflowers. Adrienne promised herself she'd hike up to the summit before she'd need to do it in snowshoes. The locals liked to joke it could snow any day now, but she knew that was an exaggeration. She smiled, enjoying the perfect late-summer morning. She'd finish her coffee, whip up breakfast in the big country kitchen and then get on with her day.

She heard someone humming and sat up straight in surprise, almost spilling her coffee. Olivia McCaffrey, Carriage Hill's owner, who lived up the road with her husband, Dylan? Maggie Sloan, Olivia's business partner?

No. Not Olivia or Maggie.

Adrienne set her coffee on the table and jumped to her feet. She was still in her nightgown and robe. Before she could leap back inside, a man, humming merrily, materialized in the side yard. He stopped abruptly, a heavy-looking sack of something on one shoulder.

She recognized him immediately.

Adam Sloan.

He was one of six Sloan siblings—five brothers and one sister. Adam was—fourth? Adrienne thought so but she'd have to consult the cheat sheet Vic had emailed her detailing the family connections of the people she'd most likely encounter in her new job. Vic Scarlatti being her birth father, a retired diplomat and her reason for ever having stepped foot in Knights Bridge in the first place.

Adam was tall, broad-shouldered, dark-haired and as sexy as she remembered from when she'd first met him last winter, when she'd house-sat for Vic. Adam was the stonemason Sloan. Quiet, she recalled.

He took her in with a quick glance. His charcoal-gray canvas shirt was rolled up to his elbows, his forearms tanned and muscled. He was dressed for physical work, including sturdy work boots. "Adrienne. Hey, there. Welcome back to Knights Bridge."

"Adam. Hi. I…um…"

Adrienne cleared her throat. She was never at a loss for words. She'd drunk wine with a European prince. She'd stocked a world-famous actor's wine cellar. Why was she tongue-tied now, with a good-looking stonemason?

Because you aren't dressed, for one thing.

She subtly tightened the belt to her bathrobe. It wasn't one of the inn's sturdy terry robes that hung in each of its guest rooms. It was a slinky, lace-trimmed black robe over a matching nightgown. Not her usual style. She felt downright exposed but did her best not to look self-conscious. "It's good to be back."

He frowned. "Maggie and Olivia forgot to tell you I was coming."

"Or I missed it. It doesn't matter." They were her employers, and Adam was Maggie's brother-in-law. No way was Adrienne saying more. She waved a hand, careful given the precarious state of her attire. "Feel free to do your thing."

"I'm just dropping off supplies."

"Supplies for…what, exactly?"

"I'm rebuilding a stone wall that was disturbed during construction of the new addition."

The addition included a first-floor suite for a live-in innkeeper, a first for the Farm at Carriage Hill. Its design, both inside and outside, fit seamlessly with the rest of the attractive antique house with its narrow, cream-colored clapboards and double-hung windows.

"It's not a big job," Adam added.

Adrienne had noticed the pile of stones and broken mortar behind the house but hadn't thought much about it. She'd assumed it was debris from construction and would be hauled off eventually. "Sounds good." She kept her tone neutral, no betrayal of her awkwardness. "Is there anything I can do for you?"

His blue eyes settled on her just long enough to make it clear he was well aware he'd caught her before she'd had a chance to get dressed. "All set." He paused ever so slightly. "Don't let me keep you from anything."

Such as a shower, clothes, shoes, breakfast. More coffee. It was tough to deal with a rugged stonemason while under-caffeinated, never mind in nightclothes. She pushed back her hair—long, dark, curly, messy—with one hand. "Sure thing." She thought she at least sounded unselfconscious. "Give me a shout if I can help with anything."

"Will do. Have you heard from Vic since you got here?"

Adrienne nodded. "A few emails."

Adam shifted the bag on his shoulder. "I won't be long right now, but I'll be back later this afternoon. That work?"

"Works fine."

He continued past her to his pile of rubble. He was muscular, fit. Made sense that a man who hauled rocks and mortar and sledgehammers and such for a living would be in good shape.

Adrienne drank the rest of her coffee. It was luke-warm but she didn't care. She'd realized pretty much everyone in Knights Bridge knew about her and Vic Scarlatti, but she still wasn't used to people mentioning him to her. She'd learned he was her biological father a year ago. He hadn't known about her, either. She'd figured that out when she'd house-sat for him last winter, not telling him that her mother had finally admitted she and Vic'd had a fling and Adrienne was the result. He'd retired after a forty-year career as a respected diplomat and was in the process of moving full-time into his country home on Echo Lake in little Knights Bridge, Massachusetts.

It hadn't been easy, but they'd made their peace with her mother's revelation. Adrienne had worked on her wine blog and consulting business while house-sitting for Vic, and then she'd taken a job at a Central California winery, owned by Noah Kendrick, a San Diego billionaire with his own connections to Knights Bridge. It'd been a great job. She'd done well. Yet when Noah and Phoebe, his fiancée and Maggie's sister, mentioned the Carriage Hill job, Adrienne had jumped at the chance.

The Knights Bridge effect, Vic would call it.

She took her mug inside, managing to keep her bathrobe secured around her. She owned flannel pajamas, too, but it was too warm to wear them. She'd bought the robe and nightgown on a whim last summer when she'd gone to Paris, where her mother and Vic had enjoyed their weeklong affair. The Left Bank, cozy cafés, liaisons in a romantic hotel near the Musée d'Orsay. Sophia Cross had returned home to California and her fiancé, Richard Portale, passing off Adrienne as their child when she was born not quite nine months later.

Her parents had divorced when Adrienne was seven. *No wonder.*

Finding out about Vic had explained so much about her mother in particular.

Adrienne set her mug on the counter in the big country kitchen. She was still obsessing about her attire. Had she made the wrong impression with Adam Sloan? Would he go back and tell his brothers about her sitting out back in a slinky black bathrobe and nightgown? The Sloans knew everyone in Knights Bridge. It could get around. Vic Scarlatti's California daughter out at Carriage Hill in a sexy black robe…she'll never fit in here…she'll get fired before Thanksgiving…

"More coffee," Adrienne groaned. "*Lots* more coffee."

She reached for the coffeepot and saw Adam through the front window. He had the back of his work van open as he lifted out another bag. He placed it on one shoulder and balanced it with one hand as he shut the van. Then he retraced his steps through the side yard to the back of the house.

Adrienne had no idea how long it would take him to rebuild the stone wall, but she'd be sure she was prepared the next time he showed up.

She put on more coffee and slipped through the old center-chimney house to the innkeeper's suite. Its wood floors coordinated with the wide-board floors in the main part of the 1803 house. Olivia Frost McCaffrey, who owned the house, was a graphic designer, her unerring sense of style and color evident in the suite's throw rugs, linens, soothing colors and woodland prints. Adrienne would have gone with white and called it a day.

She shut the door and exhaled, letting her robe come undone now that she didn't have a sexy stonemason eyeing her. She'd run into him multiple times last winter. Even as preoccupied as she'd been with her situation with Vic, she hadn't been oblivious to Adam's physical attributes. That he was the quiet Sloan only added to his appeal. A highly physical man of few words…

Adrienne groaned again. What was the matter with

her? She shook off the question and pulled off her robe and nightgown, leaving them in a heap by the bed as she ducked into the suite's private bathroom. She'd hoped Vic would be in town to greet her, but he'd left for Washington ten days ago for unspecified meetings. Almost a year of retirement hadn't settled his naturally restless soul. She got it. She was restless herself. But Vic was also driven and ambitious, a contributing factor to why he hadn't known he had a daughter until Adrienne had shown up at Echo Lake last winter. It hadn't been just her mother's doing. Vic had played a role, too. He hadn't asked questions.

He'd never married. He'd implied he'd come close at least once, but Adrienne hadn't pursued the subject with him. He was in his early sixties, and while it wasn't out of the realm of possibility, she doubted he ever would marry. Her mother hadn't remarried. She wasn't restless, but she was driven and ambitious. She'd built a successful marketing company based in San Francisco from the ground up.

"I'm a slug by comparison."

Adrienne laughed to herself as she turned on the water to the separate shower. At least her mother had never even hinted at any disappointment in her daughter. They might not have the chummiest mother-daughter relationship, but they understood each other.

Fifteen minutes later, she was showered, dressed in black jeans, a black-and-gray top and black ankle boots and on her way to the kitchen. She refilled her mug with fresh coffee. She'd more or less adjusted to East Coast time, but she needed two or three cups of coffee first thing in the morning. Getting startled by a stonemason had thrown her off her schedule.

She sat at the kitchen table by the front window. Adam's van was gone. She felt a tug of loneliness. Vic was her only connection to Knights Bridge—to the East Coast, in fact— and he was out of town. He hadn't greeted the prospect of his long-lost daughter returning to his adopted town as an innkeeper without question. "Are you sure, Adrienne?" he'd asked when she'd called him with the news.

Of course, she *wasn't* sure. She was winging it. Just as she had with her wine blog, her wine consulting, house-sitting for him. It was how she operated. She would put everything she had into the job, but she didn't know how long she'd last. A month? Six months? Six *years*?

Not six years, she thought as she drank her coffee. Right now she'd focus on six days.

Adrienne was bleary-eyed after spending the morning in the small office off her suite. By the time she entered the kitchen, she was ready for lunch and a change of scenery.

Maggie Sloan was unloading two bags of groceries she'd set on the butcher-block island. She was a whirlwind of red curls, freckles, turquoise eyes and boundless energy. Although she wore multiple hats, catering was her primary job and the kitchen, therefore, her domain. She eyed Adrienne. "Uh-oh. You've been organizing paperwork? You've got that look."

"I'm a big believer in mega-batching. I dived in and got it done."

Maggie winced. "Was it awful? Olivia and I have just been tossing stuff on the desk for weeks."

"Everything made perfect sense." Including, Adrienne thought, the Post-it note she'd discovered stuck under a pile of insurance papers: *Adam 1st thing Th. for wall.* She'd recognized Maggie's handwriting. "I only have one more drawer to sort."

"Wow. I'm impressed."

"It helps we don't have any major events until next weekend."

Maggie nodded as she set a bag of apples on the island. "Definitely. I hope it wasn't torture."

Adrienne smiled. "I opened a window and listened to the birds."

It was true. She'd appreciated the breeze, too, as she'd plowed through information on vendors, paid and unpaid invoices, business cards, catalogs, tear sheets from magazines with garden, decorating and food ideas, monthly printouts of a digital events calendar and vague handwritten notes like the one about Adam.

"Did you find our someday/maybe sheets for this place?" Maggie asked.

"I did." Adrienne grabbed a bag as Maggie emptied it. She folded it and placed it on the counter by the refrigerator. "I didn't read them. I wasn't sure if they're private."

"Oh, you can read them. Olivia and I did them one night over a bottle of wine. That's before she got pregnant. We took two sheets of graph paper and wrote down a hundred things we'd like to do with this place. All our hopes and dreams. No censoring ourselves. We just wrote down whatever popped into our heads, and we had to get to a hundred."

"I did notice purple stains on the sheets."

"That's the wine. It was terrible but we drank the whole bottle."

"And you got to a hundred?"

"Exactly to a hundred. Hiring an innkeeper was up at the top." Maggie grinned as she lifted a jar of mayonnaise out of one of her bags. "It was one of our more sensible ideas."

Adrienne helped herself to an apple. They were local apples, of course. Paula Reds, according to the handwriting on the bag. Maggie and Olivia were hardworking, creative and can-do, but they'd taken on a lot over the past year, both personally and professionally. "I'm glad to be here," Adrienne said.

"Five days and we haven't scared you off," Maggie said cheerfully. "I ran into Adam in town. I forgot to tell you he'd be here today. He says he startled you."

"It worked out fine."

"He's quiet. Stealthy, Brandon says." Brandon was Adam's older brother and her husband, an adventure travel guide and carpenter. "He swears Adam got away with all sorts of mischief when they were kids because he never looked guilty or tried to talk his way out of trouble. Brandon always dug himself in deeper. Still does."

Adrienne didn't know if she'd ever sort out the subtle personality differences among the Sloan siblings, especially the brothers. "Adam said he plans to stop by again this afternoon."

"He thinks he'll finish work on the wall before we get busy here." Maggie pulled out more groceries from her second bag. Locally-made blueberry jam, pickles, salsa. "I have Aidan and Tyler with me, and their friend Owen. They've gone out back to play dinosaurs. Have you met Owen yet?"

"I haven't. He's the new librarian's son, isn't he?"

"You're catching on. He and Aidan are both six. Tyler's eight. They all know more about dinosaurs than I ever want or need to know. Omnivores, carnivores, herbivores, raptors, this-a-saurus, that-a-saurus."

"I never played with dinosaurs as a kid," Adrienne said with a smile.

"Me, either. Zero interest. My younger sisters did. They used them for their first stage productions. No surprise they became theater majors." Maggie lifted a carton of frozen phyllo dough from the bag. "One thing I don't make from scratch is phyllo dough."

"Does anyone?"

Maggie pulled open the freezer and shoved in the phyllo dough. As the freezer door shut, she pushed back her hair, blew out a breath and then inhaled slowly. "I've been running around all morning. School can't start fast enough. The rest of today, tomorrow, Labor Day weekend and then it's Tuesday. Freedom. The boys are ready. They're bored. I think Adam's work on the stone wall is the only thing I forgot to tell you."

"We warned each other we'd be figuring things out on the fly," Adrienne said. "You've never hired an inn-keeper and I've never been one."

"But you've run a high-end California winery," Maggie said.

Not for long, and "run" was a bit of a stretch. "I straightened things out at the winery and helped get the right person in place for the job—someone more suited to what needed to be done next than I was. Noah and Phoebe made everything easier for me."

"They're quite a pair, aren't they?"

They were, indeed. Phoebe O'Dunn was Maggie's older sister and the former director of the Knights Bridge library. Now she was engaged to billionaire Noah Kendrick. Noah had made his mark with a high-tech company he'd started in San Diego and expanded with the help of his childhood friend Dylan McCaffrey, Olivia's husband. Noah had met Phoebe after Dylan's arrival in Knights Bridge. Although not a couple anyone would have put together, they were ideally suited to each other, and, from everything Adrienne had seen in her months with Kendrick Winery, deeply in love.

Knights Bridge had been on a roll lately with drawing unlikely couples together.

Was that why *she* was here? Never mind her long-lost father and her new job. Had she returned to Knights Bridge in hopes she'd find herself a man?

It'd be an unlikely man for sure, Adrienne thought, amused. When she'd left town for Kendrick Winery, she hadn't harbored a secret attraction for any of the men she'd run into during her winter on Echo Lake. She'd remembered Adam Sloan as particularly sexy but hadn't gone beyond that. She'd been preoccupied, house-sitting for a man who didn't know she was his daughter and making peace with her mother's dishonesty.

She shuddered, refusing to think about those troubled days. If she'd learned nothing else this past year, it was that she wasn't a driven mover and shaker. Not that she hadn't already known on some level, but now she knew it to her core—to her bones.

It felt right, being back in Knights Bridge, being here at the Farm at Carriage Hill, at least for now.

Maggie put a bag of fresh green and wax beans from her widowed mother's garden into the refrigerator. "Be careful with the beans. The boys helped picked them. I'd watch for anything and everything. Stems, leaves, ants."

"Thanks for the heads-up," Adrienne said with a laugh.

"I'll putter in here while the boys play out back. I won't be in your way?"

"Not at all."

"I know I have to let go around here. That's why we have you. I piled too much on my plate. Now with Olivia in her third trimester..." Maggie stopped herself. "I'm not a control freak but delegating doesn't come naturally to me."

"That's often true of entrepreneurs." Adrienne smiled as she grabbed a hunk of cheddar cheese from the refrigerator to go with her apple. "That's what my mother tells me, anyway."

"Sounds about right."

Adrienne took her lunch out to the terrace. The day had warmed up nicely but it wasn't hot. Maggie was obviously good at a lot of different things, and she liked to do them. She enjoyed the variety, the challenge—the activity. Finally, though, she'd admitted she was feeling harried and overwhelmed and needed some help. How much she'd let go, though, remained to be seen.

The apple was crisp and perfect with the cheese. Adrienne loved California, but this quiet corner of New England spoke to her. It had even through a cold, snowy winter when she'd been torn apart about so much. Part of her had wanted to hate Vic Scarlatti and blame him for not knowing about her. But she'd come to realize she didn't blame anyone. Not him, not her mother, not her dad.

She noticed the gray stone of the terrace. Had Adam Sloan built it? She shook her head in answer to her own question. It had been added by the previous owners before Adam was born, at the same time they'd installed the flower and herb gardens. She finished her apple in the garden, walking on a bark-mulched path past fragrant purple basil. Markers for various plants would be a nice touch for guests. She'd have to make sure she got the names right, but there was no rush. She had a long list of more urgent priorities.

Toward the back of the garden, she could hear Maggie's two boys and their friend Owen playing behind a small shed, apparently their usual spot. She slipped through a gap in the stone wall onto a path that led up to the McCaffrey property. There were plans to improve it. Olivia and Maggie didn't lack for plans, that was for sure.

The boys went silent. "Who's that?" one finally whispered.

"It's me, Adrienne. Your mom—Maggie's in the kitchen."

"Okay. We thought you were a giganotosaurus."

Adrienne smiled at the relief in the young voice—Tyler's, she thought. "That doesn't sound good," she said.

"It's a dinosaur," he added. "It's a theropod. That means its limbs have three toes."

"There you go," she said. "I have five toes and five fingers."

The boys giggled and returned to their play.

Adrienne noticed signs of autumn—red-tipped leaves, brown edges on ferns, yellowing field grass. Her lunch break finished, she decided to run a few errands in the village. She let Maggie know and took the ancient car Vic had loaned her. He'd kept it at his house on Echo Lake for years. It was rusted and not exactly sleek, but it ran like a top, as the saying went. She was grateful to have use of it until she figured out what to do about transportation. She'd sold her own car when she'd quit the winery and moved east. It hadn't been sleek, either.

The Farm at Carriage Hill was the last house on the dead-end country road. When Olivia's pretty house was built, the road had wound deep into the Swift River Valley, long before engineers had eyed the region for a reservoir to provide drinking water for growing, thirsty Boston to the east. By the 1920s, four small valley towns were depopulated, disincorporated and razed. Everything went. Homes, businesses, inns, camps, gas stations, general stores, factories and farms. Winsor

Dam and Goodnough Dike were finished, allowing the Swift River and Beaver Brook to flood the valley, creating the pristine waters of Quabbin Reservoir.

It was a short drive to Knights Bridge village with its classic green ringed by old houses, churches, town offices, the library and a handful of businesses. Adrienne parked on Main Street and made quick work of her errands at the post office, hardware store and country store. She didn't run into anyone she recognized and was on her way again in thirty minutes.

She parked behind Maggie's car at the inn and smiled at the sheer beauty of this place. For the first time since arriving in Knights Bridge, she didn't feel the smallest shred of doubt about her decision to take the Carriage Hill job. She got out of her car, shut the door. She could hear the stream on the other side of the road, tumbling over rocks as it worked its way toward the nearby reservoir. She breathed in the pleasant air. She could smell grass, mud and something else—a touch of mint, maybe? Was that possible this far from the backyard and its gardens?

She went inside through the separate kitchen door, painted a warm, welcoming blue, and set the bags on the butcher-block island. She noticed the mudroom door was open but assumed Maggie had gone outside to check on the boys.

A distinct moan drew Adrienne up short. "Maggie?" She ran through the mudroom onto the terrace. "Maggie—are you okay?"

She stopped abruptly, spotting Maggie sprawled on her side halfway to the shed where the boys had been playing. Adrienne leaped off the terrace and ran to her. Maggie tried to sit up but moaned again and sank back onto the bark mulch. She had one hand pressed to the right side of her face, blood seeping through her fingers.

"Easy, easy, Maggie. Let's have a look."

"I'm okay. The boys…" She leaned on her left arm and sat up partially. "Aidan, Tyler…" She couldn't seem to find the words to finish her thought. "Owen."

"They're playing dinosaurs. Did you slip on your way to fetch them?"

"I heard them yelling."

Adrienne felt a coolness inside her. "The boys? Were they caught up in their game?"

"Scared. Adrienne…"

"Hell, Maggie." It was Adam Sloan, leaping down the path to his sister-in-law. He dropped on one knee, taking her by the arm, steadying her. "Ouch. What happened?"

Her pain-racked eyes widened with unmistakable fear. "Adam. The boys. They're gone."

He looked up at Adrienne, his own eyes narrowed, mission-focused. "What's going on?"

"I just got here. I was in town. When I left, Aidan and Tyler and their friend Owen were playing behind the shed. When I got back, I heard Maggie and found her here. She says she heard the boys yelling."

Adam gave a curt nod and shifted back to Maggie. "The boys took off on you?"

"I thought they were getting carried away with their dinosaur game. I came out to give them a two-minute warning that we were going to head home." Her voice cracked. She lowered her blood-smeared hand, revealing a swelling, two-inch gash on her right temple. "They were gone. I called them but they didn't answer. I was running back to the house to grab my phone and call Brandon."

"You tripped?" Adam asked.

"I must have. I went flying and hit my head on a rock or something. I don't think I blacked out. Then Adrienne got here." Maggie started to get up, flailing her non-bloody hand, but Adam held her steady. "I'm okay, Adam. I need to find the boys."

"Whoa. You're not going anywhere. Where's Brandon?"

"He's working in town."

She tried to get up again but faltered, and Adam sat her back down on the mulched path. "You need to stay put and see to that head. Adrienne will help. I'll get in touch with Brandon and whoever else we need. We'll find the boys."

"I can't just sit here and do nothing…"

"Someone needs to be here if they come back." Adam got to his feet and touched Adrienne's shoulder. "Tend to Maggie, okay?"

"Of course."

He nodded and ran down the path. He was already on his phone as he disappeared behind the shed where the three boys had set up their dinosaurs. Adrienne figured he'd call in whatever cavalry he felt was needed. He was a local. Family. He had everyone's number.

She helped Maggie up, reassuring her as she got her feet under her. She had on wide-legged linen pants, a loose top and flip-flops, not great for charging through a garden. Blood dripped onto her shirt. "We'll get some ice for that cut," Adrienne said.

"I'm fine, Adrienne. Help find the boys."

"I don't know the woods. I'll just be underfoot, and imagine if I end up lost—"

"You'd never hear the end of it." Maggie attempted a smile. "I don't know why they took off. I need to check where they were playing again. I was focused on them not being there—I didn't notice anything else. Maybe I missed something."

"Maggie…"

She raised her chin, a stubborn look in her turquoise eyes even with blood dripping down the side of her face. "I can go on my own."

"There's no need." Adrienne put out her hand. "I'll go with you."

Two

‿ഗ⊙ഗⓔ‿

Maggie stared at a dozen dinosaur figures scattered on the stone wall. "What were those boys thinking? Where *are* they?" She spoke in a halting whisper. She'd allowed Adrienne to fetch a napkin from the kitchen and pressed it against the gash on her temple. Blood seeped through the light blue fabric. She didn't seem to notice. "I have to find them."

Adrienne picked up a green dinosaur as if it could tell her something. "Adam's looking for them." She kept her voice calm, not wanting to upset Maggie further. "I'm sure he has more help on the way."

"I can't wait around and do nothing." She adjusted the napkin. In addition to the gash, she'd suffered a bloody scrape that extended from her left wrist bone to her elbow. She'd winced with every step. She had to be bruised. "It looks as if the boys were having an epic dinosaur battle. Then what? Why did they scream?"

"Maybe they got carried away and took their battle

into the woods. Can you tell if any dinosaurs are missing?"

"I have no idea." Maggie shifted and stared out at the fields and woods. "Tyler and Aidan think they know their way around back here better than they do. Little Owen doesn't know his way around at all."

Adrienne returned the dinosaur to its perch on the stone wall. "The boys haven't been gone long," she said gently.

"It gets dark earlier these days." Maggie turned back to the array of fierce-looking dinosaurs and scanned them as if somehow they held answers—or at least clues—to the whereabouts of the three boys. She swayed slightly. "My head…"

Adrienne touched her elbow, ready to grab hold of her if needed. "We should go back to the house, Maggie."

"Yeah." She managed a wan smile. "No one needs me collapsing in the woods."

Adrienne had learned last winter that Maggie—and a lot of people in Knights Bridge—didn't mince words. "Can you make it back to the house? Do you need an ambulance? We can sit here on the stone wall in the shade if you have any doubts."

"I'll be fine. I won't pass out or anything. If I hadn't tripped…" She trailed off, no hint of a smile now, her skin ashen—probably from both pain and fear. "I'm trying not to freak out. You didn't see anyone out here, did you?"

"Just Adam." Adrienne noticed some kind of animal droppings next to a small pine tree. "Deer?"

"Moose scat," Maggie said. "It looks fresh. I didn't see a moose out here today. Did you?"

"No. Have the boys seen a moose before?"

"Not that I know of. Maybe with Brandon. Aidan and Tyler, anyway. I don't know about Owen."

"Maybe a moose came tromping through here and startled them."

Maggie didn't look convinced. "You'd think three boys playing dinosaurs would be noisy enough a moose would take a different route."

"But if he didn't hear them until he was practically on top of them—"

"They'd be startled, but they know what to do if they encounter a moose."

"Get out of the way?"

"Depends. You don't want a moose to feel threatened by your presence."

Adrienne could hear Adam calling for the boys. That meant he hadn't had any luck finding them. She turned to Maggie, who'd obviously drawn the same conclusion. "Why don't we go back to the house, Maggie? Get some ice on your injuries. You might not be feeling all of them now because of the adrenaline rush."

"Adam won't waste time. I'm sure he's called for all hands on deck."

They returned to the garden, but Maggie stopped near where she'd tripped. "What is it?" Adrienne asked her.

Her turquoise eyes showed her pain now. And her determination, her fear for her sons and their friend. "I can make it back to the house on my own. Don't worry about me, Adrienne. You go on and help find those boys."

"I will—once someone gets here to see to you. Don't waste your energy arguing with me, Maggie. I'm very stubborn once I've made up my mind."

"You'll fit right in around here, especially among the Sloans."

It was a valiant attempt at humor. "I'm an only child," Adrienne said. "I can't imagine having five siblings. The Sloans are all construction workers and first responders. I know wine and now I'm learning innkeeping."

"And they're small-town New England and you're big-city California."

"And a nomad," Adrienne added.

The distraction worked to get them closer to the terrace, but Maggie's lower lip trembled and she blinked back tears. She was struggling emotionally, forcing herself to be brave. The boys running into the woods after a moose spooked them was probably the least frightening of the possibilities racing through her mind. Adrienne had glanced around the area behind the shed for signs of adult footprints but she hadn't noticed any.

She shook off that thought. How could anyone snatch three boys without creating a ruckus?

Of course, the boys *had* yelled.

"Maggie! Adrienne!" Olivia McCaffrey waved to them from the terrace. "What's going on?"

Maggie was steadier on her feet, but blood had soaked through the napkin and dripped down her neck. When they reached the terrace, Olivia paled at the sight of her friend. "Adam texted Dylan and me. He said you were hurt, but—"

"It's not as bad as it looks."

Olivia's expression was skeptical but she made no comment. She was red-faced, breathing hard, her dark hair pulled back and matted with sweat. She wore a casual blue-knit dress and placed a palm on her rounded abdomen. She and Dylan were expecting their first baby, a girl, in November. "I walked down the road— I didn't see the boys. Dylan's checking outside at the house and barn and then taking the back way here. Come on, Maggie. Sit. The Sloans and half the town are descending. They'll find the boys."

Maggie sank onto a chair at a round wood table. "It's supposed to rain tonight. It'll get chilly. The boys don't even have water bottles with them. I haven't told Clare and Logan yet—I can't…" She sucked in a breath. "First time in ages they get away on their own for a day, and I lose Owen."

"You didn't lose anyone," Olivia said. "Don't borrow trouble, okay?"

Adrienne had met Clare and Logan Farrell but didn't know them well. Clare had taken over for Phoebe O'Dunn at the local library. Widowed with a young son, she'd met Logan, an ER doctor, not long after she arrived in Knights Bridge last fall. Vic had told Adrienne about the couple's whirlwind romance. He liked to pretend he wasn't part of the town but somehow managed to keep tabs on all the juicy gossip.

Olivia frowned at her longtime friend. "You look like hell, Maggie."

"I feel worse."

"I imagine so. Come on. Let me take a look at the cut."

Adrienne fetched the inn's first-aid kit off a shelf in the mudroom. She hadn't thought of it when she'd run inside and grabbed the napkin. The kit was fully stocked and up to date. She set it on the terrace table and opened it.

Olivia took out a packet containing a sterile bandage. She grimaced as Maggie lowered the bloody napkin. "You know you're going to need—"

"Stitches," Maggie said. "I know."

"Try to stay calm." Olivia tore open the package. "The boys can handle themselves in the woods."

Maggie looked marginally reassured. "I want to get out there and look for them."

"I know you do, Maggie," Olivia said, pulling out the bandage.

Adrienne dug out small scissors and a roll of first-aid tape. She snipped several lengths of tape while Olivia placed the bandage over the cut and Maggie automatically held it in place. "I keep worrying someone grabbed them."

Olivia shook her head. "No. We're not going there. We have zero reason to think that."

"What if—"

"Maggie, please don't do this to yourself."

She nodded but said nothing. Olivia took the bits of tape from Adrienne and applied them to the bandage to hold it in place. She and Maggie had been friends forever and obviously trusted each other and knew what to say, how to say it, what to do.

"What about the scrape?" Olivia asked.

Maggie glanced at her forearm and shrugged. "Stings. It's fine."

"Bruises?"

"A million, at least. Or maybe I've turned into one giant bruise." She gulped in a breath. "Olivia…"

Before she could respond, Justin and Samantha Sloan came out to the terrace from the mudroom. Adrienne didn't know them well, but he was the second-eldest Sloan, a carpenter and volunteer firefighter, and Samantha was a pirate expert and high-end treasure hunter. They went straight to Maggie. "Brandon's right behind us," Justin said. "Eric and Christopher are five minutes out."

Maggie nodded dully. Adrienne knew Eric and Christopher Sloan even without consulting Vic's Knights Bridge cheat sheet. Eric, the eldest of the six siblings, was a town police officer, and Christopher, the youngest of the brothers, was a full-time firefighter. The youngest Sloan altogether—the sole sister, Heather—was spending a year in London with her new husband, a Knights Bridge native and US Diplomatic Security agent, thanks to Vic's mentorship. Adrienne had befriended Heather and Brody when they were still in Knights Bridge last winter, falling in love with each other, as it turned out.

"The boys can't have gotten far, Maggie," Justin said. "We'll find them."

"Best to sound the alarm right away," Samantha added.

She wasn't one to panic. "They could turn up looking for food any minute, but you don't want to take any chances."

Maggie sniffled, blood already seeping through her bandage. "I called the boys. I don't know if they heard me. They were yelling like crazy. Why didn't they respond? Then it got so quiet…"

Justin placed a reassuring hand on her shoulder. "Look after yourself. We'll find them."

She raised her chin, a purple bruise forming on her jaw. "Do you think they decided to hike up Carriage Hill?"

"Did they express an interest in doing that?" Samantha asked.

"Tyler and Aidan told Brandon they wanted to. He said he'd take them. Maybe they got it in their heads to go on their own."

"We'll check for any sign they headed in that direction," Justin said. "Hang in there, Maggie."

He and Samantha took the same route Maggie had to the shed. She watched them, stoic. "I have no reason to panic. I know I don't." She smiled feebly at Adrienne. "Not yet, anyway."

Olivia, who'd slipped inside, returned to the terrace with a mug of hot tea that she set in front of Maggie. "It's peppermint tea from the garden. It'll do you good."

Maggie thanked her and leaned over the mug, breathing in the steam. Adrienne could smell the mint from where she stood—she was too restless to sit. Olivia offered to make her tea, too, but Adrienne shook her head and pointed vaguely at the garden. "I want to take a good look behind the shed and in the woods back there.

Maybe I'll find something that might be useful." She attempted a smile. "Besides moose droppings."

"If you see a moose, let him go on his way if possible," Olivia said. "If he sees you and reacts, tries to confront you, get out of his way. Run. Don't stand your ground or try to scare him off."

"Run," Adrienne repeated and smiled. "That works for me."

"It's rutting season," Maggie added. "Male moose can be aggressive this time of year."

"Then it's good the boys cleared out if a moose surprised them," Olivia said. She finally sat at the table, looking tired and concerned but not as out of breath and upset as she had at first.

Maggie's color was a bit better as she sipped the tea. "I guess that's one way to look at it."

Adrienne started off the terrace. "I'll text you if I find anything and I'm out of shouting distance."

"Keep in mind cell service is spotty to nonexistent in places out there," Olivia said.

"Good to know. I promise not to get lost."

The last thing she needed was a Sloan search party looking for her.

The air was still and warm, without a hint of a breeze when Adrienne eased behind the shed. And it was quiet. Justin and Samantha had disappeared, perhaps out across the fields. A few birds twittered in the trees but Adrienne heard no other sounds. No young boys whispering in the trees, caught up in their imaginary world, or returning with an uncle, an aunt, a neighbor, laughing, oblivious to their mother's fall, her fears.

Adrienne stood straight, eyeing the moose droppings. She didn't know the land back here. She hadn't grown up in Knights Bridge, hadn't been playing dinosaurs—couldn't rely on guesswork to figure out what had prompted Tyler, Aidan and Owen to yell and run off.

If that was what they'd done.

Where could they be?

She stepped past the droppings, pushing her way through ferns. She'd never been in New England during warm weather. She thought about ticks, mosquitoes, spiders. Snakes. Even if it wasn't poisonous, she'd rather not surprise a snake. In general, she didn't want to come across slithery things. A moose or a deer struck her as more manageable. Just get out of the way versus flicking it off or having it crawl up her leg.

She groaned to herself. *Just stop.*

She came to a dirt trail she hadn't realized was back here. It followed an old stone wall, perpendicular to the one where the boys had set up their dinosaurs. She had no idea where it led but suspected it eventually would take her into the abutting Quabbin wilderness, and perhaps to the reservoir's pristine waters. She planned to study maps of the area and take a few hikes herself before the cold weather. She wanted to be able to provide guests with tips, but she had a number of locals who'd be willing to step in. Maggie, Olivia, any of the Sloans.

As she walked a few yards onto the trail, she warned herself not to make any assumptions about where it led. Various trails spiderwebbed through the woods and fields, leading not only to Quabbin but across the fields to Carriage Hill, up to the McCaffreys' place, back to the inn. It would be easy for three young boys to get turned around out here, especially if they were scared.

Adrienne didn't know what route Adam had taken. She didn't hear him or anyone else calling the boys. As the trail descended slightly away from the stone wall, she noticed prints in a patch of soft dirt. She squatted down for a closer look. She could see the distinct outline of some kind of sneaker or running shoe by an exposed tree root. She stood straight, careful not to step on the print. It was small—a child's shoe? She looked around but didn't see other prints.

She didn't want to overreact and make too much of her discovery. She continued on the trail, which wound closer to the stone wall.

She didn't see additional prints—moose or human— as she continued on the path. She'd go a bit farther. She checked her phone but saw there was no service. The trail veered uphill to the stone wall. Maybe she could get out a text there.

As she came to the stone wall, she saw a dinosaur figure nestled in ferns on the side of the trail, as if it had stopped to take a nap. It was too far from the house for one of the boys to have thrown or dropped it while playing behind the shed. That meant they—or at least one of them—must have come this way.

She checked her phone. Still no service.

She stood on a rock. "Tyler! Aidan! Owen!" She paused, listening, but there was no response. "It's your mom's friend Adrienne. Give me a shout."

She stepped off the rock back onto the trail. It narrowed further, hugging the stone wall as the land dropped away to her right. She could hear a stream down through the trees, out of sight, probably winding its way to the reservoir.

"Adrienne."

She was so startled she stumbled, but Adam jumped from the stone wall and caught her by the arm, steadying her.

"Sorry," he said. "I heard you calling the boys."

"I didn't realize you were so close."

"I'd stopped to listen for them."

"Nothing yet?"

"Nothing."

Adrienne told him about the footprint and the dinosaur. "A startled moose stumbles on three boys playing dinosaurs. I can see them all bolting." She handed Adam the dinosaur. "I found it in the ferns."

He examined it. "A triceratops."

"Ah." She'd had no idea. "One of the boys must have dropped it."

Adam slipped the dinosaur into a back pocket. "There's an old cellar hole up a little ways I want to check out. Do you want to come with me or go back to the house?"

"I'll go with you." She held up her phone. "No service."

"Nope." He sounded as if he'd never expect such a thing. "There's a better trail on the other side of the stone wall."

Adrienne nodded. "Okay, let's go."

It was a *much* better trail. Since it was on the field side of the stone wall, it was wider and grassier, with fewer rocks, roots, twists and turns. Every few yards, Adam called the boys by name, emphasizing they weren't in any trouble. He never came to a full stop and moved with the ease of someone familiar with the terrain. Adrienne had no trouble keeping up with him, but she watched her footing. She didn't want to add to the concerns of the day by tripping.

"Brandon and Maggie taught Tyler and Aidan to stay put if they got lost, preferably by a stone wall or on a trail," Adam said.

"If a moose surprised them—" Adrienne broke off abruptly. "I know speculating won't help. Maggie's worried because it gets dark earlier this time of year and it's supposed to rain."

"There's still good daylight left. My brothers will organize a search party if need be. We have time to find them before dark. They can't have gone far."

"Maggie's sure she tripped. I don't think she blacked out. If she was pushed—"

"Don't go there, Adrienne," he said quietly.

It could be hard not to, but she knew speculating didn't help.

"Your mom took a tumble but she's fine," Adam called. "She's making snacks for you."

Again there was no response.

Adrienne kept an eye out for signs the boys had been this way, but she didn't notice additional footprints or dinosaurs along the stone wall, field grass, ferns, briars and brush. No candy wrappers, apple cores or anything else that would suggest she and Adam were on the right trail. In another fifty yards or so, the stone wall made a ninety-degree turn across the field, parallel to Carriage Hill Road. Off the corner formed by the turn were what looked to be the remains of the stone foundation of a small house or a shed. A number of old cellar holes could be found in the area, of homes burned and never rebuilt, abandoned for greener pastures or taken by eminent domain during Quabbin's construction.

"This is the cellar hole you mentioned?" Adrienne asked.

Adam nodded and moved closer to the cellar hole. "It's Adam, guys. Adrienne is here with me."

He sounded confident he'd found them and obviously knew this spot. The remains of the foundation and a chimney were overgrown with small trees, brush, ferns and briars. Adrienne glanced around, finally noticed spots where ferns had been recently disturbed. She breathed in the late-afternoon air, cooling noticeably as gray clouds moved in from the west, but she said nothing. Let Adam handle his young nephews and their friend.

"Aidan, Tyler—come on. It's Uncle Adam. You're not in trouble. Owen? It's okay, buddy. We'll get you back to the house."

Tyler popped up from behind a large rock. At eight, he was the eldest of the three boys, with his mother's red hair and turquoise eyes. He had on shorts, a dinosaur T-shirt and sandals and was breathing hard, his cheeks red and sweaty. "Was it a tyrannosaurus rex?"

"It was a moose, Tyler. You know that." Adam frowned

at his nephew and pointed at his lower left leg, smeared with dirt and blood. "You're hurt?"

The boy shrugged. "It's only a scratch."

"You sound like your dad. Where are Aidan and Owen?"

"Hiding. They got scared."

As if he hadn't. Adrienne appreciated his attempt to be brave.

"Well, they can come out now," Adam said. "There's no reason to be scared anymore." He put out a hand to Tyler. "Let's have a look at that leg."

Aidan shot up next to his older brother. "Tyler smashed his leg on a rock when we jumped in the cellar hole. He didn't even cry. We never saw a moose before. We thought he was going to charge us. He looked *right* at us. We ran like Dad said to. We wanted to find Dylan but we got lost."

"We didn't get lost," Tyler said. "We were hiding."

Owen stood up next to the two brothers. He was a small boy with dark, shaggy hair. It was his first summer in Knights Bridge. He and Aidan were the same age, and like the two Sloan boys, he was dressed in shorts and a dinosaur T-shirt. The shirts must have been a pact between them. He sniffled, his lower lip trembling. "We're lost," he said, barely holding back tears.

"We are *not* lost," Tyler repeated, emphatic.

Before he could continue to argue the point, Adam lifted him off the rocks and over the ferns and brush. Tyler insisted he didn't need help but his uncle had him on the ground before he could finish lodging his protest. Adam started reaching for Owen next, but the boy lurched and grabbed a dinosaur he'd dropped. He slipped as he tried to stand upright. Adam caught him but managed to smash the side of his hand on a rough gray rock in the process. He winced but said nothing, just got Owen and then Aidan out of the cellar hole and onto the field grass. He checked the boys for injuries and insect bites. Except for Tyler's scrape, all three boys were in good shape.

"Why did you run off instead of finding your mom?" Adam asked.

"The moose was running right at us, so we ran the other way," Tyler said.

"Straight up here, along the stone wall?"

He nodded vigorously. "We thought we were heading to Uncle Dylan and Aunt Olivia's house."

"Wrong stone wall," Adam said. "Good thinking, though."

"We were scared," Aidan added.

Tyler rolled his eyes. "We weren't *that* scared."

"*I* was *very* scared," Owen said, insistent.

"Yeah," Aidan said in agreement with his friend. "We thought the moose was running from a tyrannosaurus rex."

"Got it," Adam said, not belittling the boys' version of events. "Moose are big. I came on one a couple of weeks ago. I thought I'd upset him, but he was just doing his moose thing. We don't have that many moose in this area. A lot of people have never seen one."

The boys started talking in unison about their excitement at having seen their first moose, even if it had scared them—or at least Aidan and Owen. Adrienne could see Tyler wasn't about to admit he'd been scared like the younger boys. She'd seen hints of that kind of pride and stubbornness in his mother.

"What about you, Adrienne?" Adam asked. "Did you see the moose?"

She shook her head. "I had no idea a moose would get that close to the house. I haven't noticed moose or deer since I've been here, but it's only been five days. And I'd gone to town, so I wasn't here when the boys' moose turned up."

"He could have encountered a hiker and taken a detour from his usual route." Adam took the two younger boys by the hand, no indication his own injury bothered him. "Let's get you boys back to the inn. Tyler, you good to walk?"

"Yeah, no problem."

Adrienne eased to his side but didn't take his hand. "If it gets too hard to walk, you let me know, okay?"

He nodded. "Sure thing."

Owen was on the verge of full-blown tears. Adam nodded at the boy's T-shirt. "What kind of dinosaur is that?"

"It's a pachyrhinosaurus." As if Adam should know. Adrienne wouldn't have been surprised if he *did* know and was just trying to encourage the boy.

He started back to the trail with the two youngest boys on either side of him. "Omnivore, right?"

"Herbivore," Owen said. "That means he only eats plants. Omnivores eat plants and meat. Carnivores only eat meat."

"I want to be a carnivore," Aidan said. "I hate vegetables."

Their moods improved as they put their scare behind them. "We stayed together like Dad told us," Tyler said, limping somewhat but without complaint.

Adam stayed close to him. "Good job. Say the word, and I'll carry you."

Tyler shook his head. "I'm good."

Not backing off. Pure O'Dunn and Sloan, Adrienne thought. She checked her phone. Two bars. She texted Maggie: We've got them. They're fine. On our way from cellar hole.

She hit Send, and two seconds later, Maggie responded: Phew. Brandon will meet you.

Three

Aidan and Owen kept on about how big the moose was. They compared him to various dinosaurs. The words tumbled out—fueled by adrenaline, the excitement of the day. All three boys insisted they'd felt the moose's breath, he was *that* close to them. They'd clearly panicked, something Adrienne could understand.

Tyler laid claim to the dinosaur Adrienne had found. A triceratops, he confirmed. "Did you know you'd dropped a dinosaur on the way to the cellar hole?" she asked him.

He shook his head. "Maybe Owen dropped it. He was playing with it."

"He didn't notice?"

"We were running. We didn't stop until we got to the cellar hole. I figured out we went the wrong way." He looked up at her, perspiration beading on his upper lip. "That's not the same as getting lost."

She smiled. "I agree."

He didn't smile back. She glanced at his injured leg.

The blood mixed with dirt and bits of ferns, leaves and grass looked nasty, but she doubted the scrapes and scratches needed anything more than a good cleaning, maybe a bandage.

The cream-colored antique house came into view. Brandon Sloan was charging toward them. In a few more long strides, he reached his sons and Owen. The two younger boys burst into tears, their legs going out from under them. Adam scooped up Aidan while Brandon picked up Owen. Adrienne started to take Tyler's hand, but, as she'd anticipated, he shook his head, never mind he was the one with an injured leg. Just another day in the country for him.

Brandon ran his palm over Tyler's head. "You did great, buddy. Hungry?"

"Thirsty."

"Did any of you boys drink water out here—from a stream or puddle?"

Tyler didn't hesitate. "No. You told us not to."

"They're still young enough to listen to you," Adam said.

Brandon grinned, his relief palpable. He and Adam bore a strong resemblance to each other with their blue eyes, dark hair and broad shoulders. "All's well that ends well," Brandon said.

Aidan sniffled. "Did Mom get hurt because of us?"

"No way," Brandon said. "She tripped and got a little banged up, but she's doing great. She's waiting for you. She's not going anywhere until she knows you're safe."

Tyler gritted his teeth and limped, clearly determined to put up a good front and bear up under the pressure.

Brandon glanced back at him but didn't interfere with his older son's decision about how to handle himself. Adrienne eased behind the Sloans as they cut past the shed into the backyard. She wasn't surprised to see Maggie and Olivia on the terrace. They'd been joined by Dylan McCaffrey—an ex-NHL player and a multimillionaire businessman—and more Sloans: Eric and Christopher had arrived, and Justin and Samantha had returned from their search.

Brandon and Adam set Owen and Aidan on the terrace, and Tyler bolted to his mother in spite of his injured leg. "We saw a *moose*," he exclaimed.

Maggie hugged the three boys. "Did all of you see the moose?"

"Uh-huh," Aidan said. "It was *huge*."

"You did the right thing getting away from it," Maggie said.

Christopher Sloan checked Tyler's injured leg. "Need to clean it up, but it'll heal in no time." He cast Maggie a look. "You, on the other hand, need to get that head seen to."

Brandon eased next to her. "Let's go."

She relented, and Brandon helped her to her feet. Christopher followed them with all three boys. Adrienne quickly realized half the town was poised to search for the boys, with many people dropping by the inn while she'd been in the woods. Better safe than sorry, and they had the best outcome possible—three young boys safe and sound after their adventure.

Olivia and Dylan joined the remaining Sloans in checking out the spot where the boys had been playing and the moose had thundered past them. Eric, in particular, wanted to make sure nothing was amiss. Olivia would be able to confirm if anything was out of place or had been added behind the shed. She was clearly rattled. Dylan stayed close to her as they walked through the garden.

Adrienne stepped inside for a glass of water. She took a deep breath, held it and then let it out slowly, calming herself. It wasn't just the fright of losing the boys. It was all that Sloan testosterone coupled with her own newness at being here, at being an innkeeper.

Crisis averted. All was quiet and normal at the Farm at Carriage Hill.

Normal being a relative term given the company she was keeping.

After a few minutes, she heard vehicles starting out front. She glanced out the window and realized everyone was leaving. They'd cut through the side yard to the road.

Only Adam's van remained.

Adrienne found him on the terrace, eyeing his injured hand. "Do you need the first-aid kit?" she asked him.

"Nah. It's just bruised. If I got derailed by every bruise and scrape in my line of work, I'd never get anything done."

She noticed a thick two-inch scar on his uninjured hand. "Is that work-related?"

"An unfortunate encounter with a chisel blade. I was sixteen. It bled like crazy."

"Were you alone?"

"Unfortunately no. Justin was with me. I'll never live it down."

"What happened?"

He shrugged. "Hot summer evening. I was a month into apprenticing with a master stonemason and thought I knew more than I did. Tackled a job at home on my own."

"Stitches?"

"Oh, yeah." He glanced around the terrace. "I can help pick up. I promised Olivia I wouldn't leave you to do it by yourself."

"It's okay—"

But he was already grabbing the first-aid kit. Adrienne collected water glasses, napkins, a pitcher. He held the mudroom door for her. "Careful with your hand," she said.

He grinned at her. "I can hold a door."

He *had* just carried his nephew through the field. He followed her into the kitchen. He was obviously familiar with its layout—and in more pain than he wanted to admit. As she placed the dishes in the sink, she realized her legs were wobbling and her heart was racing, and not just because of the eight thousand things that could have gone wrong that afternoon and hadn't. Because of him. Her reaction to him. Damn but he was sexy.

"Were you all satisfied nothing's amiss?" she asked him.

He nodded. "The moose seems to have gone down to the road and crossed it up into the woods. No sign of a hiker or anything else that might have startled him."

"Just a moose being a moose, then."

"Seems that way. Eric's tightly wound these days. What about you? Have you seen hikers or anyone else out here?"

"No. It's been quiet."

"You'll run into more hikers out here with foliage season. Most will drive in and park down by the Quabbin gate." He got a glass out of a cupboard and filled it with water. "It's never been a problem."

"Good to know."

"It's going to be a while before Maggie and Brandon let the boys play back there, out of their sight."

"I feel pretty useless," Adrienne said, grabbing one of the apples Maggie had brought earlier. "I didn't even see the moose. Would you like some ice for your hand?"

He shook his head. "Are you worried being out here on your own?"

"Dylan and Olivia said they were in the process of beefing up security, but no, I'm not worried, certainly not about moose and such. Now, if a black bear comes knocking, we'll have to talk. They don't do locks, do they?"

Adam drank his water, smiling as he set the glass on the counter. "No bears in the kitchen yet."

"Yet," Adrienne repeated. She handed him a colander for the dinosaurs he'd collected and returned to the terrace with him. "I never played dinosaurs as a kid. I got into paper dolls for a while, but I didn't have much time for unstructured play. My mother had me in classes."

He loaded the dinosaurs into the colander. "What kind of classes?"

"Dance, music, theater, gymnastics, tennis, cooking, chess. I hated dancing and chess. The others were fine. What about you?"

He thought a moment. "Piano for a year."

"It didn't take?"

"A year was enough."

"And no other lessons?"

He shook his head. "I did track and field and played a little baseball."

"You grew up with five siblings out here in the country. Did your family have a vegetable garden?"

"Always."

"A lot of planting, weeding, hoeing and harvesting, then."

"Many hands," he said.

"Did you chop wood, too?"

His blue eyes held hers for an instant longer than was comfortable. "Yeah," he said finally. "We did cordwood from our land. Still do."

"I'm not making fun of you, you know. I'm curious, that's all."

"No problem."

"I took piano lessons. I wasn't any good at it."

He smiled. "Something we have in common."

She nodded toward the fields and woods behind the house. "Do you have old stone walls at your family home?"

"We do, and we have an arched stone bridge across Cider Brook, too."

"Same kind of rock as the walls?"

"Different. Most of the stone walls out here were

created when settlers cleared the woods for farmland. They're what we call random rubble walls."

"Sounds like my life." Adrienne waved a hand. "Kidding. How old are these old stone walls?"

"Most were built between 1750 and 1850. There's a lot of rock in this area."

"I guess you don't have to worry about a shortage."

"Not of fieldstone. Quarried stone can get tricky. I'm trying to match some up to repair stonework in the village. I'm keeping my eye on demolitions of structures with the same stone." He pushed back his chair. "It's a living."

"But it's work you enjoy?"

"Sure. No complaints. There's enough variety to keep my interest, and I like the work. Stonemasons don't specialize the way they once did. I work on my own most of the time, but I hire a crew for bigger jobs."

"Your brothers?"

He smiled. "Only if no one else is available. Not their favorite type of work."

His comment was good-natured. She'd witnessed the banter between the brothers last winter. "I noticed the stonework was all that was left in the old cellar hole where we found the boys."

"Most of my work will outlast me."

"Not mine. A bottle of wine I recommend is lucky to last the evening."

"Your guests will have good memories."

"I hope so."

They went inside with the colander. He set it in the sink and turned water on the muddy dinosaurs. He was a good uncle, Adrienne thought, and one steady, competent man. He spread out a dish towel and laid the wet dinosaurs on it. "The boys will know if I missed even one. They keep a tight inventory."

"It turned into a tense, hectic afternoon."

"You reacted well when you found Maggie. You'll handle inn crises just fine."

"I hope so. I hope there aren't any, though. But thanks for the vote of confidence." She leaned against the butcher-block island, watching as he blotted the dinosaurs with the towel. "Did you and your siblings ever take off like that?"

"Christopher and I went out our bedroom window on a sheet one night. We'd been banished to our rooms. It was just after dark. We got lost down on Cider Brook and ended up spending the night in the woods. We figure our dad knew where we were but left us out there as a lesson. He'll never admit it. It's probably not something he'd do nowadays."

"How old were you?"

"I was twelve. Chris was nine. It was Fourth of July week, so it's not like we were going to freeze."

Adrienne was fascinated by how different his upbringing had been from her own. It never would have occurred to her to go out her bedroom window on a sheet. "I hid in a closet once. Not as dramatic as spending the night in the woods. Maybe if I'd had a sibling, I'd have been more adventurous. It was just my mother and me once she divorced my dad when I was seven."

"Rough time?"

"Yeah. They did the best they could by me." She

didn't want to go there, not now, maybe not ever with a Sloan, given the family's prominence in her new town, with her new employers. "Did you and Chris slip back into your house without your parents noticing, or did you march through the front door?"

"Our folks took up the sheet so it wasn't an option. I went through the front door. I knew it would be manned but figured Chris could sneak in through the back and claim he'd been hiding all along."

"You sacrificed yourself for your little brother."

"Plausible deniability."

"Did it work?"

Adam shook his head, a smile in his eyes. "He never had a chance. It's a big family. Our folks and older brothers had all entry points covered. And Gran. She's old-fashioned. She was waiting for us with a switch." He folded the dinosaurs into the towel. "Some homecoming, huh? Lost in the woods, and we were in trouble."

"I suspect the trouble had to do with sneaking out the window on a bedsheet."

"A hazard of having a room on the second floor. We could have slipped in and out a first-floor window with no one being the wiser."

"Assuming you didn't get lost," Adrienne said. "Imagine your poor parents waking up and discovering their two youngest boys were nowhere to be found."

"Just as well they were onto us early, I guess. Heather tried the bedsheet route when she got older, but her room was in the attic, so her sheet didn't reach far enough. She had to jump a ways and damn near broke an ankle.

I heard her yell. She didn't get far before we caught up with her. Still calls us the posse."

"Well deserved, no doubt."

"Don't think she's not one of us because she's the only sister."

Having worked closely with Heather on Vic's house renovations, Adrienne wasn't under that impression. Heather was all Sloan.

Adam got two clean towels from a drawer and divided the dinosaurs into them. "Can you identify any of them?"

"A few from movies. You?"

"I think I've got them all down except this guy." He held up a fierce-looking dinosaur figure with horns. "The boys can tell me."

"Amazing what sticks from when you were eight."

"Wish multiplication had stuck."

Adrienne had no doubt multiplication had stuck just fine with Adam.

He tied the towels around the dinosaurs. "Chris went deep with his dinosaurs. He read every book he could find on them in the library. Justin and Eric never cared about dinosaurs one way or the other. Heather pretended to care but she didn't."

Adrienne pointed at a fat green-painted dinosaur whose nose peeked out from the towel. "His name?"

"Fred."

"Ha."

He grinned at her. "You didn't care about dinosaurs at eight and you don't care now."

She laughed. "I can't disagree."

He picked up the towels. "Anything else I can do?"

Her mouth went dry with awareness. Had to be the adrenaline from finding Maggie and searching for the boys. He was sexy, but she'd known that. He'd been sexy last winter. She felt heat rising into her face and quickly shook her head. "All set. Thanks."

"Okay, then." He started for the front door. "See you soon, Innkeeper Adrienne."

Four

A dam shut the front door behind him—dinosaurs and all—and walked to his van with such control that Adrienne only found herself feeling hotter. She sank against the freestanding island with such force it slid halfway to the sink. She stood straight, pushed the island back in place, ran a hand through her hair and listened to the birds twittering outside as a breeze floated through the open windows. Adrenaline. That really did explain everything, didn't it?

She had an inn to keep. She didn't need to be lusting after Adam Sloan. She was here to do a job and spend time with Vic, get to know him better now that the shock of discovering he was her father had worn off for both of them. Knights Bridge was his home. The *last* thing she wanted to do was to mess things up for him here.

The quiet Sloan.

That was what everyone said about Adam.

Quiet, maybe, but she'd seen him in action today.

She finished cleaning up the kitchen. Olivia and Maggie had put their trust in her. She wasn't going to complicate her relationship with them by letting this unsettling attraction get out of hand.

She went out to the terrace. It was quiet now, gray with the clouds and approaching dusk. A butterfly zigzagged among yellow flowers whose name she couldn't place. She didn't know what kind of butterfly it was, either. So much to learn out here, and she looked forward to every bit of it—however long she stayed in Knights Bridge.

She walked on a soft, bark-mulched path to the spot where Maggie had fallen. Spots of blood had dried on a rock. Would it draw animals to the yard? Adrienne shuddered at the prospect but decided such a scenario wasn't worth thinking about. Nothing she could do about it at this point, anyway.

Just as well the inn didn't have anything on the schedule through the weekend. She was restless, not sure what to do with herself despite having a long list of tasks she needed to get to sooner rather than later.

She returned to the kitchen and filled a pitcher with water, brought it out to the garden and poured it on the bloodstains. Maybe diluting them wouldn't help much in terms of animals but at least Maggie and the boys— and Brandon—wouldn't have to see her blood when they came out here.

Of course, it was supposed to rain tonight.

Adrienne sighed and took the pitcher back to the kitchen. She felt agitated and on edge, but it wasn't just the aftereffects of finding Maggie and discovering the boys were missing. It was the sense that she was about to spin out of control. It'd happened last winter. She'd all but stalked Vic, knowing he was her father—keeping it to herself even after she'd realized he had no idea. She hadn't been straight with him from the start.

And she'd always been restless and impulsive.

She liked to see herself as flexible, spontaneous, creative—someone who could seize the moment and make things work. Her interest in wine. Her blog. Her travels. Her consulting.

She had lots of friends. She'd done so much considering she was barely thirty.

How had she ended up at a small inn on a dead-end road in Knights Bridge, Massachusetts?

Then there was Adam Sloan. Her reaction to him.

How close had they been to falling into each other's arms after the adrenaline-fueled hunt for the missing boys?

Had she *wanted* that?

Adrienne left the question unanswered. She emptied the dishwasher and put away the dishes she'd washed by hand. She took the wet towel Adam had used to dry the dinosaurs to the laundry in the mudroom. Olivia had bought the antique house when she'd still been working in Boston as a graphic designer. She'd quit her job and moved back to her hometown a year and a half ago, expecting to live here herself as an innkeeper, freelancing as a designer to help make ends meet as she got the inn on a solid financial footing. Then Dylan had entered her life, and they'd married here at Carriage Hill on Christmas Eve. Now they were expecting their first child.

How fast life could change...

Maggie had become her business partner, and they'd managed without a full-time staff, hiring the occasional contractor for what they couldn't do themselves. Finally, though, they'd realized they couldn't do all they'd been doing—but neither could Adrienne, not with the inn's upcoming schedule. They knew that. She needed to hire people to clean, do laundry, take care of the yard, possibly handle reservations. Olivia would eventually hire someone to deal with marketing and public relations, but Adrienne would have a role. A retail shop was on the someday/maybe list. Maggie and Olivia had their own goat's milk soap-making business. There was talk of selling the products in a shop at the inn and maybe online, too. They were already used as guest-room amenities.

Olivia and Maggie had dived in without clear goals, figuring things out over the past eighteen months. That was something Adrienne could understand and appreciate. She was here, wasn't she? She'd leaped at the opportunity without any specific goals in mind for herself. Do a good job. Spend time with Vic. See what happened.

Move on when the time was right.

That was her pattern, wasn't it?

But she felt a tightness in her chest, a pang of loss and regret at the prospect of leaving.

"Give it six months. *Then* see how you feel."

She set out clean dish towels. Keeping moose out of the yard and bears out of the kitchen tonight would do the trick for her in terms of goals.

And stop thinking about Adam Sloan.

"I need to swear off men while I'm in Knights Bridge."

That was the smart move.

"Also stop talking to myself."

She smiled, feeling more in control.

Once she was satisfied the inn was tidied and she could take a breather, she walked up the quiet road. She found Olivia sitting on the front steps of the barn she and Dylan used as a base for their fledgling adventure travel business and entrepreneurial boot camps. The barn looked as if it had been there for two hundred years, but it was brand-new, built the past year and never intended to be used as an actual barn with horses or cows or anything. Olivia and Dylan had also had a new home built up the hill a bit. The Sloans had done the construction on the house and barn, both designed by a local architect... who was married to Olivia's younger sister...

More connections Adrienne had to keep track of, but she'd had a head start last winter and she had Vic's cheat sheet. She had to admit she loved the challenge and all the different ways the people in the small town, whether newcomers or born and raised there, interacted with each other.

Olivia shifted her position on the steps. "I know it'll be harder and harder to get comfortable in the coming weeks." She sounded perfectly cheerful about that prospect. "I just wanted to sit here a few minutes before it gets dark and the rain starts. It's so relaxing. I picked echinacea and phlox and put them in a vase in the barn kitchen. It's impossible to go wrong with flowers this time of year. Picking flowers was a good stress reliever after today."

"No ticks, mosquitoes, red ants, snakes, spiders?" Adrienne grinned. "I'll stop now."

Olivia laughed, stretching out her legs on the stone steps. "It's hard to believe the flowers will all be gone soon." She inhaled deeply. "I can smell fall in the air, can't you?"

Actually, Adrienne couldn't. "I'm starting to notice the seasonal nuances."

"Dylan dislikes humidity and loves cooler weather. I think that's one reason he became a hockey player. What's not to like about San Diego weather, but he appreciates New England's four seasons."

"I've never experienced a real New England fall. I didn't mind the cold weather when I house-sat for Vic, but I figured it'd probably be my only New England winter. Little did I know."

"Do you feel you're starting to get the lay of the land at the inn?"

"Definitely. It's a fantastic place, Olivia."

She looked pleased. "We've made so much progress with it."

Vic had told Adrienne how Olivia and Dylan had met, at least what he knew of it. Olivia had written to Dylan in San Diego to come clean up his eyesore of a yard up the road from her antique house, but he'd had no idea he owned a house in Knights Bridge. Turned out his father had left it to him but hadn't had a chance to tell him before his untimely death in a fall on one of his treasure hunts. Dylan had headed east to check out his property, and he and Olivia had swooped into each other's lives. In the process, they'd discovered that

Duncan McCaffrey had bought the property from a retired high school English and Latin teacher who'd given birth to him in her late teens. His birth father, a British RAF pilot, was killed early in World War II, never to return to Grace Webster, the young woman he'd fallen in love with across the Atlantic.

According to Vic, Grace had never held her and her British lover's baby before he was adopted.

Duncan had met his birth mother before his death and bought her house on Carriage Hill Road. Grace, in her nineties, had moved into the town's assisted living facility and was looking forward to being a great-grandmother.

Adrienne smiled to herself. Little Knights Bridge did have its secrets.

While Dylan and Olivia were figuring out why his father had bought Grace's house, Vic was working in New York with no idea he had a secret baby of his own.

Why her mother hadn't told him would never make sense to Adrienne, but that was Sophia Portale. She was the type who had the answer before anyone had asked the question. Come up pregnant after a Paris fling, weeks before her marriage to another man? Pretend the fling never happened. Pretend the baby was conceived on your honeymoon. Don't tell anyone the truth, including your daughter, even when she's an adult—unless she corners you and you have no other choice.

There was something to be said for that level of guts, gall and certainty, Adrienne supposed.

Once she'd admitted her affair with Vic, her mother

had hinted her decision to keep silent hadn't been impulsive or without cost. It must have been a lonely plight, even for such a strong, successful woman. Her marriage had failed. Vic had gone on to a stellar diplomatic career. She'd launched a marketing business and had thrown herself into the work, doing well, never remarrying. These days she was in a relationship with a corporate executive, but there didn't seem much passion involved. Adrienne sometimes wondered if her mother had learned to keep such a thing at arm's length.

It wasn't as if she still carried a torch for Vic Scarlatti after all this time.

If she ever *had* carried a torch for him.

What's done is done, Adrienne.

Vic had endured a few dark nights of the soul when he'd learned he had an adult daughter last winter. *I never had a clue you were mine. Never. I swear, Adrienne.*

She believed him.

She became aware of Olivia eyeing her. "Are you okay?"

"Sorry. Mind wandering."

"Understandable after this afternoon," Olivia said without hesitation. "I'm glad you and Adam found the boys before nightfall. Maggie held it together pretty well, but I know she was worried they'd end up spending the night in the rain, even with the entire town out looking for them. We didn't find any sign of a hiker or camper who could have startled the moose. That's just as well, in my opinion. It's unlikely anyone's out there pitching a tent for the night."

"That works for me," Adrienne said.

"Camping's not allowed on Quabbin land, or ours without permission. I'm sorry Maggie got banged up. And Tyler. He's going to have a good bruise on his leg to start school."

Olivia was obviously tired. "I should get back," Adrienne said.

"Do you want Dylan to give you a ride?"

"It's not far. I'm happy walking."

"Dylan can walk with you—"

"I'm fine, thanks. I'm just relieved all's well."

Olivia started to get up but paused, taking a moment to find her balance, breathe, steady herself and then straighten. She smiled happily. "I used to bounce to my feet, but best I take my time."

"Especially when there are stone steps involved."

"I got dehydrated earlier this summer and keeled over. I didn't get hurt, but it was a wake-up call to drink more water. I'm not a hothouse flower, just mindful of where I am with this pregnancy." Olivia stood upright and placed a hand on her lower back, stretching. "Maggie and I are thrilled to have you here, Adrienne. Speak up about anything you need, any ideas you might have. Don't hesitate, okay? Dylan's around, too."

"I will. I'm thrilled to be here. Thanks."

Adrienne waited as Olivia went inside. Everything about the house and barn from materials to landscaping was designed to blend into the quiet area of rolling hills, fields and woodlands. She couldn't imagine a more perfect spot for the McCaffreys to welcome their first child.

Halfway back to the inn, the rain started, just a few drops at first. Adrienne ducked inside and watched out the window above the kitchen sink as more rain fell, soaking into the lush lawn.

She didn't see so much as a chipmunk, let alone a moose.

During a break in the rain, Adrienne dashed outside and picked a few sprigs of parsley to add to her leftover minestrone soup. She loved the idea of having herbs growing in her backyard. Somehow fresh parsley made her meal seem more festive. It was dripping wet but she rinsed it off anyway and blotted it dry with paper towels.

She'd just found kitchen scissors in a drawer when Olivia called to invite her to dinner. "I'm so sorry. I should have said something when you were up here."

"Not a problem. We're all worn out. I have on my fuzzy slippers."

Olivia laughed. "Do you really own fuzzy slippers?"

"A half-dozen pairs of wool socks. I'm working on the fuzzy slippers." She stirred the soup. "Thanks for the invitation."

"Rain check," Olivia said.

After she hung up, Adrienne snipped the parsley and added a handful to her soup. Maggie had dropped the soup off earlier in the week as a welcome. Much appreciated on Adrienne's part. She'd finish it off tonight.

She poured the rest of a Willamette Valley pinot noir she'd opened last night and sat at the kitchen table with her soup. Maggie had added late-summer vegetables from her mother's garden. The inn had a small vegetable garden that she and Olivia wanted to expand. Adrienne loved their imagination and energy. Right now she was focused on getting day-to-day operations more under control.

The soup was even better tonight, if only because she was starving after the adrenaline rush of the missing boys. She'd spent many evenings alone house-sitting for Vic last winter, but she'd been so caught up in her emotions at having discovered he was her father that she had paid little attention to the quiet and beauty of the small town he'd made his own.

The rain picked up. A breeze fluttered through a maple tree in the front lawn.

Adrienne smiled. What a spot Olivia had chosen for herself when she'd bought this place. As imaginative as she was, she hadn't pictured herself meeting a man like Dylan McCaffrey, marrying him...having a baby with him...

As much as Adrienne wanted to be here in Knights Bridge, tackling innkeeping, she could feel her old restlessness stirring. She'd always been a tumbleweed. She'd probably always be a tumbleweed. Olivia and Maggie had known that about her when they'd hired her. Had they thought their attractive hometown would work its magic on her?

She saw she had a text message from Vic. He'd be

back in the morning. Any excitement in sleepy Knights Bridge?

Ah…what to tell him? She realized how much she was looking forward to seeing him and typed a quick response. I'll tell all when you get back.

Intrigued.

Safe travels.

But as she finished her wine, she knew she wouldn't tell Vic *everything* about today. She'd skip the part about her attraction to Adam Sloan. All in all, she was proud of how she'd handled herself today, and that was all Vic needed to know.

She finished her soup, locked all the doors and headed to her suite, appreciating the peacefulness of her surroundings. She'd change into her warm, comfy pj's, pour another glass of wine and enjoy the quiet, rainy evening.

Only her mother called.

Adrienne tied her flannel pajama bottoms. "Mom," she said, answering her phone.

"What's wrong?"

She smiled. Leave it to Sophia Portale to zero in on her daughter's state of mind. "Nothing. Just pouring wine and settling in for the night. We're three hours later here. But it has been a day." She explained what had happened. "It all worked out. Just about everyone in town was ready to get out in the woods."

"That's great. About the town, I mean, not the situation itself. And you haven't been there a week. Well, no wonder you've poured wine. Is Vic joining you?"

"He's out of town. I haven't seen him since I got here."

"Oh. I see. Well." Her mother cleared her throat. "None of my business."

"I'm not abandoning you for him—"

"Of course you aren't. That never occurred to me. I was surprised you took this job, but it's your choice. You like it so far?"

"Yes." No hesitation. Her mother would have noticed. "It's cool and raining."

"And you're not feeling restless."

"Not really." *Not yet*, she almost said.

Her mother sighed. "It's been quite a year for you," she said.

"It sure has. How are you?"

"I've joined a CrossFit gym. I need to work on strength training. It's two blocks from the house. That'll help me be consistent."

"Good for you, Mom. I'm working on adding some fitness equipment at the inn, but it's not a priority."

They chatted for several minutes. A few highlights of her life suited her mother in phone conversations. She preferred deeper in-person talks, not that any were planned. Her life was filled with work, work-related socializing and exercise. But she and Adrienne were close in their own way.

"I'm glad you called, Mom."

"It's always good to talk with you. Call anytime."

After they hung up, Adrienne pulled the shades,

Five

Adam dropped off the dinosaurs at Brandon and Maggie's house, a fixer-upper off South Main in the village. It was raining when he went inside. His hand hurt like hell but it'd be okay. He'd had a mad urge to kiss Adrienne Portale when they were together in the inn's kitchen but it was just as well he hadn't. She was Vic's daughter. Carriage Hill's new innkeeper. He didn't think she'd have turned him away. Washing the dinosaurs in the kitchen, drying them and bundling them up, he'd sensed she'd been thinking about kissing him, too. But it'd been a weird day, so maybe not.

Brandon gave him some ibuprofen for his hand. He and Maggie were just back from the hospital where she had her head looked at—she got stitches but there was no concussion, at least. Christopher had hung out with the boys but had now left for the firehouse. Maggie was raging. Adam wasn't surprised given her personality and the scare she'd had. The boys were watching a movie while she "rested," but she was at the kitchen table, barely able to stay seated. "I've had it with those damn dinosaurs. Next time the boys can pull weeds for entertainment. They get lost in their fantasies. If they'd been doing something useful, they wouldn't have freaked out about a moose and taken off in the wrong direction."

"They might have freaked out more if they were bored out of their minds pulling weeds," Brandon said.

Adam wasn't getting in the middle of this one. Brandon dumped the dinosaurs out of the towels onto the table. He unearthed a velociraptor and stood it on the table in front of Maggie. "I don't know. The boys would come across worms and slugs weeding. That could fire up their imaginations, too, maybe more so than this baby since worms and slugs are real. Might run into a snake while weeding, too. You come across snakes in your work, don't you, Adam?"

"Sometimes."

He decided not to mention he'd almost stepped on a garter snake in the pile of rocks and old mortar behind the new addition at Carriage Hill. He hadn't said anything to Adrienne, either. Moose and bears were enough to have on her mind without adding snakes.

Maggie was unmoved. "I don't care. The boys wouldn't think a slug is a dinosaur."

Her eyes were sunken, the toll of her head injury evident—if not to her. Adam spotted a saltasaurus with his name printed in black marker on its belly and edged it deep into the pile of dinosaurs. He saw a couple of others from his boyhood days. He hadn't saved them. His mother, maybe? Christopher? Heather? Didn't matter. Adam wasn't going to expose more Sloans to Maggie's wrath.

"The boys can't live in a bubble," Brandon said. "They knew what to do when the moose saw them and then when they realized they made a wrong turn. It worked out."

"Imagine if they'd come across a fox or a bear or a fisher cat—"

"Or a pissed-off squirrel."

Maggie glared at her husband. "Do not make fun of me, Brandon Sloan."

"I'm not. I've stumbled on pissed-off squirrels. They can get nasty."

She sputtered into a reluctant laugh and shoved the velociraptor at him. He grinned at her and returned the dinosaur to his pals on the table.

"You haven't had stitches in years," Adam said. "There was that time in high school—"

Maggie moaned. "That was Brandon's fault."

Of course. Adam smiled. "Figures."

"It *was* your fault, wasn't it, Brandon?"

He shrugged. "It was an accident but yeah—my fault. I've got to own that one. Hatchet slipped out of my hand while I was trimming cordwood and the blade embedded itself in your thigh."

"Ten stitches," Maggie said.

"Could have been worse," Brandon said.

They'd be fine, Adam thought. He left them in the kitchen and stopped in the living room to check on the boys. They were engrossed in their movie—no surprise it was about dinosaurs. Their favorite topic these days. He cleared out. The rain had faded to drizzle but would pick up again.

Brandon followed him out to the street. "Thanks for today, Adam."

"Sorry I wasn't there when the boys ran into the moose."

"One of those things. Adrienne seemed to handle the situation well."

"Yeah. She was steadier than I'd have expected after the drama last winter with Vic."

"Pretending she was just the daughter of an old friend who was willing to house-sit for him. I guess I don't blame her for wanting to see what he was like before telling him she was his daughter. Think she'll last at Carriage Hill?"

"I haven't thought about it."

"I wonder how Vic feels about having her here."

Adam shrugged. "He's out of town. He hasn't seen her since she arrived. Seemed fine about it when he left."

"Maggie's happy with her. Olivia, too. Guess that's what counts."

"Maggie will have a hell of a headache tomorrow."

Brandon nodded, rubbing the back of his neck. "You got that right. Thanks for everything today. Good you found the boys. What made you think they were in the cellar hole?"

"It's where we'd have gone at their age."

"No moose around here back then."

Brandon went back inside. Adam headed to his van. He could feel the ibuprofen starting to work on his hand.

It'd be fine by morning. He hadn't realized Brandon had harbored similar reservations to Adrienne's return to Knights Bridge—as someone more likely to cause trouble than to resolve trouble. He took her actions today as a positive sign. Olivia and Maggie needed someone with enough confidence and backbone to get the workload at the inn organized and delegated. Maggie in particular wasn't what anyone would call a master delegator. Her tendency to take on too much had contributed to a months-long separation and near-divorce, but Brandon, an adrenaline junkie with dreams, had made his own contributions. Adam appreciated his sister-in-law's can-do nature and his brother's high energy. He was glad they had decided to stay together. Today hadn't seemed to stir up old grievances between them.

He got in his van and started the engine. He pictured Adrienne as she'd pushed back her dark hair with one hand, her eyes shining, her mouth full and...

Yeah. Best he'd resisted. He didn't need to be the one causing trouble. Brandon was still on high alert. He'd have figured out what'd happened in a heartbeat, and Adam didn't need that. Neither did Adrienne.

The drizzle changed to rain again on his drive out to Echo Lake, past the small farm where Maggie's widowed mother, Elly O'Dunn, had extensive vegetable gardens and kept a dozen or so goats. She had a tendency to overdo, too. She and Vic Scarlatti had become friends over the years, even more so since he'd retired and moved to Echo Lake full-time. If it was more than a friendship, they were doing a good job keeping it a secret. Adam doubted it was, at least at this point. Vic and Elly both needed friends, good neighbors. They would be hesitant to risk what they had by introducing romance.

His take, anyway, Adam thought. But what did he know?

He made the tight turn onto Vic's winding driveway. The classic 1912 Arts and Crafts lake house was silhouetted against the stormy sky, situated above the lake amid evergreens and mature shade trees. Vic had owned the property for twenty years but had only gotten around to much-needed renovations after he retired. He'd hired Sloan Construction. Heather had overseen the initial work, and Adam had restored and rebuilt much of the stonework at the house and added a wine cellar—per wine expert Adrienne Portale's specifications.

He'd had some pleasant conversations with her before she'd headed west to work at Noah Kendrick's winery. He'd definitely noticed she was attractive, energetic and sorting out her life. He figured the sorting out had to do with her career, maybe a romantic breakup. He'd been as surprised as everyone else in town that she was Vic Scarlatti's daughter, unbeknownst to Vic.

Work on the sprawling lake house had been a fun project, and Vic an easy client. The renovations had gone faster than expected, in part because Vic had moved into his guesthouse and let the construction crews do their jobs without micromanaging and time-intensive changes. *Do your thing, ladies and gentlemen* was Vic's mantra. He'd moved back into the main house in early August, ahead of schedule. That had turned out to be perfect timing for Adam. He'd just flipped a house in town and was bunking with his folks until he figured out whether he wanted to flip another house or settle down somewhere. Vic offered to give him a break on rent in return for looking after the place and repairing a stone wall by the driveway that a delivery truck had slid into after a summer deluge.

Their arrangement hadn't been part of any grand plan but instead a spur-of-the-moment decision. Adam had stopped by to check on a stone wall that needed repairing and found Vic playing Scrabble on his iPad on the front porch overlooking the lake, and they'd struck a deal.

Done, just like that.

Adam parked at the guesthouse, tucked among evergreens close to the lake. It was small, only about forty years old. It had never been much structurally. He didn't consider the two-bedroom cottage worth renovating, but if Vic ever got to the point of sinking some money into it, Justin would make that decision. He was the head carpenter with Sloan Construction. Adam knew carpentry but he didn't have his brother's expertise. He looked after the company's finances and he did stonework. Full stop.

He greeted Violet, his eight-year-old golden retriever. He usually took her with him on the job but hadn't today. She'd woken up lazy and he'd let her have a day on her own. He got a beer out of the fridge and took her down to the lake. The rain had let up again, at least for the moment. She chased a few leaves and dug up a small stone while he drank his beer. He had a long list of things he should have gotten done today and hadn't, but he was good with that.

He glanced back at the guesthouse, a perfect spot any time of year but particularly through summer and into fall. Vic had encouraged him to have friends and family visit. He'd figured he didn't have to worry about wild parties with Adam. True enough. He'd had Brandon and Maggie out here with the boys to swim. He and his brothers had enjoyed a few beers by a fire on the beach, or what passed for a beach—a thirty-yard stretch of sand along the water's edge.

A smattering of stars peeked out from the shifting clouds but Adam knew they wouldn't last, not tonight. Although he'd lived in Knights Bridge most of his life, he'd never spent much time on Echo Lake. He'd heard an ambassador owned a place in town but hadn't gotten to know Vic until the past year.

If Vic had known he had a daughter growing up in California, would he have been a part of her life? Adam wanted to think so, since he liked Vic, but it wasn't any of his business. And his mind was on other matters—such as just how much he'd have enjoyed kissing Adrienne.

"Damn."

She had proved more competent today than he'd have expected, not out of meanness, he thought, but because of her background and newness to her innkeeping job. He'd been pleased to hear Maggie and Olivia were hiring an innkeeper but surprised when he found out it was Adrienne Portale. But no one had asked his opinion and he hadn't offered one. A good thing, since Adrienne had done well today. She'd been calm, focused and on her game despite her unfamiliarity with the woods or the missing boys themselves.

He and Violet returned to the guesthouse. A quiet evening was in order. The rain started up again, and he listened to it hitting the roof and deck as nightfall descended. He got another beer and threw together some dinner. Meaning he microwaved a burrito. He took it into the living room and went over his work for the next few days.

He had a lot to do before winter. Best he focus on that instead of the new innkeeper in town. He was relieved he hadn't tried to kiss her. Between Vic, the guesthouse, the friends who owned Carriage Hill and his own history with women who weren't suited to the kind of life he wanted—yeah, he thought. He wasn't going to be kissing the new innkeeper anytime soon.

Vic Scarlatti returned to Echo Lake while Adam was drinking coffee and taking a look at the section of a stone wall, original to the property, that had taken a hit a few weeks ago. It'd be an easy fix, but he also noticed a section where the mortar was crumbling. New England was rough on mortar. Last night's rain had ended. The grass, still wet, glistened in the morning sun.

He watched Vic climb out of the rear passenger seat of a sleek black sedan. The driver got Vic's bag out of the trunk and set it on the stone walk. Vic thanked him and the driver got back behind the wheel. In a moment, the car eased down the driveway. Adam wasn't surprised Vic had arranged for a car to drop him off. Vic wasn't one to endure unnecessary trouble or discomfort. In his world, driving himself to and from the airport or even enlisting a friend to do it was out of the question. Frugality wasn't his thing. He'd spend his last penny on his deathbed.

For all Adam knew, though, the private car was covered by whatever entity had whisked Vic off this past week. He hadn't explained but Adam had deduced from the available evidence that this trip wasn't a mini vacation. It had come up at the last minute, and Vic hadn't exactly thrown golf clubs into the trunk of the car that picked him up. Whatever he'd been up to, it was likely related to his diplomatic experience.

He walked over to the stone wall and greeted Adam with a cheerful good-morning. He was wiry, with thick gray hair and dark eyes that reminded Adam of Adrienne. He hadn't noticed a resemblance last winter. Vic wore lightly rumpled but expensive clothes. Sport coat, polo shirt, khakis, walking shoes. Given his decades of experience as a foreign service officer, he was accustomed to travel. He'd said he didn't miss it. Adam wondered about that. "Morning, Vic," he said. "How was the trip?"

"Fine but I missed the lake. I stopped by Elly's place to see about Rohan." Rohan being Vic's rambunctious golden retriever, not yet a year old. "She said he'd been into the thistle. She was grooming him. I told her to have at it. I'd have begged her to tackle the thistles if he'd been here instead of with her. She'll drop him off later."

Adam had de-thistled a number of dogs in his day, including Violet. Rohan would have been a challenge.

A puppy, but also Vic Scarlatti's puppy—his first one. Training had been haphazard. "I don't mind looking after him next time you're out of town."

"Violet wouldn't mind?"

"She and Rohan get along fine."

"Golden retrievers. They get along with everyone and everyone gets along with them. I'm not planning a 'next time,' at least not soon." Vic glanced at the damaged stone wall before shifting back to Adam. "Elly told me her grandsons took off yesterday at Carriage Hill. Adrienne found Maggie injured."

"It all worked out," Adam said without elaborating.

"Yeah. That's what Elly said. She's on Maggie's case about resting but doubts she'll listen. Busy time of year with school starting and fall coming up. Did the boys really see a moose?"

"A big one, apparently."

"I've seen moose out here. I can understand mistaking one for a dinosaur."

Adam couldn't and the boys hadn't mistaken their moose for the dinosaur. That had been their sense of drama in overdrive. He tossed the remains of his coffee in the grass. "The boys got away from the moose and got turned around in the process. It's easy to do out there, even without a moose."

"And Adrienne—she's okay out there by herself?"

"No reason to think otherwise." Adam kept his expression neutral. No point letting Vic start wondering about the local stonemason, too. "Olivia and Dylan are just up the road. Adrienne can always give them a shout if she needs to. She's not as isolated as you are here."

"That's for damn sure."

"How was your trip?"

"Interesting if only to me but no complaints. Good to be home."

"I bet. No problems here while you were away."

"Excellent." He narrowed his eyes on Adam. "What's on your mind?"

A perceptive man. "It can wait. I don't want to spoil your reentry home."

"Go ahead. Spit it out. I've had three cups of strong coffee since my flight landed in Boston and then I sat in a car for two hours with nothing to do but twiddle my thumbs. I'm jittery. Might as well talk to me before my caffeine crash."

"Okay. Did you tell Adrienne I'm living in your guesthouse?"

Vic rubbed the back of his neck and made a face. "I haven't gotten around to it."

"She's been in Knights Bridge for almost a week, Vic."

"That's correct."

"Vic."

"What?"

"Tell her. It's not up to me to tell her. Why risk turning nothing into something? She'll wonder why you kept it from her. The longer you wait, the worse it'll get. I don't want to get stuck in the middle."

"Yeah, well, I don't blame you for that. She can be a hothead. Reminds me of my mother." He blew out a

breath and lowered his hand, looking tired and preoccupied. "I didn't tell Adrienne about you because I had
this trip come up and had to pull things together. She
was busy getting ready to head east. Then she was getting settled at the inn. And I didn't tell her because it
is nothing. You're living in my guesthouse while you
look for a new place and help out here. Why should
Adrienne care?"

"Not buying it, Vic. You know you should have told
her."

"Yeah, yeah. You're right."

Adam brushed loose dirt off his right thigh. He
didn't know much about Vic's relationship with Adrienne, but it wasn't any of his business. Now he wished
he'd kept his mouth shut. That was his default. "Did
you know she was returning to Knights Bridge to take
the job at Carriage Hill before you offered me this
place?"

"Yeah, but so what? I told her she could stay with
me here at the house, but she wanted to go all in and
decided to move into that brand-new innkeeper's suite
at Carriage Hill. I haven't seen it yet. Have you?"

Adam nodded. "I helped paint the walls and woodwork and move in the furniture."

"I hate painting," Vic said with a shudder. "Bores the
hell out of me. It's a good thing I didn't have to make a
living in construction. I'd have starved. I'm all thumbs.
I don't even know how to hang a picture. What do you
think about when you're painting?"

"Painting."

"Ha. Stay in the moment. Smart, I guess. Or just not

going to tell me? Never mind. I warned you I'm jittery. Don't you have a job out at Carriage Hill?"

"I'm reconstructing an exterior stone wall that was dismantled when they did the addition. That's why I was out there yesterday when the boys took off."

"You could have mentioned the guesthouse to Adrienne yourself."

"Nope. That's your job. Not taking you off the hook, Vic."

"Think she was waiting for me to offer it to her instead of just a room up at the house?"

"Ask her."

"I could do that." Vic toed cracked mortar in the wall. "You don't think she *wanted* to move into the guesthouse, do you? She's not mad at me, is she?"

Jittery covered it, Adam thought as he watched Vic mess with the mortar. A good walk along the lake would help him settle down, but Adam wasn't handing out advice. He glanced toward the lake, the water choppy, shimmering in the sunlight. He turned back to Vic. "I talked stonework with Adrienne when she was out here this past winter, and I spent a short time with her yesterday searching for the boys. I couldn't say what she wants."

"That's the point, isn't it? I don't know, either. I didn't ask." Vic stood straight and blew out a breath. "Hell."

"If she does want to stay at the guesthouse, I'll move out. It'll only take me a couple of hours to pack up. I don't have much stuff."

Vic rubbed the back of his neck again, as if he were

in pain. "Then I'd have to pay cash for anything you do around here."

"We'll figure something out."

"You could stay at the house. There's room. You can't go back to your parents' attic. How long were you there?"

"Two weeks. It was always a temporary arrangement. It's my sister's old room. She had it decorated to her taste at nine."

"It still has her rosebud wallpaper."

Adam grinned. "Elly told you that?"

"You did. You were grumbling about it one day when you were up here, and I overheard you. You weren't sure you could cope."

Adam remembered now. "Heather would have my head. She still likes those rosebuds. I probably could handle morning glories or ivy or something. I couldn't deal with the rosebuds, though. But it's the canopy bed that got to me. She painted it black when she turned thirteen. I feel like I'm at my own funeral."

"A black canopy bed in an attic, and rosebud wallpaper." Vic laughed in amazement. "Your parents must have kept the room as is to keep any of you from staying for too long, including Heather given how her tastes have matured. Air-conditioning?"

"No AC, Vic. Come on. It's New England."

"I had AC added here when I redid the house. I can't deal with heat and humidity. I know you'd managed in Heather's old room in the attic, but living out here while you repair the stonework makes sense. Enjoy the lake before cold weather sets in. Figure out what's next for you. Let me worry about Adrienne."

"Works for me," Adam said.

From what he'd heard and had witnessed himself, Vic liked playing the benevolent country gentleman. Before he retired, he'd blow into Knights Bridge for a few days, maybe a couple of weeks in summer and over Christmas, and then blow out again, back to wherever he'd been assigned. He'd admitted having difficulty adjusting to retirement. He was only in his early sixties and could have continued working, but he'd passed up assignments, given up his apartment in New York and moved to the country full-time.

Adam set his mug on the stone wall and squatted down for a closer look, aware of Vic not moving on to the house. Adam glanced up at him. "You're hopelessly bored, Vic."

"I've only been back here five minutes."

"You're used to more drama in your life. Only so much drama beating iPad Scrabble."

"That's why I'm writing my memoirs."

"Ha. Right."

Adam wasn't about to ask Vic for details on his memoirs—or his latest Scrabble game, either. He'd already dodged questions about this trip he'd been on. "I have to run out to Carriage Hill." Adam flicked a chunk of loose mortar off the wall and stood straight. "I won't volunteer anything about the guesthouse to Adrienne, but I'm not keeping secrets."

"Didn't ask you to," Vic said.

"Just so we're clear."

"You might be the quiet Sloan brother, but you're as hardheaded as the rest of them. I'll tell Adrienne you're in the guesthouse next time I see her—probably later today. Okay? I don't think she's going to care one way or the other. She's doing well, getting settled, learning the job. She's never been an innkeeper. I didn't want to distract her, but at the same time, I don't know why you living here would be a distraction."

Adam wasn't going there. "You look guilty, Vic, just for not telling her in the first place."

"I look oblivious. There's a difference."

"Fair enough." Adam figured he'd made his point. He didn't want to be a source of tension between Vic and his daughter. "Honesty is always the best policy. Isn't that what you diplomats say, or is that too simplistic?"

"It's a decent cliché. Discretion is sometimes the better part of valor. That's another good one."

"We could go on all day." Adam grabbed his jacket off the wall. He would need it today. "I'll see you later."

"Have the whiskey ready if Adrienne chews me out and I need a drink."

"I only have beer."

"Beer will do," Vic said, stretching and then heading up to his lake house, walking as if he dreaded every step.

Drama, Adam thought. Vic was used to more going on in his life than he'd had in Knights Bridge, even with discovering he had a daughter from a thirty-year-old fling in Paris.

Six

Adrienne was at her laptop on the terrace when Adam arrived with a golden retriever at his side. *Not* what she'd expected. Olivia and Dylan had dropped off their dog, Buster, earlier that morning. He was part German shepherd and had adopted Olivia during her first weeks living on her own at Carriage Hill, which meant he pre-dated Dylan. He leaped up from his spot in the shade and bounded off the terrace, but he and the golden retriever were obviously not strangers. Adam petted the big dog. "Hey, Buster. You do love it here, don't you, buddy."

"Who's your friend?" Adrienne asked, nodding to the golden retriever.

"This is Violet," he said. "Violet, meet Adrienne. Adrienne, meet Violet."

She got up from her laptop and stepped off the terrace, kneeling down to pet Violet. She was an older dog, not a puppy like Vic's golden retriever, Rohan. "Hello,

Violet. Do you help carry rocks, or do you leave that to Adam?" She looked up at him. "She's your dog?"

"She is."

"I don't remember meeting her last winter."

"I didn't have her with me that much when I was up at Vic's place then. He and Rohan were new to each other. Violet's used to a quieter life."

Adrienne stood straight. "She's lovely."

Violet strained on her leash to follow Buster back to the terrace, but Adam held her tight. "Settle down, girl." He eased up and smiled at Adrienne. "She and Buster can get each other worked up, but they'll be fine."

"I've no doubt."

He nodded to her spot on the terrace. "Keeping up with your wine blog?"

"Inn work. My blog's still on hiatus. I might resurrect it occasionally when I have something to say. Maggie, Olivia and I want to come up with a wine list for the inn. Simple, good wines."

"Doesn't have to be expensive to be good?"

"Not at all."

"I was hoping you'd say that." He paused, glancing at the garden, where so much commotion had happened yesterday. He had on another canvas shirt, this one a deep maroon that echoed the first tints of color in the surrounding landscape. "Has Maggie been in touch today?"

"Not with me. Have you heard from her or your brother? How's she doing?"

"I texted Brandon. He says she had a good night."

"It could have been so much worse yesterday. I try not to think about that."

"Yeah." He unsnapped the golden retriever's leash. "She won't bother you, but if she does, let me know."

Adrienne promised she would and returned to her laptop. Buster flopped on the terrace next to her. Violet collapsed into the grass by the addition where Adam was working. It was a perfect, lazy late-summer day to be a dog. Adam started to head in that direction but stopped when Maggie came out to the terrace from the mudroom.

Adrienne was surprised to see her this soon after her injury yesterday. "Maggie...you're looking well."

She groaned. "Better than I feel, I hope."

Adam frowned at her. "Did someone drop you off?"

"I drove myself. You didn't hear me? I parked behind your van. It's okay—I'm cleared to drive. I don't have a concussion. The gash looked scary because of the blood. Sorry about that. I hope you all left the mess for me."

"We did no such thing," Adrienne said.

"I'm so embarrassed. The boys feel guilty but it wasn't their fault I fell. I shudder to think how far they'd have gone if you two hadn't come along."

"Damn right," Adam said with a wink. "They found a good spot to hunker down. They'd have managed if they'd had to spend the night."

"If they'd run into some dangerous creep instead of a moose—"

"Maggie, don't," Adam said. "You can drive yourself crazy with what could have happened."

"I should know better, shouldn't I?" She smiled, a

spark in her turquoise eyes. "I'm an O'Dunn married to a Sloan."

Adam turned to Adrienne. "Small towns. Our two families go way back."

"That's an understatement," Maggie interjected with a wry smile.

"It's special to have such connections," Adrienne said. "You two have known each other since grade school."

"Since forever," Adam said. "I remember Maggie in pigtails."

"Ha. I remember you pulling them. You were a cute little devil, though."

Adrienne could imagine the two of them as children, here in their little hometown.

Maggie teetered slightly, and Adam swooped to her side and helped her into a chair. She mumbled a thank-you. Her jaw had discolored below the bandaged gash, and she looked stiff and achy—she had to have some decent bruises from her fall yesterday. "Everything is under control here, Maggie," Adrienne said. "I have plenty to keep me busy before we need to put our heads together again. Why not just rest today?"

"The girlfriends' weekend is coming up."

Adrienne pointed at her laptop screen. "I'm going over the schedule now."

"I need to meet with Felicity MacGregor to go over plans."

Felicity was a local event planner who'd also grown up in Knights Bridge. "You have me now, Maggie," Adrienne said. "I can meet with Felicity. I'm sure she'll know what questions to ask if I don't, and we'll report back to you."

Maggie hesitated. "Are you sure I'm not throwing too much at you at once?"

"Absolutely. It's not too much."

"Oh. Good, then. Thanks."

Maggie seemed slightly taken aback. Adam grinned at her. "You'll get used to having help." Buster rolled onto his back with a dramatic yawn. Adam rubbed his foot on the big dog's stomach. "Buster would have deterred that moose yesterday."

"I don't mind having him here," Adrienne said.

"You could do worse than a big ugly dog." Maggie started to lean over to pat Buster but grimaced in pain and sat back. "I'm not incapacitated, but I do have to remember I have stitches in my head. I'll check on Olivia while I'm here and see how she's doing."

Olivia didn't easily or naturally delegate, either, but she'd promised Adrienne she would give her space, especially with a baby on the way. Marrying a wealthy man had forced her to recognize she couldn't do it all. Dylan was a regular guy in most ways, but he did have a lot going on.

Maggie couldn't sit still and lurched to her feet too fast, swore, breathed, held up a hand to indicate she was okay and then headed back to the mudroom. "Don't rat me out to Brandon," she told Adam. "I'm *fine*."

"Just don't pass out," Adam said. "I'm calling him if you do."

"Deal."

Adrienne waited until Maggie shut the mudroom

door behind her before returning to her laptop. "I'm chipping away at getting more help here. It's been quite a year of changes in town."

"That's for sure. You're okay after yesterday?"

"I am, thanks. No bug bites, cuts or scrapes."

"Slept okay, then?"

"I made sure I locked all the doors. Obviously I wasn't worried about a moose breaking in, but yesterday reminded me I'm alone out here on the edge of the woods. Olivia said Buster could stay here anytime. Of course, I was at Vic's over the winter. Not exactly your metropolis." She smiled up at Adam from her laptop. "At least bears hibernate during the winter."

"Not something I've thought much about. I'll be here about an hour. Give a shout if you need a hand with anything. As a friend. Off the clock."

"Oh. Right." *Again* getting tongue-tied with him. She beamed him a smile. "Thanks." She hit a few keys on her laptop. "Hope the work goes well."

"I'll be up at Vic's this afternoon."

"He texted me a little while ago to let me know he's home. What are you working on at his place?"

"A section of the driveway wall hit by a delivery truck."

He didn't elaborate. Adrienne noticed his golden retriever wag her tail. "Nice to meet Violet. There's a story to go with her name, I assume?"

"A lot of Violet stories."

He patted Buster and went on his way, moving with the ease and control of a man in good shape, accustomed to the kind of often technical, often heavy work he did. Violet had settled into a spot in the shade next to the pile of rocks he was turning back into a wall. She wagged her tail again. It took some effort, but Adrienne managed to turn back to her laptop and get to work.

Maggie inched her way onto the terrace as Adam finished up for the morning. He sighed at her. "You look miserable, Maggie."

She plucked a spent purple blossom from a terra-cotta pot. "I had grand fantasies of harvesting herbs today."

"They'll keep."

"Not for long. They'll go to seed, there'll be a frost—"

"And you can do without them," Adam said.

She tossed the spent blossom—catmint, he thought—into a raised bed off the terrace. "I guess. How's your hand today?"

He shrugged. "Hurts."

She smiled at him, easing painfully toward the table. "You are a man of few words."

"It's not my first bruised hand and won't be my last. How's that?"

"Very stoic of you." She eased into a chair. "Adrienne's gone into the village to pick up a few things at the store. She's a great self-starter. I hate to think what would have happened if she hadn't come along yesterday when she did."

"I'd have found you."

Maggie gave him a feeble smile. "Lucky you."

"I'm heading up to the lake for lunch. Why don't I

drop you off at home? Adrienne and I can get your car back to you."

Her jaw set firmly. "I'm good to drive."

Adam frowned at her. "You don't look good to drive."

"I look worse than I feel."

He didn't bother hiding his skepticism but he wasn't going to argue with her, either. "Let me know if you change your mind. Violet and I will be taking off in about ten minutes."

But Maggie didn't linger on the terrace and headed inside by the time he finished work for the morning. He was climbing into his van when Adrienne returned from town in Vic's old Ford. She parked under Olivia's hand-painted The Farm at Carriage Hill sign, featuring a clump of chives. The homey sign and antique New England house didn't coordinate that well with the woman who jumped out of the car. Dressed in black, dark hair pulled back, sleek, hip and tempting as hell.

Adam offered to help her with her bags but there was only one.

"Will you be back this afternoon?" she asked as she shut her car door with her hip.

"That's the plan."

"See you then."

She didn't so much as glance back at him as she glided up the walk to the kitchen door. She had no problem opening the door despite her groceries. It shut behind her as she disappeared. Adam started his van. He'd watched her from behind the wheel. He gritted his teeth and started up the quiet road. Adrienne Portale was a woman he had no business wanting to touch.

He found Vic down at the lake, throwing a stick in the water for Rohan. Violet sank into the sand on the strip of beachfront, panting, eager to jump into the water herself but holding back, as if she knew Rohan might overwhelm her in his excitement to get to the stick. Vic's golden retriever puppy was obviously delighted to be home on Echo Lake. He swam eagerly out to the floating stick.

Vic, on the other hand, hardly gave Adam a glance, just stared at Rohan and the rippling lake water.

Adam shoved his hands in his jacket pockets. "Hell, Vic, you haven't been back here a full day and you're already bored."

"Not bored. Thinking."

"About what?"

"Who to get to write the foreword for my memoirs."

"Wouldn't it make sense to write your memoirs first?"

Vic shrugged, still without looking at Adam. "I figure getting someone interesting to do the foreword would inspire me to dive into the writing. I've been fiddling."

Adam had no idea if Vic was sincere about the foreword or rationalizing his procrastination. Either way, he still looked bored. "I guess that's something to think about while you throw a stick for Rohan."

"Rohan loves the water. I know I shouldn't stand out here thinking about who can write my foreword. I should live in the present, not launch myself into the future or back to the past." He kept his gaze on Rohan, who'd caught up with the stick. "That's the problem with memoirs. Reliving the past. Thinking about what might have been if not for the mistakes, the betrayals, the distractions and the nonsense."

"That's life." Adam pointed up toward the guesthouse. "I need to grab some lunch."

Vic turned, grinning knowingly. "I would, too. I wouldn't have wanted to talk about memoirs at your age, either. I don't want to now. I'm probably wasting time. My life wasn't that interesting."

"Then why are you bothering with your memoirs?"

"It's something to do besides play Scrabble on my iPad and throw sticks for Rohan."

"And why say your life wasn't that interesting? You're still in your prime, Vic. Shouldn't you wait another twenty years to make that judgment? Maybe you're writing your memoirs too soon."

Adam regretted his comment immediately. He absolutely didn't want to have a heart-to-heart conversation with Vic Scarlatti about his memoirs, his past, his future, any of it, especially not after lusting after his daughter most of the morning. Vic had friends who better understood him and the issues at hand. Let him talk to them.

"Fair points," Vic said.

Adam watched Rohan swim toward shore with his stick. "I'll be working on the wall this afternoon."

Vic grinned at him. "Go on. You don't need to listen to me. You have a living to make."

Rohan emerged from the lake, ran to Vic and deposited the stick in the sand. The puppy shook off, water spraying everywhere. Vic didn't seem to mind. He wouldn't have been so easygoing six months ago, but life on Echo Lake seemed to be growing on him. Despite his bouts of boredom and restlessness, he was settling in. He and Adrienne had restlessness in common, Adam thought as he headed up to the guesthouse with a reluctant Violet. He didn't know if Adrienne had picked up on Vic's restlessness when she'd house-sat for him last winter or if it was somehow genetic, or just a coincidence.

Didn't matter. He didn't need to figure out Scarlatti father and daughter.

Violet settled in her spot by the glass doors out to the guesthouse deck while Adam microwaved another burrito. He wasn't restless. He hadn't been restless even when he'd signed up for a stint in the Marines. He'd returned home to his work as a stonemason. It and restlessness weren't compatible, but he wasn't wired for restlessness. He was patient, thorough, focused and outcome-oriented, and he tended to live in the present. He'd never stand on the lakefront thinking about something like who to get to write a foreword for his memoirs.

After lunch, he left Violet sleeping in the living room and walked up to the main house. He grabbed work gloves out of his wheelbarrow, which he'd left by the wall he was repairing, and pulled them on. Maybe Vic's fantasies of retirement weren't stacking up with the reality. He liked having people out to the lake, but summer was winding own. Fall kayaking was still possible, but he wasn't much of a kayaker. Adam was. He'd go out whenever he could. Did Adrienne kayak?

He shoved such thoughts out of his mind. He glanced down through the trees. Vic and Rohan were walking up

to drive. She'd texted a few times about the upcoming girlfriends' weekend. She'd assured Adrienne she would be fine to do the catering. Adrienne had promised she'd get in touch if she had any questions. She understood it wasn't easy for Maggie to throttle back control. Her mother was like that, but not as much fun as Maggie O'Dunn Sloan.

And her mother couldn't cook for a damn.

Adrienne smiled, thinking of her generous, energetic, hard-driving mom. If Sophia Portale ever organized a girlfriends' weekend—an unlikely prospect on its own—it wouldn't be at a place like the Farm at Carriage Hill. Adrienne appreciated that her mother hadn't thrown obstacles and objections at her about her move east to take an innkeeping job and spend time with Vic. *If there's anything I can do to help, you let me know, okay, Adrienne? I don't know much about innkeeping but I do know marketing and business.*

What would her mother say about the sheet Adrienne was drafting for guests on what to do if they encountered wildlife? Moose, bears, wild turkeys...

She laughed and set the water bowl in the mudroom. At least she'd stopped thinking about Knights Bridge's favorite stonemason. Probably its only stonemason.

Buster lapped up the water, and Adrienne walked him up to the McCaffreys' barn. It was a beautiful afternoon, neither too hot nor too humid. Olivia and Dylan weren't around, but Russ Colton, a security consultant with California roots, was in the front garden and welcomed Buster back home. Adrienne had met him when she'd first arrived at the inn, and they'd gone over various security procedures. He was on Vic's Knights Bridge cheat sheet. He'd landed in town after she'd left for Kendrick Winery and had promptly fallen for Kylie Shaw, a popular author and illustrator of children's books who'd been living anonymously out on the river.

Another of those Knights Bridge stories with myriad tentacles, Adrienne thought. Russ was ex-navy and no-nonsense, and she was happy to have him on the case with everything from stray hikers to stray moose.

"Never hesitate to get in touch with me if you have any concerns," Russ said.

Adrienne promised she wouldn't. "Fortunately Knights Bridge is a low-crime town," she added.

"Fortunately."

It was the best she was going to get from him.

As she walked back down the road, she breathed in the woodsy smells and listened to the stream that ran mostly out of sight along the road, and she smiled at what a fish out of water she was here. When she arrived at the inn, she couldn't resist taking a peek behind the garden shed. All was well. No fresh signs of a moose. She smelled a hint of mint in the garden. She was accustomed to city life and was aware of how isolated she was on the dead-end country road, but that was part of its appeal. And it wasn't *that* isolated. It was quiet right now, but soon there would be a constant stream of contractors, guests and Maggie and Olivia's family and friends. Sloans, O'Dunns, McCaffreys, Flanagans, Frosts. It was quite a list.

She wasn't worried about intruders—human or animal—but she was feeling agitated and restless. She couldn't put her finger on why. Getting used to her surroundings, maybe. Her role, the number of people she was trying to keep straight but who all knew each other and her story.

She returned to the house, got the keys to Vic's old car and went out through the kitchen door, locking it behind her. She leaped behind the wheel and quickly yanked the door shut. She had no reason to suspect anything afoot in the woods adjoining the antique house. If she did, she'd talk to Olivia and Dylan—and Russ Colton.

But had she felt better having Adam around that morning?

It's not that, she told herself.

She wasn't used to not having neighbors on one whole side of where she lived. Just endless woods, and whatever was in them.

Adrienne drove to Echo Lake and parked next to Vic's much nicer new car. She didn't see Adam working on the damaged part of the wall. Vic had texted her about the delivery truck hitting it, before she'd arrived in town. This is what passes for excitement around here.

She'd thought he'd seemed amused, pleased, even, that his life wasn't as intense as it had been during his decades with the US State Department. Now...well, she had her doubts and couldn't help but wonder if he was as enthralled with retirement as he wanted to be.

She found him on the sprawling porch of his lake house, seated in a comfortable old chair with his iPad on his lap. She grinned at him. "You're playing Scrabble, aren't you?"

"Caught me. I'm losing and I have it on an easy setting." He set the iPad on a small side table he'd painted years ago and rose, taking her by the hand and kissing her on both cheeks. "Hello, love." He stood back, smiling at her, eyes crinkling with what she took as real affection and pleasure at seeing her. "Welcome to Knights Bridge."

"Thanks, Vic. It's great to be back."

"I'm sorry I wasn't here to greet you upon your arrival."

"No problem. How was your trip?"

"Frightening." He sat back down while she leaned against the wide rail. "I was asked to share my expertise at a seminar and a few private meetings and found myself almost wanting to go back to work."

"Key word being *almost*?"

"You got that right. How was your first week on the job?"

She wasn't convinced at the sincerity of his denial about not wanting to go back to work but let it go. "Everything's going great. I'm glad it's a quiet week—meaning no guests. Yesterday wasn't quiet."

"Ah, yes. Elly told me about the boys. She took their little adventure in stride. She knows her grandsons and found out after the fact. I think she's more worried about Maggie. Doesn't trust her when she says she's fine."

"The O'Dunns aren't easily thrown off their game from what I've seen."

"Had to be a scare for you, finding Maggie injured

and then discovering the boys were missing. She must have been terrified."

"She was. I didn't have much of a chance to focus on my own emotions."

"And Adam was there?"

"He arrived just after I found Maggie."

"I can see you doing what you had to do. That's one reason you'll make a fine innkeeper." Vic pointed at the iPad next to him. "I've been wrestling with voice-activated software all morning. Thought I'd like dictating my memoirs, but it'd be more fun dictating to a human being. I feel like I'm talking to myself, and the software's still adapting to my voice. I said 'gardening' and it typed 'regarding.'"

"I can see that happening."

"I should stick to typing. I swear I think through my fingers."

Adrienne noticed his iPad was open to the last of a Scrabble game between it and Vic. "Looks like you're playing Scrabble to me."

"I'm not procrastinating," he said. "I'm taking a break. I'm pondering the first chapter of my memoirs."

"Start with something exciting. Held at gunpoint, interrogated by cutthroat thugs. Then go back to how you got there and what's next."

He smiled up at her. "Being in a tense meeting won't cut it?"

"You mean you were never held at gunpoint?"

"I'm a diplomat, not ex-CIA."

"Well. Okay. Good luck."

"Disappointed?"

"No, nor surprised."

"But you don't know who'd want to read my memoirs."

"I didn't say that—"

"Doesn't matter. It's not an exercise in ego. It's… processing the past."

"I think I can understand that."

"I did intellectually at your age. Now it's at the gut level. Most of what I did isn't terribly interesting but some of it mattered. Rohan, did you say hi to Adrienne? Watch out. He's been rolling wet in sand."

"So I see," she said as Vic's adorable, rambunctious puppy came up to her, his tail wagging. Vic had cleaned him off but he was still wet, with sand stuck to his soft coat. She petted him and said hello. "Golden retrievers do love the water."

"I told him he could have a swim in the lake provided he *didn't* roll in the dirt afterward. I need to remember he's still a puppy."

"At least he didn't run off."

"Small favors. He ran off often enough as a little pup."

Rohan had been dropped out by the lake as a ten-week-old puppy, and Vic, who'd never had pets, had adopted him. Adrienne had been house-sitting then and had done what she could to help, including collecting puppy-training books from the library. She'd missed the rascal while she'd been in California.

Vic watched Rohan flop beside his chair and then eyed her. "What's on your mind, Adrienne?"

"Nothing. Well, life in the country. Do you ever get nervous up here by yourself?"

He shrugged. "I was here for a nasty thunderstorm about fifteen years ago. It scared the devil out of me." He got to his feet again and stood next to her. They looked out at the impressive view of the lake glistening in the late-summer midday sun. "You and I are used to different lives than the ones we have here."

"That's the idea, isn't it? We wanted something different."

"Life in small-town New England is definitely different," Vic said.

Adrienne spotted a pair of ducks out on the lake. So peaceful. "Knights Bridge was a break for you for twenty years. Now it's—"

"Forever."

She shot him a look. "Come on, Vic. You sound as if you've just been sentenced to life in prison."

"Do I? I don't mean to." He sighed at the view. "I'm an ungrateful sod. I couldn't ask for more than what I have here. It's perfect."

"The renovations worked out well."

"The Sloans did a great job," Vic said. "The plans kept everything that works about the house and zeroed in on what needed to be updated and changed. It kept the character."

"The Sloans are good at what they do."

"So are you. I'd have skipped the wine cellar but I'm loving it."

"See? Told you."

"Yes, you did," he said with a laugh.

Adrienne left him to his iPad and puppy and went inside to prepare lunch. Vic had everything organized. Maybe he was bored, but if he was, she thought it was largely because he was adapting to retirement more slowly than he wanted to or had expected he would.

He'd set out a nice New Zealand sauvignon blanc for lunch. She decided a small glass wouldn't ruin her for work that afternoon. She set lunch on a tray and took it out to the porch. Rohan was passed out in a sunny spot. Vic helped her set up lunch on a small table. They enjoyed the chicken salad, grapes, cucumbers, pickles and wine while chatting about the latest goings-on in town—weddings, babies, new businesses—and how her new job was shaping up. She told him about the innkeeper's suite and the busy fall season ahead, and what she planned to put into place to ease the burden on Maggie and Olivia—and ultimately herself as their first-ever innkeeper. Vic listened with interest.

"And you, Vic?" she asked him. "What are your plans now that cooler weather is upon us?"

"I can watch the leaves turn while I write my memoirs and play Scrabble."

"You went from assignment to assignment for forty years. It's an adjustment to go from that kind of life to being settled in one place. I think I inherited your nomadic spirit. Any regrets about your career as a diplomat?"

"Besides not knowing I had a daughter?"

"That wasn't your fault."

"It's not a question of fault, or maybe it is. I'm glad you're here now. I'm glad I'm here with you. How we got here…" He smiled wistfully, raising his wineglass. "The stuff of memoirs."

"It beats describing how you burned up fax machines and glared like no other diplomat in US history."

"We did have a fax machine start smoking on us once. Had to buy a new one."

They laughed together, and when they finished lunch, they cleaned up the dishes together. Adrienne could have sat out on the porch with him and finished the bottle of wine, but they put the rest of it away—"for later," Vic said.

He returned to his chair on the porch. "I take a twenty-minute nap after lunch as a rule and have for decades, but I think it'll be longer today. Tiring flight. I don't sleep on planes the way I used to."

"I'll leave you to it, then."

She wasn't ready to go back to the inn and Rohan wasn't about to let Vic nap. She took him down to the lake. He didn't have the ambition to go into the water and found a rock to chew on instead. She'd been surprised how much she'd missed this place after she'd moved back to California to work at the winery. As she came to the lakefront, she realized she shouldn't have been surprised. It was beautiful here. She'd come to love Vic, Rohan, the lake itself—and the town, this pretty blip on the map.

A breeze blew across the lake, strong enough to lift the ends of her hair. Rohan leaped up without warning and charged into the water. Something had caught his eye but she couldn't see what. Then he did a wide turn and swam back to her, a sodden chunk of wood in his mouth. He must have spotted it floating in the choppy water.

"Now, don't shake off on me." She got him to sit, at least more or less. He dropped the stick on command, if only to get her to pick it up and throw it for him. He was so eager, how could she resist? "Here you go," she said, flinging the stick out into the water.

He bounded off after it, spraying sand and water from his soaked coat. Vic had threatened to have Rohan's long golden hair clipped after catching him on the couch one time too many, but Adrienne and Elly O'Dunn had persuaded him not to. Puppy training wasn't on the list of Vic's many skills, but Rohan was doing fine, if not about to win any dog-obedience awards.

"He never gets tired of chasing sticks, does he?"

Adrienne recognized Adam's voice and turned as he strode down to the lake. "I didn't realize you were here," she said. "I didn't see your van up by the house."

"I parked at the guesthouse."

"Are you working on a stone wall there, too?"

He picked up a stone lodged in the sand and flung it into the water, far enough from Rohan and the stick he was fetching not to distract him. Adam watched the ripples from where his stone hit the water. "No," he said. "Just the one on the driveway."

Adrienne frowned. "I see. Collecting rocks down here? Taking a break?"

He shook his head and turned to her, his blue eyes steady. "I live here. Worked it out with Vic."

She stared at him. He lived here? She took a moment to absorb his words. "In the guesthouse?"

"Right."

"Since when?"

"I moved in a few weeks ago."

"I see. I didn't realize."

He kept his gaze on her. "Do you mind?"

She shifted from that penetrating gaze and watched Rohan swim back to shore. She was at a loss. It was Vic's property, not hers, but couldn't he have said something? But why should he? Why *would* he? She'd told him she planned to live in the innkeeper's suite when she took the job. He'd been getting ready to go out of town. He hadn't said much about it but it had to have been on his mind.

"Sorry." She cleared her throat, pushing back her surprise. She was more taken aback no doubt because it was Adam who was at the guesthouse, not someone else from town or even one of Vic's former colleagues. "Whatever you and Vic worked out is between you two."

"I assumed you knew. I'm repairing the stone wall and doing a few other things for him, and looking after the place when he's away. It's temporary but I like it out here."

"Who wouldn't? It's up to Vic. He can do what he wants."

"You mind," Adam said.

"I'm surprised. That's all. I love this spot. It's obvious you do, too."

"I can't imagine anyone not loving it. Vic said he'd tell you about our arrangement, but it probably slipped his mind." He paused, as if to let it sink in that he was being charitable about Vic. "I was bunking with my folks after flipping a house. It was a fixer-upper. I fixed it up and sold it. I was here to check on the wall that got hit and Vic suggested I move into the guesthouse until I figure out what's next."

"Makes sense." It did, didn't it? Why was she feeling so ridiculously off balance? It had to be Adam. She wouldn't have been nearly as frayed if Vic had offered the guesthouse to one of Elly O'Dunn's younger daughters, or Eric or Christopher Sloan—or anyone else in Knights Bridge.

Rohan capped her sudden sense of not belonging here by running up to Adam instead of her, wagging his tail, stick in mouth. Adam patted the eager puppy, who wasn't relinquishing the stick. "Rohan's a great dog," he said.

"I missed him when I was in California." Adrienne smiled past her weird sense of hurt. "I missed Vic, too."

"You have family out there, don't you?"

"In Northern California. My mother is on the go with her business and my dad—he didn't know Vic was my father, either. We're sorting out a few things, as you can imagine."

Adam nodded without comment. Definitely a man of few words. He got Rohan to be still and let go of the stick, but he didn't throw it into the lake. Rohan didn't object and flopped into the grass at the edge of the small sandy beach, then promptly rolled onto his back.

"Where's Violet?" Adrienne asked.

"Napping. She's not as young as Rohan." He left it

at that. "I'll be back at the inn in a little while. That okay with you?"

"No problem. It's been quiet. I haven't seen anyone or anything out back, including the moose."

"Having Buster and Violet around probably helps with the wildlife."

She smiled, brushing windswept hair out of her face. "I can always take Rohan with me."

"Rohan, huh?" Adam managed a quick smile. "He'd be a big help."

"He'd charm hikers and moose alike."

Adrienne thanked Adam—although she wasn't sure why—and convinced Rohan he needed to go with her back up to the house. She returned him to the porch and started to say goodbye to Vic, but he was snoozing, iPad on his lap.

She stood by her car a moment, watching the waves on the lake, stirred up by the wind. She loved this place on the small, quiet New England lake, but she felt no sense of entitlement to it whatsoever. If Vic wanted to work out an arrangement with Adam Sloan for the guesthouse, that was their business. She had no say or interest and probably shouldn't have an opinion, but she did wish Vic had told her. It wasn't as if he'd chosen a stranger over her. He knew Adam better than he knew her.

The suite at Carriage Hill could be used for guests. She didn't *have* to live there. It wasn't a requirement.

For sure she would feel less awkward and on edge if Vic had someone other than Adam living in the guesthouse.

"For sure," she repeated out loud.

"For sure what?" Vic asked as he came out to the driveway.

She turned from the lake and smiled at him. "Just talking to myself. I hope I didn't wake you."

"Nah, not at all. Restless?"

"Not at the moment. Adam told me he's living at the guesthouse."

"For now." Vic paused, looking guilty. "He's handy to have around."

"I'm sure he is. All the Sloans are handy. I'm better at finding people to do things than I am at doing them myself."

"You and me both. I remember the stonemason Adam apprenticed with. Crusty old loner but damn good at his work."

"You've known the people around here for a long time," Adrienne said.

"I have, yes. I got busy and didn't get around to telling you about Adam. I should have, but it wasn't a thing. I wasn't hiding it. I just didn't think to tell you."

"Not a problem." She opened her car door but didn't get in. "Let me know if I can help with your memoirs."

"You could end up being my only reader."

She noticed an edge to his voice despite his attempt at self-deprecating humor. "I understand you've agreed to speak at one of Dylan McCaffrey's entrepreneurial boot camps. You have a lot to offer on how to navigate the world."

"A good Scotch, a good pair of walking shoes and a good heart."

"There you go. That could be the subtitle for your memoirs."

He responded with what sounded to her like a genuine laugh. His dark eyes sparkled. "Good one." He motioned up toward the house. "I'll get back to it. See if I can teach that software to understand my voice. I'm in better spirits since I made a seven-letter word in my Scrabble game."

Relieved at his good mood, Adrienne said goodbye and got in the car. As she drove away from the lake, past Elly O'Dunn's farm and through the village, she felt at once a stranger in Knights Bridge, and at home.

Eight

⊰∙⊱

Adrienne found Maggie back at Carriage Hill, in the garden, assessing a half-dozen tall, bushy basil plants. "It kills me they might go to seed before I can make pesto," she said, sighing. "Basil doesn't like cold weather. A few cold nights, and these plants will be done for. It's almost Labor Day…"

"There's time," Adrienne said. "I've never made pesto but I bet I could."

"I freeze batches in ice-cube trays."

"It must be like having summer in the freezer."

Maggie smiled then, reluctantly. "I want to have a look at the cellar hole where you and Adam found the boys. It'll help me sleep, being able to picture it. I'm not an anxious person by nature but—" She licked her lips. "Let's just say last night wasn't good."

"You had a scare yesterday, and getting banged up yourself can't have helped. Are you up to walking out there?"

She stood straight, squaring her shoulders. "I am. Absolutely."

"I'll go with you."

"Would you? That'd be great."

Maggie was eager to go. Adrienne followed her through the garden to the spot behind the shed where the boys had played, encountering the moose, and then onto the path on the edge of the field. Maggie didn't move fast but she wasn't as unsteady as she'd been that morning, whether because she'd taken something for pain or was feeling better.

"Russ Colton has been overhauling security but a moose isn't anything to worry about," she said, slowing slightly as she brushed past ferns. "He wants to add an alarm system to the inn, but without overdoing it. Most of what he has in mind are passive steps we won't see. He's good." Maggie smiled back at Adrienne. "Buster doesn't count as passive anything, in case you were wondering. He was our security before Russ. But with Dylan's ventures—it makes sense to take reasonable precautions."

Adrienne agreed. They continued in silence along the stone wall. Maggie paused a few times to gather herself, but she never complained or turned ashen. Adrienne hoped the fresh air and exercise would do them both good.

They were about a hundred yards from the cellar hole when Adam eased in next to them. Maggie looked surprised. "How did you find us?"

"Vic's car, Maggie's van, no caterer and no innkeeper at the house."

"You put two and two together," she said.

He winked at his sister-in-law. "I also heard you."

Maggie grinned at him. "I hope you didn't think we were a couple of moose." She motioned vaguely ahead of her. "I want to see the cellar hole."

"Understandable. How's Tyler's leg today? I meant to ask earlier."

"It aches when he has to do his chores and isn't a problem when he wants to play outside."

"Sounds about right." Adam nodded back toward the inn, now out of sight. "I left Violet in the kitchen."

"She's a good dog," Adrienne said.

"She is," Maggie said. "I brought fresh bread from home. Violet won't steal it off the counter. Buster would."

"You didn't make bread this morning, did you?" Adam asked her.

"Got it out of the freezer."

There was no hint of defensiveness in her tone. Adrienne again could feel the tight bond between them, not just as siblings-in-law but as two people who'd known each other all their lives. He joined them as they continued on to the cellar hole.

Maggie immediately climbed onto the remains of the old foundation. Adrienne stood next to Adam by a birch tree. "Do you know who lived here?" she asked.

"No idea," he said. "You could probably find out at the library or historical society. Thousands of houses were torn down to make way for the reservoir and its watershed. This could have been one of them, but I'd guess it was abandoned before then."

"Someone who cleared out of New England and headed west in the nineteenth century."

"Possibly."

Maggie descended deeper into the cellar hole, to the spot where the boys had taken refuge from their moose. The rock on which Adrienne was standing wiggled slightly. "I don't want to collapse what's left of the wall."

"You won't," Adam said.

Despite his certainty, she decided not to take any chances and jumped off the rock into ferns. She did *not* want to break an ankle and have Adam carry her back to the inn, or even just skin her knee and look like an inept city girl.

"Are the cellar holes and stone walls protected?" she asked.

"Not by law, no."

"I guess it's not worth the effort and expense to mess with them unless you're developing the property. Do you ever scavenge them for your stonemasonry work?"

He shook his head. "There are other places I can get what I need." He pointed down the hill through the woods. "That's one of the small streams that feed into Cider Brook, which empties into the reservoir."

Maggie rejoined them. "Cider Brook used to empty into one of the branches of the Swift River before Winsor Dam was built. It's a north-south valley. That added to its attractiveness for a reservoir. This area was so different back when this house was built."

She stepped up onto a boulder and wobbled, but Adam caught her by the arm. "Steady."

She blew out a breath, shut her eyes a moment, then opened them as she smiled. "Phew. We don't need me to pass out and hit the other side of my head." She grinned at him. "Then I'd have matching scars."

"Not funny, Maggie," Adam said.

"Shall we count your scars?" She laughed and turned to Adrienne. "Don't mind us. Sloans and O'Dunns aren't known for being overly cautious, but I like to think we're not reckless."

"You know your own minds," Adrienne said.

"Yes, there you go. That's it, right, Adam?"

"Right. Sure thing, Maggie."

She sat on a boulder, catching her breath. She looked up at Adrienne. "Samantha was following Cider Brook when she and Justin met last fall. She ducked out of a storm into an old nineteenth-century cider mill he owns. It got struck by lightning and caught fire. Honestly. It's been through *hundreds* of storms without getting struck by lightning. Meant to be."

"Vic told me that story," Adrienne said. "Samantha was hunting for buried pirate treasure, wasn't she?"

Maggie nodded. "She worked with Dylan's father on his treasure-hunting expeditions. She was convinced a notorious New England pirate had ventured out here from the coast with his treasure and suspected he'd buried it along Cider Brook."

"Did you two ever follow the brook as kids?"

"Not Cider Brook," Maggie said. "Adam, you and your brothers followed it into Quabbin a few times, didn't you?"

"Yeah," he said. "I tagged along with Eric and Justin when I was seven or eight. They say I bitched and moaned the whole way."

"I would have, too," Maggie said. "Heather was never

interested. I remember that. Maybe if she'd had sisters like I did instead of you lot."

"She was always the smart one," Adam said.

Maggie got carefully to her feet. "No argument from me."

"Following brooks." Adrienne smiled. "Something to do growing up here. Do you still enjoy walking in the woods?"

"Today," Adam said. "Not yesterday with the boys missing."

"That's an understatement," Maggie muttered.

That was Adam Sloan, Adrienne thought. A man of understatement.

"I'm glad you found the boys before it got dark and rained," Maggie added. "It feels safe here. Safer than what I envisioned last night."

"Ready to head back?" Adam asked her.

"Yeah. Yeah, I think so."

"Head?"

She swallowed visibly. "Pounding."

He stayed close to her as they returned to the trail through the field back toward the inn. Adrienne glanced behind them at the cellar hole. "Do you just see the stonework when you look at the remains of an old house or stone wall, or do you picture the people who lived there—the people who built them?"

"Hard to picture them since I don't know who they were."

He was being intensely literal. It was probably deliberate. She doubted much he did *wasn't* deliberate. "Could any of them have been Sloans?" she asked.

"Maybe."

"Well, I'm envisioning cozy nights by the fire in days gone by instead of early death through infectious disease and such. I can smell a steaming pot of New England baked beans and see children contentedly reading poetry by candlelight while Dad fills the wood box and Mom darns socks."

Adam looked amused. "Would you know how to darn socks?"

"I hear skepticism in your tone."

"Not for no reason," he said.

"Mm. Yes. Your suspicions are correct. I have no clue how to darn socks. I'm not sure I even know what darning is. But I can read poetry. You?"

"I can load a wood box."

Adrienne laughed. "I can do that, too, and I expect I'll have to soon enough with summer winding down. What made you decide to become a stonemason?"

"Opportunity," Adam said. "I apprenticed with a master stonemason in high school. The work took."

"I remember him," Maggie said. "He was a third- or fourth-generation stonemason, wasn't he?"

"At least that."

"Your work will outlast you. Mine doesn't outlast the night. Well, unless there are leftovers. Then it lasts for a few days."

"But it tastes better than rocks," Adam said.

She turned to Adrienne. "Adam also handles finances for the family business. Justin and their dad hate it and Adam doesn't mind."

"Justin's not as cranky with Samantha in the picture,"

Adam said, good-humored. "She's as stubborn as he is. Someone else he can butt heads with besides me."

Adrienne could imagine the strong-willed Sloan siblings having epic disagreements, even as tight-knit as they were. She noticed a dinosaur figure lying on the side of the trail and scooped it up. "Know what it is?"

"I have no idea," Maggie said. "I'm not sure I want to know."

Adam glanced at it. "It's a gorgosaurus."

"You remember that from when you played dinosaurs as a kid?" Adrienne asked him.

"No. I recognize it from the movie *Walking with Dinosaurs*. Tyler and Aidan had me watch it with them one snowy Saturday afternoon while I was looking after them."

"You're a good uncle," Maggie said.

"It's a good movie, and they kept up their end of the deal and helped me shovel snow after it ended."

"Was it dark out?" Adrienne asked.

"Not that dark. Maggie and Brandon have lights at their place."

"We have streetlights, too, in the village," she added.

Adrienne pushed through tall field grass on the edge of the path. "I shoveled snow at Vic's on my own a few times. I often wondered what would happen if I tripped with no one out there. I always had my cell phone with me."

"Vivid imagination," Adam said.

"Very vivid when it's ten degrees, icy and dark." She held up the gorgosaurus figure. "Carnivore?"

He nodded. "Big-time."

She handed the dinosaur to Maggie, who slid it into her vest pocket. Adrienne glanced back across the fields, out toward the hill that gave both the inn and the dead-end road their name. Colorful wildflowers lit up the landscape. "It's so pretty out here," she said. "Maggie, have you and Olivia considered doing nature trails? We could make up guide sheets and markers. It's not a priority, of course—"

"It's a great idea. We just haven't had the time. We're *so* glad to have you, Adrienne."

Adrienne thought she noticed Adam smile ever so slightly, as if he were pleased with his sister-in-law's comment, but she couldn't be sure. "I'll see what I can do to get a start on walking routes. Keep it simple for now. Planning upcoming events and finding someone to do the towels and sheets are priorities."

"Makes sense to me," Maggie said, then went pale and sank—but Adam caught her by the waist before she collapsed. She rallied, insisting it was a momentary lapse, but he and Adrienne got her between them as they finished the rest of the walk to the house.

Maggie sighed when they cut through the garden to the terrace. Adrienne followed her gaze and saw Brandon Sloan pacing from the catmint across to a pot of yellow mums and back again. Adam glanced at his sister-in-law. "You did tell him you were going out to the cellar hole?"

"I figured we'd be back before he got here." She waved to her husband. "Where are the boys?"

"Up with Olivia and Dylan," Brandon said. "How did you do tramping through the woods?"

"We stuck to the field." As if that made a difference. "I could use a glass of water."

He motioned to a pitcher on the table. He'd also set out glasses and a plate of sliced apples and cheese. "I anticipated that when I saw you limping back here."

"I was not limping. I hurt my head not my legs or hips or—"

"Staggering. That better? I saw you, Maggie. You almost passed out."

"Almost passing out isn't actually passing out."

He studied her. "You look ready to keel over." He shifted to his younger brother and Adrienne. "Justin said she'd insist on going out there. Thanks for going with her."

"I already thanked them," Maggie snapped. "Honestly, Brandon, I'm not one of the boys."

He sighed. "I know."

She sighed, too. "I'm sorry if I worried you." She set the gorgosaurus figure on the table and scowled at it as she sank onto a chair, Brandon hovering at her side. "I'm tempted to throw the damn thing in the garbage. I guess it wasn't the dinosaurs' fault. The boys could have been weeding and the moose still would have startled them."

"It wasn't one thing that led to yesterday," Brandon said, handing her a glass of water.

"Yeah, I know. I'm trying not to get lost in all the bad things that could have happened but didn't." She picked up the dinosaur again. "Ugly fellow, isn't he?"

"I'm not sure it's a he," Adam said. He took the pitcher from his brother and filled two glasses, handing Adrienne one.

"Tyler mentioned they were one dinosaur short. He'd know," Maggie said, setting it back on the table. "I guess I'll look back fondly on their dinosaurs one day." She looked up at Brandon and Adam. "I should ask your mother if she does."

"Or maybe you shouldn't," Adam said.

She laughed, wincing. "It still hurts to laugh."

Brandon touched her shoulder gently but said nothing. Adrienne drank her water and half listened as Adam and Maggie chatted comfortably about family goings-on. The latest from Heather in London. Concerns about Eric, who apparently had been surly lately. Adrienne thought she had everyone they mentioned clear in her mind, but she didn't have Vic's cheat sheet memorized yet. She'd have to figure out how to manage her work with people coming in and out with little or no warning. Maggie and Olivia were used to a fluid schedule, but they had different roles.

Violet wandered out to the terrace. Brandon had left the mudroom door open. The golden retriever yawned and plopped at Adam's feet. "Lazy day," he said affectionately, petting her.

"I should have followed Violet's lead and taken a nap instead of tramping up to the cellar hole." Maggie helped herself to cheese and apple. "Don't say you'd have told me so if you'd had the chance."

Adam grinned at her. "Never."

"I wouldn't, either," Brandon said. "I'd have done the same thing and gone out there if it'd been me. You okay, Maggie? For real?"

"Yeah. Headache. Wobblier than I want to admit.

Getting rehydrated will help." She nibbled on her apple slice as she shifted to Adrienne. "I'm more outnumbered with the Sloan men than usual with Heather in London. Helps to have Samantha now. I thought Christopher and my sister Ruby might get back together, but she's still in Hollywood with stars in her eyes. He's not leaving Knights Bridge. He loves being a firefighter. And Eric…" She sighed. "I don't know what's up with him. Maybe nothing. It can be hard to tell with a Sloan."

"Saying we're hard-hearted as well as hardheaded?" Brandon asked cheerfully.

"Reluctant to show emotional pain," she said, clearly tongue-in-cheek.

"Ah. That." Brandon shrugged. "Eric and Christopher are fine."

Maggie smiled at Adrienne. "See what I mean?"

Adrienne wasn't getting mixed up in that one. She grabbed some apple and cheese. "Can I get you all anything else?"

Brandon shook his head. "Sorry for the trouble yesterday."

"The boys are safe," Adrienne said. "That's all that matters."

Maggie perked up. "I finalized the menu for next weekend."

"What's next weekend?" Adam asked.

"Eight women will be here. They've been friends since college, and they're all turning forty this year." Maggie turned to Adrienne. "I really should be here for your meeting with Felicity in the morning."

Brandon refilled his water glass. "But you don't need to be here, do you?"

Maggie adjusted her ice pack. "I trust Adrienne and Felicity completely, but I'm responsible for the catering, and with Olivia taking it easy—"

"You want to be helpful," Brandon said. "Adrienne, you and Felicity will let Maggie know if you need her for anything, right?"

Adrienne didn't answer right away. She read Brandon as trying to do his own part to help without being overly solicitous toward his wife and annoying her—a balancing act he hadn't always succeeded at maintaining, apparently. But Maggie smiled, setting her water glass on the table. "Don't worry, Adrienne. You won't get between Brandon and me. He's got a point." She shot him a look. "This time."

Brandon grinned at Adam. "Did you hear that? First time since fifth grade Maggie admits I have a point."

Adam held up a hand. "Adrienne isn't walking into that trap."

"I like staying busy and having a bunch of different things going on," Maggie said. "But I have a pounding headache just from doing a few things here. I don't want to end up back in the ER for overdoing it."

Brandon brushed a hand on his wife's pale cheek. "You're doing great, Maggie. It's easy for any of us to crank ourselves into overdrive."

"Sometimes I don't think I have a pause button, never mind an off button."

Neither Sloan brother responded. Adrienne had worked as a solo entrepreneur enough to appreciate

Maggie's drive and her sense of responsibility to clients and guests. She wanted the women arriving next weekend to have a wonderful time. If anything went wrong, let it not involve the food, the accommodations or the service. Maggie was good at so much but catering was her vein of gold. Having an innkeeper—even an inexperienced one—would help her concentrate on what she did best. Olivia loved design, color, painting and strategizing. Leaving the day-to-day operations of Carriage Hill to someone else made sense for both of them.

Adrienne glanced out at the flowers and herbs, a perk, for sure, for guests. "Eight women who've been friends since college meeting at an out-of-the-way country inn for a weekend. I have friends from my college days but not *eight*." She spoke lightly, but it was true. She doubted she could round up eight women friends, period, for a weekend get-together. "Maybe I'll have enough friends for a weekend get-together by the time I turn forty."

"You've been on the go since college," Maggie said. "You probably have friends all over the world."

"I try to make friends wherever I drop my anchor." *Why* had she gone there? She got up from the table. "I have a few things I should get to. Give me a shout if you need anything."

Maggie watched her head to the mudroom door. "It's an adjustment being out here on your own. If you'd like someone to stay here until you get your feet under you, we can arrange it."

"Thanks, but I'm fine. I love the quiet. Listening to the birds." Adrienne deliberately avoided glancing at

Adam, standing by the table, drinking his water. "I'm not nervous on my own here."

"Excellent," Maggie said.

Brandon helped her up. She admitted she was dragging and not up to driving. They decided to take her van and get Adam or Dylan to drive his truck back to the village. Maggie turned to Adrienne. "Adam will be here for a while. Let him know if you need anything. Thanks for going with me to the cellar hole. It was good for me."

"Same here," Adrienne said. "I was focused on the boys yesterday. It was good to get another look at it."

"I needed to do it for peace of mind. I'm sure I freaked out more than I would have because I took that tumble. I realized in the middle of the night that I really thought someone had pushed me…" Maggie stopped, her turquoise eyes narrowed with obvious pain. "But no one did."

She and Brandon left through the kitchen. Adrienne decided not to go straight inside after all and instead gathered the dishes from the terrace table. Adam helped carry them inside. She pointed vaguely toward the sink. "I'll clean up. Thanks."

"Need a hand?"

"That's okay. I've kept you from your work long enough."

"No problem." He went into the mudroom for Buster's water bowl. He filled it at the sink and set it back in the mudroom. Violet dived into it. "You'd think she went on our walk instead of lazed around here," he said, returning to the kitchen.

"Thirsty dog."

He picked up a dish towel. "Maggie and Olivia enjoy the work here, but it's good they recognized they needed more help and someone to figure it all out. How are you faring as an innkeeper?"

"So far, so good, but it's only been six days." Watching him dry his hands was proving to be ridiculously distracting. She tugged open the dishwasher. "I've learned the hard way I'm at my best when I focus on the things only I can do. It's not always possible, but it's a good place to start when deciding what to delegate. In other words, I know how to wash sheets and towels, but it's not the best use of my time."

"Makes sense." Adam placed the towel on the counter. "Going to straighten things out here and move on? You could be the Mary Poppins of innkeeping."

"At least she'd been a governess before taking on the Banks kids."

"Imagine those two confronting a bull moose." Adam worked his injured hand a bit, as if it was stiff. His bruise from yesterday had turned into a mix of purples and blues. "It's your first job as an innkeeper, but you're the type who likes to keep things fresh."

"A restless soul," she said with a smile.

He lowered his hand. "An unconventional innkeeper for an unconventional inn."

She loaded glasses into the top rack of the empty dishwasher. "You're a steady type, aren't you? That must be a plus with your work. What do you think about while you haul rock and such?"

He leaned against the counter. "Hauling rock and such."

"I suppose a wandering mind can be dangerous for a stonemason."

"Not always."

She felt his gaze on her as she rinsed off plates and added them to the dishwasher. "Do you think about your hopes and dreams? You know. Places you want to visit. Things you want to do. Do you keep a someday/maybe list or something similar?"

"Why wouldn't I just visit the places I want to visit and do the things I want to do?"

"Time, budget, work, family commitments." She shut the dishwasher. "Maybe you want to go to Paris *and* San Francisco. You can't be in two places at the same time. Maybe you want to build a house on Echo Lake but don't have the funds saved."

"So I'm supposed to keep a list of everything I might want to do someday?"

"Or might want to learn. Learning Spanish is on my someday/maybe list, for instance."

"Was becoming an innkeeper on it?"

He hadn't missed a beat. Adrienne sighed and grabbed the towel he'd used, noticed where it was damp from his hands. She didn't know why that felt sexy to her but it did. "Spending time with Vic was on it. Having a someday/maybe list helps. Seriously. Your mind isn't always at you, whispering *Paris* in your ear. It knows you're not going to forget. Your energy goes into where you need to have your focus, and things start to fall into place in your life—"

"And next thing I'm in Paris?"

She ignored his sardonic tone. "Something like that."

"I'm not making fun of you," he said.

"It's new territory for you."

He stood straight. "What else is on your someday/maybe list?"

"It's so long, I divided it into categories. Travel, purchases, experiences, learning. I go through them regularly and ditch what no longer interests me. It works that way, too. Writing something down makes it more concrete without taking action, and you look at it and go—*nah, I don't really want a new car.*"

"You don't want a new car?"

"I wasn't being literal," she said.

She saw the slightest smile and spark in those blue eyes. "I know," he said.

She grinned at him. "You're teasing me. Well, as a matter of fact, I *do* want a new car, or at least a good used one. Vic's loaner isn't going to last."

"That car has a lot of miles left in it."

"You're a waste not, want not Knights Bridge Sloan," Adrienne said. "Do you make *any* lists?"

"Groceries and supplies."

"What about tasks?"

"We keep track of jobs on the company computer. You're into lists?"

"I love lists. I have list templates. My generic packing list, for instance. I don't have to come up with a new list every time I drag out my suitcase—not that I'll be going anywhere anytime soon with this job."

She looked around the kitchen for something else that needed her attention. "What would you like to do if you took a trip?"

"Go someplace I could do a lot of walking and dig into the history and sights."

"Paris is great for that," she said. "It's a fantastic walking city and there's loads to see."

"Sounds good. I'll set up a savings account for Paris."

Adrienne eyed him. "You're not serious."

"Sure I am. Who doesn't want to see Paris? Jess Flanagan wanted to go to Paris for ages. She finally got Mark to go with her last fall. You know who they are, right?"

"I do. Jess is Olivia's younger sister who works for their family millworks. Mark's a local architect. He designed the addition here as well as Olivia and Dylan's new house and barn." Adrienne smiled. "Vic did a cheat sheet for me."

"Why am I not surprised? Another way to procrastinate writing his memoirs." Adam smiled, reaching down to pet Violet as she wandered in from the mudroom. "Jess and Mark's wedding was the first big event here."

And now they were expecting their first child, a boy, due not long after Olivia's baby girl.

Adrienne chose an apple from a bowl and polished it on her shirt, just to have something to do with herself. Adam didn't show any indication he was affected by the romantic changes among his family and friends. The man was steady, she thought. Definitely steady.

"Up for another winter in Knights Bridge?" he asked her.

"I haven't thought that far ahead. Last winter I was caught up in sorting out my relationship with Vic—if I even wanted one. I managed not to get arrested, but I can't say I enjoyed my first winter here."

"Hard to discover things weren't what you thought they were."

"And that my mother knew all along and didn't tell my dad or Vic."

"Vic's cool, though. It wasn't like she had a fling with some hapless jerk."

"That's true."

"Yeah." Adam left it there and stood straight. "I'll be by in the morning to work on the wall."

"Okay. I might stop by the lake later to see Vic."

"Sure thing."

He snapped his fingers at Violet. She hesitated, as if she wouldn't mind hanging out in the kitchen for a while longer, but she followed him out the front door.

A strong, patient man and his dog, Adrienne thought with a smile. She went out to the terrace. Maggie and Brandon had forgotten Tyler and Aidan's gorgosaurus. Adrienne picked it up. It was a fierce-looking fellow. "You can be my guard dinosaur for the night. Scare off any critters."

She set the figure on the table. She'd get it back to

its owners tomorrow. In the meantime, she'd work on plans for the upcoming fall events at the inn. *That*, after all, was what she was being paid to do.

Nine

⧸⧹

Instead of going to Vic's that evening, Adrienne indulged in a bath in her suite's new tub, sprinkled with Carriage Hill's goat's milk bath salts, and collapsed into bed early. She dreamed about bears and moose turning into dinosaurs and awoke in a sweat, heart pounding as she realized... *I'm okay. I'm in a quaint New England inn on a beautiful late-summer morning.*

Five thirty on said beautiful morning.

She moaned. "Ugh."

Couldn't she have dreamed about the Sloan brothers? Why not the good-looking stonemason brother? Muscular, blue-eyed, capable. Played with dinosaurs as a kid.

Dreaming about Adam wouldn't have been a nightmare, but that didn't mean getting carried away with her attraction to him wouldn't turn into a real-life nightmare. Dinosaurs were scary in a dream, but they were extinct in real life. Adam Sloan was *not* extinct. He was real, and he and his family were interwoven into Knights Bridge—into Vic's new life.

All of which made a certain sense at the crack of dawn.

She wasn't going back to sleep. She was wide awake now that she'd started thinking about Adam.

"You'd be better off having another nightmare about dinosaurs."

Muttering to herself, she threw back the duvet and rolled out of bed.

Best just to get up and on with her day.

The windows had insulated shades rather than drapes, but that was fine with her. She'd left them raised the first couple of nights since the windows looked out on the backyard and there were no neighbors. Who'd peek in on her, an owl? Bats? She wasn't worried. But she'd pulled them since Adam had turned up to work on the stone wall. What if she overslept? Wandered in from the bathroom and he was right there, hauling rocks and such? She'd decided she'd sleep better with the shades pulled.

She raised the shades and looked out at the yard in the early-morning light. Adam had made progress on the wall but probably not as much as he'd intended given yesterday's jaunt to the cellar hole. She pictured him working patiently, deliberately. What would happen if he became impatient, a bit less deliberate?

Adrienne groaned at the intrusive thoughts and forced them aside. She got cleaned up, pulled on clothes—black jeans, black top, sandals—and headed to the kitchen. She made coffee, poured a mug and took it upstairs. She immediately felt the soothing effect of Olivia's blend of contemporary and traditional furnishings coupled with the wide-board floors and other original features of the early-nineteenth-century house. Given her experience as a graphic designer, Olivia had a great sense of color, but she also had a natural instinct for how to make a room homey and inviting and yet feel unplanned. The previous owners had renovated the house with its becoming a bed-and-breakfast in mind, so the guest rooms all had private bathrooms, featuring, of course, Olivia and Maggie's goat's milk bath products.

As she sipped her coffee and shook off the last of her nightmares, she peeked into each of the guest rooms. She looked for anything she might want to bring up in her planning session with Felicity MacGregor later that morning. All the rooms were attractive, decorated with prints of herbs and New England wildflowers, embroidered pillows, painted furniture and Olivia's collection of antique linens. Two had fireplaces. Adrienne would happily spend a few nights in any of them.

She started back to the stairs but paused at a series of simply framed black-and-white photographs of old stone bridges and stone walls. They were beautiful, even haunting. A small typewritten note at a bottom corner of each frame identified the photos as spots in Knights Bridge. *Along Cider Brook. The Sloan Farm. Out to Carriage Hill. Echo Lake.*

She recognized the cellar hole where the boys had hidden from the moose. The image captured the sense of history she'd felt there. It wasn't signed, but the notes indicated all the photographs were the work of Adam Sloan.

"No kidding," Adrienne said aloud, in complete surprise.

Well, then. That sure was something to wrap her

head around, wasn't it? Adam was not only into photography but very good at it. Not that she was an expert.

But maybe she shouldn't be so surprised. He was a stonemason. He probably knew all the old stonework in the area, never mind just Knights Bridge, and given the nature of his work, he would have the patience to pull off such great photographs. She could see him getting together the proper photography equipment, figuring out the perfect angle, waiting for the right light—the time, the conditions, the moment. Then doing any necessary touch-ups on the resulting shots and choosing only the best ones to show to anyone.

But these stone walls...these stone bridges...

Looking at the photographs, Adrienne wanted to visit each place and touch the stones, the moss and lichens and leaves—to breathe in the smells of the New England fields, woods, lakes and streams.

Her own photography skills began and ended with her smartphone. Ninety percent of her shots were spontaneous and not worth saving or retouching. She seldom took the time to delete them. They just piled up in her cloud storage. If any were frame-worthy, it would be the result of serendipity, not patience or skill.

She returned to the kitchen and finished her coffee while she scrambled a couple of eggs with herbs from the garden. She made fresh coffee and took her breakfast out to the terrace. It was a glorious morning with no sign of unwanted or unexpected two-legged or four-legged guests, just bees humming in the flowers.

Adam didn't show up early.

Just as well, Adrienne thought as she got on with her day.

When Felicity MacGregor arrived a few minutes before ten, they decided to meet on the terrace. Felicity was an expert event planner with her own business in Knights Bridge—a definite plus for a new destination inn, entrepreneurial boot camp and adventure travel business.

Fifteen minutes into their meeting, Adam came around from the front of the house and headed to the rock wall with a quick wave of his free hand. "Don't let him fool you," Felicity said, her laptop open on the table in front of her. She was around Adrienne's age, a professional comfortable in her own skin. "Adam's as rough and tumble as his brothers. He just gets on with things. Don't think he's a pushover because he doesn't have a lot to say."

Adrienne smiled. "A word of warning?"

"An observation. Gabe and the Sloans have stayed friends since we were kids. The Sloans are a tight-knit crew." Felicity paused and grinned at Adrienne. "You have no clue who Gabe is, do you? Gabe Flanagan. Mark's younger brother. Mark is Olivia's brother-in-law—"

"The architect. Her sister Jess's husband." Adrienne thought back to Vic's cheat sheet. "Gabe just moved back to Knights Bridge?"

"Right. He's joined Dylan and Noah's venture capital office in town. They've brought in a friend from California—a woman, quite the entrepreneur. They're renovating a Victorian house by the library. Supposedly it's haunted." Felicity seemed inordinately pleased at that prospect. "Gabe and I are getting married. We've been friends since we were tots, and it turned into romance over the summer. Short version of *that* story."

"Another Knights Bridge happy-ever-after?"

"Yes. Another one. Mind you, I wouldn't have even imagined Gabe and me together a few months ago. More likely I'd have said I'd drown him in the river the next time I saw him."

"I understand there's a swimming hole on the river out by your place."

"It's heaven. Come out before the water gets too cold."

Meaning it was always cold, just not *too* cold. Adrienne thanked her for the invitation. She loved all the various small-town connections, but she had to work at it to keep track of them—who was related, who had deep roots in Knights Bridge and who had only just arrived. Vic fell into a gray area. He lived in town but wasn't completely a newcomer or someone with generations of relatives in a local cemetery. She didn't have even his tenuous ties to the town.

She and Felicity got to work. Felicity was organized and could grow her business and take on employees, but she liked being a solo entrepreneur and hiring freelancers when she needed more help. "My mother has her own business," Adrienne said. "She's achievement-oriented in a way I'm not and never will be."

"I thought I'd follow in my family's footsteps and end up in finance," Felicity said, matter-of-fact. "I hacked away in that world for a while. It wasn't my thing but it's helped me with my own business. I figure nothing's wasted. Does your mother give you a hard time about your career choices?"

Adrienne shrugged, aware of Adam working nearby. "She was more optimistic when it looked like I'd be a wine guru. Now she's given up, I think. We don't talk about it that much. She's happy I pay my own bills."

"Not one for a girlfriends' weekend at an out-of-the-way country inn, is she?"

Adrienne shook her head. "No."

"Thought not," Felicity said lightly. "What about you? Are you one for a girlfriends' weekend?"

"Well, I'd have to have girlfriends." Adrienne matched Felicity's lighthearted tone. "I do have friends, mind you, but I've moved around a lot and traveled a lot. So do most of them. We're scattered."

"The group coming next weekend are scattered, too. They met when they were students at UMass. Three live in the Boston suburbs and the rest are in Austin, Tampa, Chicago, Reno and Seattle. They've stayed in touch all this time."

"We'll make it a special weekend."

"Are you feeling ready?"

"No, but that's where you come in, and if I waited to be ready before I did anything, I wouldn't be sitting here with you, in this beautiful spot, planning a great weekend for a small group of friends."

They cruised through Felicity's event bible and applied the various steps to the upcoming weekend, breaking it down into simple, manageable tasks. The friends had left the details to her and Adrienne, with straight-forward guidelines. By the time they finished, they had a solid schedule in place, with times, who did what—anything and everything needed to make the weekend fun for the guests. Felicity had contingency plans for almost every potential emergency, from injuries and illnesses to fires and floods. "You don't want to have to think on your feet in a crisis," she said. "Of course, you can't plan for or predict everything."

Maggie Sloan recovering from a head injury, for one. She was still down to handle food but nothing else, and there was a backup if she wasn't up to it—although there was no reason to think she wouldn't be. Brandon would lead the friends on a hike. The atmosphere of the inn and the local area appealed to the women, and they wanted to spend time together as well as have time on their own. Felicity was setting up keepsake books for each guest. They'd arrive Friday afternoon and leave Sunday afternoon. They understood New England's fickle weather but Felicity and Adrienne had accounted for the possibility of a rainy weekend.

By the time Felicity left, Adrienne felt more in control of her first big weekend as Carriage Hill's innkeeper. Olivia and Maggie had known she was new to the work, but they'd put together a solid notebook of information, templates and protocols. Adrienne liked to think *not* being a local had its advantages. It was possible she'd see opportunities, holes and problems where someone who lived in town wouldn't.

Bears and moose in the yard, for instance.

At the moment only Adam Sloan was here. He walked from his work site across the lawn to the terrace. "You can come inside anytime you want," Adrienne told him.

"Use the facilities, whatever. It's shorter to get out front by going through the kitchen. I don't mind."

"Thanks. Not a good idea today. I'm sweaty and dusty."

Which somehow managed to add to his sexiness. She found herself noticing the sweat and dust on his muscled forearms. She cleared her throat. "Do you often see bears, moose, bobcats and such out here?"

"Rarely."

"What's rarely to you?"

Using a folded black bandanna, he wiped mortar or some other kind of dust off his forehead. "It means I don't see them often enough to think about it. I see deer a fair amount."

"In the yard?"

"On the edges." He tucked the bandanna into his back jeans pocket. "Why?"

"I want to get a better idea of what to expect—for guests more than for myself."

"Animals tend to keep their distance when a lot of people are here."

"Makes sense. If guests walk into the woods on their own?"

He shrugged. "I've never had a problem."

"Right. Okay. Good to know."

She gestured toward the rock wall he was rebuilding. "Work's coming along okay?"

"On schedule."

"Do you need anything from me?"

Just the slightest hesitation as his gaze settled on her. "I'll let you know," he said finally.

Heat spread up from her neck into her cheeks, but she decided best to blame the late-summer weather rather than her intense physical reaction to him. "I didn't get out to see Vic last night. I'll stop by later today."

"He'd like that. Come down to the lake. You two can throw sticks for Rohan."

"He really is bored, isn't he? Vic, I mean. Not Rohan."

"Writing his memoirs isn't enough for him."

She thought Adam might elaborate, but he didn't. "Maybe when he's eighty. Do you think he likes having me here? Never mind. That's not your problem. Are you sure you don't want a glass of water or something?"

"All set."

No chitchat. She almost brought up the photographs, but he took advantage of her hesitation to leave. She watched him cross to the side yard. He was one sexy man. No question about that, and she couldn't be the only woman in Knights Bridge to have noticed.

She shook off *that* thought and, after hearing his van start, went inside.

Adrienne took the back way along the stone wall to the McCaffrey barn. She spotted two gray squirrels, a chipmunk, a robin and chickadees. As she went through a gap in the stone wall to the barn, two butterflies swooped past her into the field.

She found Tyler and Aidan Sloan on the barn deck, lining up dinosaurs on the rail, table and chairs. She said hello and went through the glass doors. Maggie was in the kitchen area, apron on as she stood at the sink. "All dinosaurs present and accounted for?" Adrienne asked.

"That's what they tell me," Maggie said. "Brandon and I aren't letting the boys out of our sight. All we need is for them to wander off again. Eric will have us arrested." She smiled at Adrienne. "*Slight* hyperbole."

"That'd be quite the local scandal."

"Wouldn't it? I know I probably shouldn't be here but I couldn't sit home. I haven't been overdoing it. The boys were thrilled to get that last whatever-a-saurus back. Thanks."

"Gorgosaurus. No problem."

"How was your meeting with Felicity?"

"Great. I emailed a brief report to you and Olivia."

"Awesome, thanks. Olivia asked me to tell you that if you get spooked being at the inn on your own, you can always stay here. You'd be on your own, but at least it's closer to Olivia and Dylan than the inn. It's an alternative to Buster staying with you. Don't hesitate, and don't be shy, okay?"

"I'm fine. I love staying at the house, and the suite's fantastic."

"It can't be spookier than being at Vic's on your own last winter. That was before renovations, too. I suppose you could stay up there. You know Adam's living in the guesthouse, right?"

"Mm. It's temporary."

Maggie turned water on in the sink to wash off a colander filled with tomatoes. She looked better today, more rested, not as stiff. "The boys and I picked these at my mother's place this morning. I can't decide what to do with them. So many options." She turned off the water. "The boys want to be independent and think they don't need supervision. Phoebe and I wandered off a few times as kids but not as much as Ruby and Ava—the twins. They're the youngest. They were completely impossible. Phoebe and I went after them loads of times. Mom—well, you've met her."

"Not a worrier."

"To say the least. My sisters and I had a lot of freedom even when my dad was alive. I don't want the boys to be fearful, but I want them to take proper precautions. But enough of that. Do you want me to wait and read the email or do you have time to go over your meeting with Felicity?"

They sat at the table—with a good view of the boys on the deck—and Adrienne filled her in on the highlights. "That all sounds great," Maggie said. "I'm still good for handling the food. There's a backup plan if I had been injured worse. Felicity insisted we have backup plans once she took over our event management."

"So she said. Makes sense. We'll stay in touch, then."

"Olivia and a few of us are planning a movie night before the baby comes."

"Do you want to have it at the inn?"

Maggie sat back against her chair and smiled. "We want you to join us."

"Oh."

"Sorry. Olivia would have done a better invitation. We'll figure out a good time and let you know. We always have fun. You can advise us on wine, but only if it doesn't feel like work. We don't want to take advantage."

The casual invitation wasn't unusual for Knights Bridge, Adrienne had discovered. For a small town, it wasn't cliquish, but people weren't intrusive, either. If you wanted space, you got space. If you wanted to do things, you could do things. Maggie was particularly social. No surprise there. Adrienne appreciated the tight friendships and deep bonds among people who'd grown up in town, but they were open to newcomers, too. They didn't have to fit into a tidy box, either. That didn't mean there weren't disagreements, hurt feelings, outright fights and changes, some welcome, some unwelcome.

She walked along the road down to the inn. She wasn't sure when or if Adam would be back. He seemed to work when it suited him. She supposed she could press him for a schedule, but she didn't need to know, provided he didn't intrude on guests. She grabbed her laptop and immersed herself in work, wanting to finish the basic planning and list-making she needed to do this first week on the job. She saw she had an email from a friend in Montana who was an innkeeper: You give me tips on wine and I'll give you tips on innkeeping, beginning with smile, smile, smile.

Adrienne laughed to herself. The last time they'd gotten together, she'd been in the throes of breaking up with her boyfriend and figuring out what to do about Vic Scarlatti now that she knew he was her father. Forget him? Write to him? Was she sure her mother was right and hadn't skipped or forgotten about another lover around the time Adrienne had been conceived?

In short, she had been miserable.

I owe you a selection of your favorite wines for putting up with me last winter. I'm off to a decent if not uneventful start as a Knights Bridge innkeeper. What's a good time for you? I'll call. Let's talk.

Her friend responded an hour later, and they agreed to talk that evening.

Adrienne switched to a spreadsheet to work on Carriage Hill's finances. They were in good shape but it was yet another reminder of all Maggie and Olivia had managed to take on the past year.

Shortly before five, Adrienne shut down her laptop and put away her files and notes for the day. She looked forward to having dinner with Vic and wanted to enjoy the gorgeous weather while it lasted. If Adam was there, fine, but she didn't want to make life awkward for him. But she was probably projecting. *She* was the one who felt awkward, but she knew she didn't need to. It was her newness in town and to being here openly as Vic's daughter—and her uncertainties about her job, how long she'd last, if she was as up to it as Maggie and Olivia believed. Noah and Phoebe had given her a glowing recommendation. She'd worked hard and done well at the winery, but it was…well, a small California winery. Her main task had been to get the right people into place, the true experts who could take the winery to the next level.

It was a quiet, beautiful drive through the village and out to Echo Lake. She found Vic on the front porch, having wine with Elly O'Dunn and Adam. Rohan was the first to greet her. The puppy leaped up and jumped on her, nibbling her hands when she petted him. "He's excited," Adrienne said. "You didn't give him wine, did you?"

"He's just happy to see you," Vic said. "I told you he missed you."

Adam stood with his wine. "I'll leave you all to chat."

Vic looked disappointed. "You're not staying for dinner?"

"I have a few things I need to do."

Adrienne avoided watching Adam head inside with his wineglass. She worried Vic or Elly would notice her attraction to him for sure if she watched him, but maybe it was obvious that she was trying not to. She was surprised how off balance she was, but there was no denying he was under her skin. Maybe she was just experiencing the aftereffects of finding Maggie injured and the boys missing—and of having Vic back in Knights Bridge—and she would feel more herself in a day or two.

"Here," Vic said, handing her a tennis ball. "Would you take Rohan down to the lake and let him burn off some energy before dinner?"

"I can help with dinner—"

"We're fine. It's nothing fancy. Rohan's run my legs off today and he's still not tired."

Adrienne smiled. "Puppy energy. I'd love to take him down to the lake."

"Did you bring your swimsuit?" Elly asked. "You could take a swim before dinner."

She hadn't brought a swimsuit. She hadn't left one behind after she'd house-sat for Vic. She hadn't exactly needed a suit over the winter, but she'd imagined herself swimming in the lake on a hot summer day. When she'd taken the winery job, she hadn't known when, or if, she'd be back to Echo Lake.

"Do you want to take a glass of wine with you?" Vic asked.

"No, I'll wait. See you in a bit."

Rohan trotted by her side, occasionally jumping up to try to get the tennis ball. When they reached the lake, he plopped next to her expectantly. She tossed the tennis ball across the sandy beach. He fetched it and ran into the water with it, circling back around to the shore with the ball in his mouth. Adrienne laughed, and while he was swimming proudly to her, she glanced at the guesthouse. Violet lumbered down to the beach, but she was alone. No Adam.

When Rohan ran out of the water with the ball, he got Violet energized and chasing after him on the sand. Adrienne found a stick and threw both it and the ball into the lake. While the dogs bounded into the water, she kicked off her shoes, rolled up her pants to her knees and waded in. The air was cool, but the water was relatively warm—at least warm enough.

She noticed Adam on the sand by the trees. She didn't know how long he'd been watching her and the dogs. He smiled as Adrienne joined him. "Now I'll have a wet dog at my feet all night," he said.

"Does Violet sleep with you?"

"On the floor at the foot of the bed. No dogs in bed with me."

Adrienne dropped that conversation thread right there. "How old is she?"

"Eight. She was ten weeks old and sick when I took her home. Eric told me about her. We're a dog family and he thought we might be able to help each other. I was just out of the military." Adam paused, a distance coming into his eyes. "Violet and I were both in rough shape. I named her when she woke me up to go out at dawn one morning. I knew she'd be okay then. The sky was a violet color that morning. It fit."

"Violet's a great name. She seems to like it out here."

"Water, sand, Rohan, rocks to chew. What's not to like?"

Adrienne laughed. "True enough. Do you like it here?"

"I don't chew rocks but I enjoy Rohan and the lake. I get along with Vic, too."

"He's more down-to-earth than I expected when I first came here last winter," Adrienne said. "I wish I'd known him when he was active as a diplomat. He told me ninety percent of what he did was paperwork, but I don't believe him. Do you?"

Adam shook his head. "Not a chance."

"Tough to write your memoirs if you can't tell half the good stuff because it's classified. Are you sure you don't want to join us for dinner? Violet could join us, too."

"She's tired tonight. Rohan's wearing her out. Enjoy your dinner." He paused, those blue eyes connecting with hers. "I'll see you tomorrow."

* * *

Adam sat out on the guesthouse deck after Adrienne and Rohan headed back up to the house for dinner. Violet had collapsed in happy exhaustion after her frolic with the puppy. Rohan had seemed as pleased as Vic was to have Adrienne back in town. Adam couldn't say the same for himself. He'd complicated his life by moving into Vic's guesthouse. Wanting to kiss his daughter wasn't helping. He'd expected to have it be a passing urge, but it wasn't. At least not yet. He was attracted to her, and it was a problem.

He reached down and patted his golden retriever's wet coat. "We're set in our ways, aren't we, girl? No upsetting our applecart."

Adrienne Portale was a wanderer by nature and upbringing. She'd never stick in Knights Bridge. Her first week as an innkeeper had gone okay, but it hadn't been uneventful. It wasn't her fault the boys took off, but she and "eventful" went together, didn't they?

Adam didn't need to complicate his life. He didn't need trouble.

But hell...he *was* attracted to her. He couldn't deny or explain it.

"Don't need to."

He got up and ushered Violet back inside. He toweled off her paws and wiped off as much mud as he could. He'd brush her when she was dry, probably in the morning. It was getting dark now. Summer was winding down. He had a lot to do before it did, and not one item on his task list involved romancing the new innkeeper in town.

He microwaved a burrito. He could have joined Vic, Elly and Adrienne for dinner, but he didn't think it was a smart idea. As if to confirm his good judgment, his brothers turned up at the lake wanting to enjoy a last fire on the beach and beer before Labor Day and the unofficial end to summer. But Adam knew it was more than that. He, Justin, Brandon and Christopher had their eye on their eldest brother, Eric. He wasn't himself. He'd been quiet and even withdrawn for much of the summer—and, lately, often sported a permanent three-days' stubble, not his usual style. Something up with his police work? Adam had no idea.

They built a fire, settled onto blankets and logs and watched the flames as Justin handed out bottles of beer. "Samantha picked it out," he said. "It's classier than the usual stuff we drink by a fire."

"But is it as good?" Christopher asked.

Eric took a swallow of his beer. "Who cares?"

That was their opening. Justin pounced first. "You want to tell us what's going on, Eric?"

He stared at the flames. "No."

Adam remained on his feet. He tried the beer. It was Belgian. He liked it. "You're getting hard to be around, Eric," he said finally. "It's obvious something's eating at you."

"But it's okay if you don't want to talk to us," Christopher added.

"The hell it is." Eric popped to his feet, creating a long shadow in the firelit sand. "You'll all hound me until I cough it up. Trish and I broke up. She moved to Atlanta."

He and Trish Vargas, a paramedic in nearby Amherst, had been engaged for months. Adam was the first to respond to the news. "Why Atlanta?"

Eric shrugged. "New job."

"When did she leave?" Brandon asked.

"Three weeks ago. Took the job two weeks before that. Gave notice, packed, left."

Justin put another log on the fire. "That sucks. Did she invite you to go with her?"

"We both knew it wouldn't work even if I could find a law enforcement job in Atlanta. I should have seen it coming. Her mother moved to Atlanta in the spring. Nothing keeping Trish here."

Except her fiancé, Adam thought. He noticed Christopher sinking cross-legged onto a blanket they'd spread on the sand. He'd been dealing with his own breakup with Ruby O'Dunn. He'd followed her out to LA thinking he might come home with her. He hadn't. "Best this happened before you two got married," he said.

"I haven't told Gran yet," Eric said. "She likes Trish."

"She likes you better," Brandon said.

"She'll remember that after she tells you that you let your engagement go on too long." Justin stood back from the fire as it crackled with the fresh log. "You know Gran."

Eric gave a mock shudder. "She called it the everlasting engagement."

Justin grinned. "Don't you love how she holds back, doesn't say what she thinks?"

Adam couldn't suppress a grin of his own at the thought of their father's widowed mother. In another thirty seconds, Eric grinned, too. As the firstborn, he held a special place in their grandmother's heart. He also liked to tease her.

"You could have said something to us," Brandon said. "We've had our own go-rounds with women. Look at Maggie and me. We almost split up last year. I had to sleep in a damn tent for a while before I could soften her up."

Justin handed out more beer. Two each was the limit, but they nursed them for another hour before they let the fire die down. Eric perked up, his relief palpable now that his younger brothers had dragged his secret out of him. It wasn't just the embarrassment of his broken engagement that had compelled him to hold back. Next to Adam, Eric was the most contained of the siblings, and he'd needed time to absorb the big change in his life. Trish was smart, attractive and dedicated to her work, and she was no longer going to walk down the aisle as his bride.

By the time his four brothers were ready to leave, they had tackled a wide range of topics, including Knights Bridge's pretty new innkeeper. Adam stayed neutral but he realized he wasn't. If not for Vic being just up the hill, he'd have kissed her tonight. With her consent. He wasn't a jackass. But she'd have said yes, and he'd have regretted it, because she had wanderlust just like Ruby O'Dunn and Trish Vargas.

Eric hung back as Justin, Brandon and Christopher started up to their trucks. "Staying here's working out?" he asked Adam.

"So far, so good. Violet likes it."

"Only female you have to keep happy. Hell, maybe I'll get a puppy."

After Eric left, Adam doused the remains of the fire with lake water and collected the bottles. No sister-in-law Trish after all. Not meant to be, he thought, heading back to the guesthouse with Violet.

Ten

Adrienne settled in at Carriage Hill for the long Labor Day weekend. With no guests, the antique house was quiet, but she noticed a handful of vehicles—more than usual—on the dead-end road, presumably hikers on their way into the Quabbin woods. No one ventured close to the inn's backyard or startled a moose or a bear or anything else that affected her.

She had Vic to dinner on Saturday and showed him around. "The addition's quite nice," he said. "It blends in beautifully with the house. It's not easy to tell it's two hundred years newer."

"Mark Flanagan did the design and Olivia's family millworks matched the windows."

"Excellent craftsmanship, not that I'm an expert." He stood by the back window in the innkeeper's suite and nodded at the yard. "That's the wall Adam's redoing?"

"Mm, yes," Adrienne said.

"He could redo a cathedral. He's that good. He does quality work. He trained with the best, studied hard, worked hard to learn his craft. He does things on Adam time, but he does them well."

"What's Adam time?"

Vic smiled as he turned to her. "It's not an insult. He's deliberate. He works with the weather and juggles multiple projects, and he does things right the first time."

"Not a bad way to be."

Adrienne continued the tour, leading Vic up to the second floor. He liked what he saw here, too. She didn't point out the stonework photographs—that would be too much talk of Adam and she didn't want Vic to get the wrong impression. But he noticed anyway. "That's a bridge at the lake," he said, stopping at the last of the photographs. "Recognize it?"

She shook her head. "Where at the lake?"

"Opposite the house. I used to walk out there, but I haven't in ages. I should again. I need some exercise." He peered more closely at the photograph. "Adam's work? I didn't know Adam was this good a photographer. How did I miss that? Did you know?"

"Not until I saw these."

"They're good." Vic stood straight and nodded in agreement with himself. "Very good."

"I think so, too. He's a solitary sort, isn't he?"

"That's not possible for a Sloan."

Vic led the way downstairs and into the kitchen. It was a beautiful evening, and they decided to have dinner on the terrace. They worked together to set the table and carry out the simple fare of summer squash, local tomatoes with fresh basil, avocado and olive oil and rotisserie chicken from the country store.

Vic placed the salad on the table. "When I first started coming to Knights Bridge twenty years ago, I couldn't find a decent avocado in town."

"Life is full of changes." Adrienne smiled at him as they sat at the table. It was a pleasant evening, with a slight, cool breeze. "I've even seen decent-looking artichokes at the country store."

"Imagine that. That must please your West Coast soul."

"Well, I'm sure not everyone cares whether we can get avocados and artichokes at all, never mind good ones. There are things I couldn't get in California." She poured the Kendrick Winery chardonnay she'd chosen for the evening. They raised their glasses. "To good times in Knights Bridge, and to time together."

Vic clinked her glass. "Cheers, Adrienne. Great to have you back."

They talked about innkeeping, Scrabble, how much he was enjoying the renovations at his lake house, the upcoming foliage season, Rohan—everything except their personal lives, his as a retired diplomat, hers as a single woman in little Knights Bridge. He dodged talking about his recent trip to Washington. Adrienne didn't pursue it. They cleaned up after dinner together, and it was dusk when he finally said good-night. She stood on the kitchen steps as his car lights disappeared up the road.

As she started inside, she could hear a rustling in the underbrush across the road. An animal of some sort but not a big one—not a moose or bear or even a deer, she decided. A squirrel, maybe. She shut the door behind her and noted the quiet of the old house. She didn't mind being on her own for the rest of the evening. She wanted to settle in and get comfortable in this new space, and make sure she had a handle on its ins and outs as well before she started welcoming guests. She'd clean tomorrow but she was meeting with a local cleaning service first thing on Tuesday. She had a green light from Maggie and Olivia to get someone to clean the place on a regular basis, not just after events.

By dark, she was tucked in bed with a book, windows open and more rustling sounds out back. She finally threw back the covers and peeked behind the shade, catching two deer running into the fields from the wall Adam was rebuilding. She smiled, left the shade open and crawled back into bed, pulling the covers around her, picturing what it would be like not to be here alone. But that got her nowhere, and she resumed reading her book.

Dark clouds and rain moved in on Sunday. Carriage Hill was damp and chilly enough that Adrienne was tempted to light a fire in the cozy living room, but it felt way too early in the season. She'd also have to fill the wood box. Which made her wonder…where was the cordwood? The garden shed? Surely Olivia hadn't hauled wood that distance when she'd lived here.

Well, it was something to do on a rainy Sunday morning.

Adrienne donned her raincoat and made her way through the backyard to the shed. Sure enough, she discovered the remains of last season's cordwood. That meant someone had to shovel a path to the shed in the winter. Sand it when icy. Make multiple trips out here to fill the wood box. Vic had a fireplace and had stored his cordwood on the front porch. During renovations, he'd had a lean-to built for the wood, easily accessible from the kitchen door.

Something would have to be done about the wood, Adrienne thought, mentally adding it to her task list. Olivia and Maggie must have put it off given all the "musts" they had to figure out. An out-of-the-way wood box was probably a minor inconvenience to them. To Adrienne—she was out here in the rain, wasn't she? It had to be moved.

She collected six good-sized logs into her arms and started out of the shed. Her hood fell off the top of her head, but she didn't mind—at least until she felt rain going down her back. She navigated a puddle in an area on the path that needed re-mulching. Then she stepped in another puddle she hadn't seen given the wood in her arms.

She heard a sound off to her right, by the field, and stopped short.

A moose. Big, antlers, standing still on the other side of the stone wall, gazing at her as if she'd just landed from Mars.

He won't cross the stone wall, will he?

Adrienne took a step on the path, toward the terrace, but the moose turned and moved on, lumbering into the woods and out of sight.

She exhaled, shaking as much from being startled as actually encountering her first moose. She adjusted the logs in her arms—they were getting heavy—and took two steps toward the house, then slipped in the mud. She managed not to fall, but in the process of maintaining her balance, she dropped four logs. She held on to the two remaining logs, although she wasn't quite sure how.

"Not bad for a city girl," Adam Sloan said, appearing in front of her in the rain.

Adrienne gaped at him. He did have a way of turning up out of nowhere. "Where did you come from?"

"Side yard. Just got here." He walked to her—he had on a battered rain jacket—and picked up the dropped logs. "Did you hurt yourself?"

"No. Did you see the moose?"

"Yep. Big guy. He must be the one the boys saw."

"I'd have bolted, too, if I'd been in their shoes."

"You're soaked," he said.

"Getting there."

He pointed to the logs in her arms. "Want me to carry those, too?"

"I can manage. I can manage the ones you have—"

"Not a problem."

They weren't, either. She could see that. It wasn't just a question of his size and strength but his familiarity with hauling cordwood. And he had the advantage of not being drenched. And not having slipped in the mud. And not having just done a stare-down with a bull moose.

She followed him into the mudroom. He wasn't as soaked as she was. He hadn't been outside as long, but she wouldn't be surprised if the rain just bounced off him. A *joke*, she told herself. She let him take her two logs. He set them on the floor by Buster's dishes and stood straight. "There are towels—"

"On the shelf above the dryer. I see. Thanks." She peeled off her raincoat and hung it on a hook to drip-dry. "Carrying the logs was a last-minute decision. I wasn't prepared. I was just checking where Olivia stores wood and figured I might as well grab some while I was out there. It's my first time here in the rain."

Adam took a folded towel off the shelf and handed it to her. "First time for everything."

He didn't strike her as amused or condescending, just trying to help if he could. Adrienne shook open the towel. "Not bad for a city girl, huh? Good point."

"And one from California at that." He smiled. "I'm not laughing at you."

"Well, if you are, it's fine, because…" She blotted her hair and dried her neck, but she couldn't hold back and finally sputtered into laughter. "I can see the humor in my situation since I didn't break an arm or twist an ankle. Rain, wood, moose, mud, puddles. Rugged local. I had it all, didn't I?"

Adam picked a bit of wood off her arm. "Life in the country."

She wasn't cold now, she thought. "Thanks for your help."

"Sure. Are you chilled? Do you want me to make tea or something?"

She shook her head. "I'm okay. I'm already warming up." Thanks to his touch, even just his presence. "I should change into dry clothes."

"And buy a proper raincoat."

"That, too. Is there anything you need from me?"

"I stopped by to check on the wall. We're getting more rain than I expected. I won't be long."

"Take your time."

"I can fill your wood box if you'd like."

"Thanks, but I'll just throw these logs into the wood box and leave it at that. I won't be building a fire today."

He glanced at the logs at their feet. "There's enough wood here at least to take the dampness out of the air. Do you have kindling?"

She hung her towel on a hook. "I have no idea."

"Makes sense it didn't come up yet. You've only been here a week and it's still summer."

But he'd have considered kindling, cordwood and the rest of it. "I do know the chimney's been cleaned for the season."

"That's a plus," he said. "I'd be glad to check things out. Give me five minutes."

He ducked out of the mudroom back outside. Adrienne left the wood where it was and went through the kitchen and down to her suite to change. The heat from being near him quickly dissipated. She *was* chilled. She pulled on leggings, a long-sleeved shirt and dry socks and ran the hair dryer on her wet hair for two minutes.

She found Adam in the living room with the logs she'd grabbed in the shed. "Wall's in good shape," he said, placing the logs in the wood box by the fireplace. "You need a few things if you're going to have a fire. I'll drop them by when I'm back here on Tuesday. Can you wait until then?"

"Sunny and in the upper seventies by then. I can wait. I can pull everything together myself, though."

"I know what you need and where to get it. It won't take any time at all. It's no trouble."

She nodded. "Okay, thanks."

"You look cold," he said.

"Warming up. I did get a bit chilled. I'm going to make tea. You're welcome to join me."

"I should be getting back. I wiped my feet but I still might have left a trail. If you have a mop—"

"I'll take care of any muddy trails we left."

"Right."

His gaze settled on her as if he knew she was reacting to him physically—maybe was happy about it? Awkward, she thought. She spun into the kitchen, and he followed her, opening the door as she filled the kettle with water. "Call if you need anything." He seemed to want to say something else, but he didn't and left, shutting the door softly behind him.

He was all business. No drama. He'd stopped by because of his work. As Vic had pointed out, juggling his various projects on his own time was what Adam did.

Adrienne made tea and sat with it at the kitchen table. If anything, the rain intensified, pelting onto the stone walk and the lush, green lawn. She noticed a few spots where she and Adam had tracked mud on the floor. She'd let them dry before she swept them up.

Halfway through her tea, she was warm again, and almost back to normal after the wood, the rain, the moose and Adam Sloan.

* * *

Her mother called that night, and Adrienne told her about her little adventure earlier in the day but left out any mention of Adam's arrival. Knowing Sophia as she did, there was no doubt in her mind her mother would ferret out the sparks between her and the local stonemason. She'd warn Adrienne not to get in over her head, remind her she'd only just arrived in Knights Bridge—and then insist she didn't want to interfere. Now that Adrienne knew about her mother's Paris fling with a handsome young diplomat, her cautions about keeping her wits about her with men had taken on a new meaning. She wasn't just being controlling. She was speaking from experience.

My mom, Adrienne thought with a smile. They did know each other well.

"I'm sore from my first CrossFit classes, but I love the program," her mother said. "I'm going to be lifting small houses before you know it."

Adrienne laughed. "I wouldn't put it past you. I'm gearing up for a girlfriends' weekend. Would you ever do one?"

"A what?"

Adrienne smiled to herself. "Never mind. I'm glad you called."

"Of course. It's always great to talk with you. And Vic? How's he?"

"Rohan's still getting the better of him."

"That's his dog, isn't it? A Lab or something."

"Golden retriever."

"Right. Well. You always wanted a puppy."

One of the bones of contention between them over

the years. And yet, somehow, they had never had a truly contentious relationship. Her mother was straight-forward and didn't leave Adrienne wondering about her opinion. She would never pretend she wanted a dog just to placate her daughter. *I love dogs when they belong to someone else. I can't take on the responsibility of having a dog of my own.*

It would be our dog, Mom.

Mm. That's what you say now. Wait until you want to go away for a weekend with your friends. Or wait until you go to college. Then it'll be my dog.

No beating around the bush. That was her mother. Direct to a fault.

Except about Vic being her only daughter's biological father.

Almost three decades she hadn't been direct and straightforward about *that*.

"Water over the dam," Adrienne said, checking the wood box. As Adam had observed, she had logs but not much else. She'd need tinder, kindling, matches, fire starters. The fireplace screen needed a good cleaning.

There *was* a fire extinguisher.

She dutifully added "fire stuff" to her to-do list. Ten to one, Carriage Hill's autumn guests were going to want fires, and she didn't want to leave it to Adam. If he helped, great. If not, she'd head to the country store with a list and get their advice. Done.

In the morning, Adrienne awoke to drizzly skies and an email from her mother with a recipe for hot mulled apple cider attached. From my grandmother. I haven't made it in years. It strikes me as perfect for your new life.

Adrienne remembered the recipe but she was positive her mother had never made hot mulled cider. Her grandmother had, though, one Thanksgiving when Adrienne was ten. She'd died the following year after a stroke. Adrienne felt a wave of nostalgia for her, and then guilt at wishing, even for that brief spurt, her mother was more like her. It wasn't fair to wish she was something she wasn't. Adrienne typed a quick reply.

Thanks, Mom. I was hoping you had saved it. Fond memories.

She hit Send and took her mug of coffee outside. It was too wet to sit at the table, but the weather was starting to clear. She could hear birds twittering madly. They sounded happy to her.

She went inside and whipped up eggs and toast made with Maggie's oatmeal bread. Adrienne loved good bread but she'd never made any from scratch in her life. But how could Maggie keep up with homemade bread for the inn on top of everything else she did? Her workload wasn't sustainable.

"That's why I'm here," Adrienne said aloud, and got busy.

By noon, it was warm and sunny, and she had arranged for a local cleaning service to do a deep-clean of the entire house. Adrienne met with the owner on the terrace and started to explain about the new addition—

but she already knew. Lisa Zalewski was her name. "I'm from Knights Bridge," she said, as if that explained everything.

"Ah. I see."

"The Sloans did the addition. I graduated high school with Christopher Sloan. He helped out when he had a free minute, but he's a full-time firefighter. But you know that, right?"

"Yes," Adrienne said.

Lisa squinted out at the yard from her seat at the terrace table. "Adam's redoing the stone wall, I see. Violet's helping?"

"She comes with him. I don't know how much help she is."

Lisa laughed, her eyes crinkling up. She was good-humored, with a sturdy build and a passion—her word—for her work. She promised Adrienne she wouldn't regret "for a millisecond" hiring a cleaning service. "I quit my job at the bank and started the service two years ago. I've never looked back." She grinned as she got to her feet. "What can I say? I love to clean."

She was chuckling as she left.

Adrienne sat outside for lunch and was helping herself to a brownie she'd thawed out of the freezer—one of Maggie's apparently famous brownies—when Olivia arrived. She'd walked down the road from her house and kept a hand on her lower back, presumably indicating discomfort. "I want to gather herbs and cut back perennials for the season," she said.

"Could you use a hand?" Adrienne asked.

"I'd love it. My lower back's been giving me fits. I

thought a walk and a bit of work in the garden would at least be a distraction."

She explained how she and Maggie had started making their own essential oils, but they'd put their grand plans for them aside for now, relying instead on a local source for anything they needed for their goat's milk products. They were getting help with that venture, too, but they had enough of an inventory for now. They also loved to paint and refurbish old furniture, but Olivia was taking a break while she was pregnant.

"I'm focusing on my design work," she added as she placed an armload of fresh basil into a basket. "Maggie and I love having a variety of things to do. I used to worry I wouldn't be good at anything because I like to do so many things, but then I realized most of them fall under the same umbrella."

Adrienne added sprigs of parsley to the basket. "You make life more pleasant. Attractive designs, lovely goat's milk soaps and bath salts and such, a comfy inn in a beautiful setting where people can relax and enjoy themselves. The adventure travel and entrepreneurial boot camps fit in with what you started here. They all mesh."

"Maggie and I both just dived in with dreams more than specific goals."

"You're figuring things out as you go along, adjusting based on experience. It works. I've met people who have thick notebooks and extensive spreadsheets of plans that gather dust."

"Better to take action sometimes than to plan."

"How's Maggie doing?"

"Much better," Olivia said, pausing to stretch her lower back, then moving to the parsley patch. "She and Brandon are getting the boys ready to start school tomorrow."

They picked more herbs and then took their baskets to the terrace. Olivia left half for Adrienne to do with as she pleased. "Including turn them into compost. I'll never know."

Adrienne laughed, but she loved the idea of making pesto. She'd done it once somewhere she'd lived. Provence, she thought. She'd stayed with friends in the wine business and she'd gotten into cooking for a bit.

Pesto, however, entailed a trip to the village for everything but the fresh basil.

She had work to do this afternoon. She'd make a list of what she needed in town and go in the morning. A good excuse, she decided, for indulging in pancakes at the village's only restaurant.

Naturally three Sloan brothers were at a table when Adrienne entered Smith's at eight the next morning. Justin, Eric and Adam. The restaurant was located in a converted house off Main Street, with bright mums in pots on its small front porch. She sat at the counter and acknowledged the brothers with a quick wave. Justin and Eric finished before she put in her order and said hello as they headed out. Out of the corner of her eye, she saw Adam leave a few bills on the table and get to his feet.

He stopped at the counter on his way out. "I'll be at Carriage Hill later this morning and will stay the rest of the day. I should be able to wrap up work there by tomorrow at the latest."

"Great. It'll be nice to have the wall finished before weekend guests arrive. Thanks for letting me know."

His gaze settled on her. "Enjoy breakfast."

"They don't have avocado toast, so I'm having pancakes."

He grinned. "That's one of the better excuses I've heard for having pancakes. Do you actually like avocado toast?"

"I do. I thought about adding it to the inn's breakfast menu but decided to stick to a New England theme." She pointed at her menu, flat on the counter in front of her. "I can still change my mind and skip the pancakes."

"Go for it."

"I suppose I have all day to burn them off."

"Yeah," Adam said, clearly amused. "There's that."

Only after he left did Adrienne realize the sexy nature of his remark. She felt heat in her face, her neck—she had to be beet red. She quickly ordered coffee but talked herself out of pancakes. Instead she ordered scrambled eggs and sliced tomatoes. Local eggs, local tomatoes. She liked that. She'd indulge in pancakes another time. She didn't need to have burning them off on her mind. She skipped toast but couldn't resist a house-made apple-streusel muffin when the waiter brought out a batch and set them not a foot from her.

A warm muffin slathered in butter…

She'd have to burn it off, too, but she didn't care. She ate every crumb.

After breakfast, she decided to walk down the street

to take a look at Red Clover Inn. The Sloans had bought it after she'd left Knights Bridge for Kendrick Winery. It was a rambling, empty old place in desperate need of renovation or a bulldozer.

"Enter the Sloans," she whispered to herself.

Vic had explained that Justin and Samantha were living at the inn while they organized and supervised its major overhaul. Built in 1900 as a classic New England inn, the building had narrow white clapboards and black shutters, many with peeling paint and cracked or missing sections. The property bordered a field dotted with wildflowers, including—of course—red clover. The lawn was dotted with beautiful shade trees and stone walks. There was a detached garage, and a rope hammock was tied between two trees in the side yard.

Adrienne noticed Justin's truck and Samantha's car in the driveway.

And then she spotted Adam on the front porch.

For no good reason, she felt as if she'd been caught spying on him. She started to about-face and bolt back to her car, but he waved to her. "Come on up. I'll show you around the place."

Samantha came through the screen door onto the porch. She, too, waved and invited Adrienne inside. Short of being rude or saying she had to keep moving to burn off the streusel muffin, she had no graceful way out. But she realized she didn't want one. She wanted to see Red Clover Inn, and to be a part of this small town.

She also had time to kill until the country store was open for her pesto ingredients.

Eleven

Adrienne followed Adam and Samantha through the entry and down a hall past a large living room, library and reception area. They entered a country kitchen with an adjoining pantry. Samantha explained that she and Justin lived in a suite in back. There were a few other rooms on the first floor. It was a sprawling place that hadn't been updated in decades—perfect for the Sloans to take on. From what Adrienne had learned from Vic at dinner on Saturday, Adam handled the "big picture" finances for his family's business rather than day-to-day bookkeeping. His father and Justin oversaw the day-to-day construction work and crews. Brandon preferred to stick to carpentry and his occasional guide work. Heather, the youngest, was studying interior design while she was in London and as much a part of the family business as her brothers.

It would be easy to go overboard with renovations, but Adrienne doubted the Sloans were wired that way. They'd stay within reasonable boundaries. Samantha was a big thinker. She was the granddaughter of renowned explorer and adventurer Harry Bennett, whose death was one reason she'd ended up venturing to Knights Bridge last fall. She fantasized about staying on as the innkeeper after renovations were completed, but as far as Adrienne could tell, no one believed that would happen.

Samantha leaned against a kitchen counter, its worn top cracked but spotless. "We're only just getting started with renovations. We'll be lucky to have figured out what windows to replace by Thanksgiving, but my cousin Charlotte still wants to have her wedding here."

Justin shrugged. "Everything works. It's just old."

"Charlotte and Greg have an emotional attachment to this place," Samantha said. "They stayed here together by accident when Justin and I were on our honeymoon. One of those right hand, left hand situations. You remember Greg, don't you, Adrienne?"

"Definitely."

She left it at that. Greg Rawlings, a senior Diplomatic Security agent, hadn't been her biggest fan. He'd turned up at Vic's last winter when she hadn't exactly been on her best behavior. Vic had included him on his Knights Bridge cheat sheet because of the upcoming wedding. Charlotte Bennett was a marine archaeologist, in true Bennett family tradition. She'd recently moved from Scotland to Washington, DC, to open an office there for a marine archaeology institute, and to be close to Greg, who'd taken a position at DSS headquarters.

"All's forgiven," Justin said. "Greg said to tell you good luck up here in the sticks."

She laughed, relaxing. That sounded like Greg. "This is a wonderful spot for a wedding. Let me know if I can help in any way."

An elderly woman appeared on the back steps, but Adam had spotted her and opened the door. She had her cane poised to knock. "I see you have company," she said, returning the cane to her side. "Mind if I come in?"

She entered the kitchen before getting an answer. "Good morning, Gran," Justin said.

"Good morning." She paused and peered at Adrienne. "You're Vic Scarlatti's daughter, aren't you?"

Before Adrienne could answer, Adam jumped in. "That's right, Gran. This is Adrienne Portale, the new innkeeper at Carriage Hill. Adrienne, this is my grandmother, Evelyn Sloan. She lives next door. She knows everything that goes on in town."

She eased onto a chair at the large pine table. She was in her eighties, with snow-white hair and the lines and sags that came with her advanced age. She wore a tunic, wide-legged pants and sturdy walking shoes. "Lovely to meet you, Adrienne. I didn't speak out of turn, did I?"

Obviously she wasn't concerned if she had. "Not at all," Adrienne said. "Yes, I'm Vic's daughter."

"He's a good man. I hope my boys are treating you well. They can be a rough bunch."

"We learned at your knee," Justin said with a wink, turning to Adrienne. "Don't think Gran's a sweet little old lady. She ran a nursery school in town for forty years. She's tough as nails."

Adrienne laughed at the banter between the Sloans. Samantha smiled, too. "You'll get used to them," she said.

"I lost my husband a few years ago," Evelyn said. "I still live on my own but most of my friends are in assisted living here in town. I walked over—I take a shortcut through the yard." She leaned her cane against the table. "I keep it in case my knee acts up. I don't need it."

Justin started to argue with her but instead filled a glass with water from the faucet. "You know one of us would walk over here with you, Gran. Just call."

"I know how to text."

"Text, then. And drink up," he said, setting the water glass in front of her.

"I will, I will." She picked up the glass and addressed Adrienne. "When one gets older, one doesn't always feel thirst the same way one used to."

Justin grinned at her. "One. I like that, Gran. As if we're not talking about you."

"It's proper English. Perfectly fine." She sipped her water, shifted again to Adrienne. "I understand Adam's working out at Carriage Hill and living up at Echo Lake. Did he tell you I'm flying back to London with Heather and Brody when they come home for Thanksgiving and Greg and Charlotte's wedding?"

"I didn't," Adam said.

"You mean my name didn't come up?" Her blue eyes twinkled as she kept them focused on Adrienne. "It'll be my first trip to England. I'm making plans."

"Gran, you don't leave until late November," Justin said.

"Half the fun of taking a trip is the planning. I've

been reading biographies of Henry the Eighth's wives. He had two of them executed. Two! I've known that since I was in the sixth grade but it never fails to shock me."

"Henry the Eighth is dead, Gran," Justin said. "You won't be having dinner with him."

She leveled her gaze on him. "Don't get smart with me, Justin Sloan. You're getting as bad as your brother Eric." Clearly it wasn't a problem, but she turned to Adam with an approving smile. "I'm glad I have one nice grandson."

"Ha," Justin said. "You have to watch out for the quiet ones."

Adam rolled his eyes, good-humored, and shifted to Adrienne. "Samantha's helping Gran with her research for her trip. You've been to London, haven't you?"

"A few times."

His grandmother set her glass down after the tiniest of sips. "Henry the Eighth was a bastard but he was responsible for quite the building boom. He oversaw the construction of incredible, iconic places. St. James's Palace, Whitehall Palace, Sandsfoot Castle—there are more but I won't bore you. I got a stack of books out of the library and I'm perusing various websites on my iPad."

"You're going to be in England for a week," Justin said. "You won't have time to see everything."

"I'm winnowing down the list and getting a sense of the possibilities, the history, the ambience. I'm studying maps, too. Gardens, parks, squares. Didn't you do that when you and Samantha decided on Scotland for your honeymoon?"

He shook his head. "No."

"Curmudgeon."

"Heather will take you wherever you want to go," Adam said. "What do you recommend, Adrienne?"

"I'm not an expert on London—"

"I'd love to hear your ideas," Evelyn said.

"Keep it simple. Don't try to do everything. I'd leave time for rest and serendipity. That said, I love walking through the parks, and I was blown away by Churchill's War Rooms."

"They're across from St. James's Park, not far from Westminster Abbey," Evelyn said knowledgeably. "They're both on my list. I remember Churchill. This is my one chance to visit England. I want to see as much as possible but I don't want to come back in an urn."

Even Justin was shocked at her bluntness. "Gran."

"What? Okay. I'll allow for rest and—what was it?"

"Serendipity," Adrienne said. "Give yourself time and permission to duck into a cute shop that catches your eye or a pub that's not on a strict itinerary, or to walk down a pretty street that catches your fancy."

"I'm bringing my cane, although my knee's much better."

Justin smiled at her. "Imagine that."

According to Vic, a chronic knee ailment had kept Evelyn Sloan from attending Justin and Samantha's wedding in England that summer, but her grandchildren believed she'd used it as an excuse not to make the trip—and regretted it later. "Serendipity sounds like a great idea," Evelyn said, ignoring Justin's remark.

"Plan on staying with Heather or Brody the whole time you're there," Justin said. "Don't go off on your own. We don't need a call from Scotland Yard about you going missing."

"Brody is an FBI agent. He won't allow it."

"DSS agent, Gran."

Her mischievous look suggested that subject was part of the ongoing banter between her and her grandsons.

Adam smiled at Adrienne. "Want to see this place? Come on."

"Sure," Justin said. "Go off with the pretty innkeeper and leave me with the old lady." He winked again at his grandmother. "I'm a lucky guy."

"You both are," Evelyn said. "Neither of you is Henry the Eighth."

Adam's first stop with Adrienne was the inn's library, complete with a large fieldstone fireplace, floor-to-ceiling bookcases and a cozy, old-fashioned atmosphere. She noticed board games tucked onto shelves. *Clue, Monopoly, Risk, Scrabble.* From the library, they headed upstairs to a long hall with guest rooms on either side. Adam explained they'd be doing some restructuring when they renovated but wouldn't lose any rooms in the process. "The building is sound. That helps," he said. "Heather is helping with the interior design plans from London. She likes to remind us it's not the same as interior decorating."

"You prefer rocks and finances?"

"I have the patience to work with them but none

when it comes to traffic flows and deciding on things like bathroom fixtures."

"Do renovation plans involve new or existing stone-work?"

"Some of the stonework out back has a few problems. All the stonework inside is in great shape. Here. I'll show you."

He stood close to her and pointed out the window to a patio and firepit that required his attention.

"I saw your photographs at Carriage Hill," she said.

"Photography's a hobby." He stood back from the window. "I've been working on a series of photographs of old stone bridges and stone walls in the area. I'm in no rush." A small smile. "The bridges and walls aren't going anywhere."

"Vic noticed the photographs at Carriage Hill, too. They're a nice touch."

"I appreciate that."

They went downstairs, back to the kitchen. Justin had left to walk Evelyn Sloan back to her house, and Samantha had catalogs for bathroom fixtures open on the table.

Adam led Adrienne through the kitchen door to the backyard with its mature flower beds and expansive, if weed-prone, lawn. "You're still parked at Smith's?" he asked her.

She nodded. "I have a few errands to do in town. The back door's unlocked if you need to get into the house."

"I have a key. You don't need to leave it open on my account."

"I'm used to locking up everywhere else."

"Vic says you've never lived anywhere six months."

"And a lot of places not that long. I house-sat, dog-sat, did short-term rentals and all sorts of things while I was learning about wine and traveling the world. Well, some of the world. Lots of places I've never been. Have you traveled much?"

"When I was in the military."

"Right. Thank you for your service."

"It was a privilege," he said, pulling open the driver's door to his stonemason's van. "See you later."

She thanked him for the tour and headed out to the sidewalk. He waved as he passed her in his van. She continued past her car up to Main Street, arriving at the country store as Maggie was leaving. She carried two bags and flinched when she said hello. "My head's pounding. I think I overdid. This damn thing is taking longer to heal than I thought it would."

"Here, let me help," Adrienne said.

"I walked over here from the house. I can manage to get myself home." Maggie took a shallow breath, obviously in more pain than she wanted to admit. "You don't need to take the time to go back with me."

"I don't mind. It's a beautiful day. I'd love to walk with you."

Adrienne took the heavier of the two bags. She'd have taken both but Maggie hugged the smaller one tight to her chest, as if it was helping her to stay upright. Adrienne offered to get her car, but Maggie insisted she could walk home. They crossed the street to the common. She seemed better when they reached South Main and crossed it. It was a short distance to the side street where Maggie's house was located.

The boys were in school, and the house was quiet as they set the bags on the kitchen counter. Adrienne unloaded the cold goods and put them in the refrigerator and freezer. Maggie sank onto a chair at the table.

Adrienne found a glass, filled it with water and handed it to her. "Do you want me to call Brandon?"

"No, I'll rally. All set for the weekend?"

"Felicity and I have everything in hand."

"Olivia will help. I will, too. The food—"

"We can go with our backup plan for food, Maggie."

"No need. I pushed it this morning. I felt okay over the weekend. I just came down with this headache. I thought walking would help. Actually, I think it is—it's not as bad as it was at the store. I'm not worried. The cut and my bruises are healing well. I'm lucky I didn't get a concussion."

"Are you picking up the boys from school?" Adrienne asked.

"Clare will walk them back here."

Owen's mother. "Good."

Maggie smiled, looking wan but somewhat better. "I prefer to do the worrying than to be worried about."

"Maybe seize the moment with the boys at school and rest. Why don't I pick them up when they get out and take them to the inn? They can hang out there until Brandon gets off work. That'll give you the afternoon to rest."

"If you don't mind…"

"Not at all."

Reassured Maggie was okay, Adrienne left her stretched out on the sofa in the living room and walked back across the common. She bought her pesto ingredients at the country store and collected her car by the restaurant.

When she arrived back at the inn, Adam was deep into his work on the wall. She didn't disturb him. A few minutes later, Maggie texted her: Adam will pick up the boys and bring them to the inn. Is that okay?

Why not? She wanted to help. She typed her response: Of course.

Adam disappeared for lunch. Adrienne huddled in the small office to work, but she was in the kitchen when he arrived with the boys and about five thousand dinosaurs they'd gathered on a quick stop at home. She suggested the boys set up on the terrace while he finished work. They liked that idea. "Uncle Adam's going to take us to the lake after he gets done with his work," Tyler said. "You'll come, too?"

"If I can," she said vaguely.

"Adam said it's okay. Didn't you, Adam?"

He set their backpacks by the mudroom door. "I did."

"I meant if I finish my work here," Adrienne said, pushing back an image of him in a swimming suit, herself in her tankini...

"Oh," Tyler said. "I hope you finish."

"We won't run away even if we see a moose," Aidan said. "Promise."

She smiled at them. "Good plan. I'll be in the kitchen. Shout if you need anything."

Violet stayed on the terrace with them while Adam

returned to his work on the wall. Forty-five minutes later, he entered the kitchen, not too dusty and sweaty, all considered. "I'm all set. We'll head out. It's warm today. A last swim of the season sounds good. See you at the lake?"

Adrienne hesitated. "I think so."

"Think—"

"Yes." She smiled past her uncertainty. "Yes, I'll see you at the lake."

She followed him outside. Dinosaurs were spread out on the stonework, table, chairs and a bench and perched in the catmint. The boys were stalking them from the garden, but they didn't balk at picking up and getting out to the lake.

After they left, Adrienne slipped into her swimsuit. She didn't want to have to change at the lake. She pulled shorts and a T-shirt on over her suit and stuffed underwear and an extra change of clothes into a canvas tote.

"Prepared for everything," she said to herself, taking a deep breath as she headed to her car.

Sloan uncle and nephews had changed into swim trunks by the time Adrienne made her way down to the lake. She'd already noticed Vic wasn't home. He'd mentioned he wanted to bring Rohan to Elly O'Dunn's farm and help her pick the last of the season's tomatoes.

Adam had on a T-shirt and his swim trunks. Adrienne tried not to stare at his bare legs and feet. He nodded toward the lake. "Swim?"

"Not sure. I mean, I *can* swim, but I'm not sure I want to. I'm sure the water's nice, but the air—it's not as warm out as it was. I don't want to freeze getting out of the water."

"That's half the fun of swimming this time of year."

"Any time of year in New England," she said. "And you *would* look at it that way."

"You want to do it. Go on. Don't talk yourself out of it." He leaned closer to her, a spark of humor in his eyes. "I'm encouraging you, not goading you."

The boys, already in the water, called to her. "Come on, Adrienne! It's not that cold."

That cold. She nodded to Adam. "I notice you haven't gotten in the water yet."

"Waiting for you."

She had no idea if he was serious.

"You already went to the trouble of getting into a swimsuit," he added.

"Yes, but getting into the water, getting out dripping wet—goose bumps, chattering teeth, purple lips. Scrambling for a towel and jumping back into my clothes before I freeze—" She sighed. "You think that's what I want?"

"Put it that way, yeah, that's what I think."

She grinned. "I will if you will."

"You're on."

He pulled off his shirt, tossed it on a blanket spread out on the sand and ran into the water. He dived without breaking stride. Adrienne breathed once he had his bare chest and legs under water, out of sight, but he popped up quickly, flipped onto his back and waved to her. She figured a chilly swim was in order given her reaction to him. She pulled off her shorts and T-shirt and tossed them onto the blanket. She would have preferred a more gingerly approach to getting into the water, but she wondered if Adam was checking her out, too.

The water was *not* that warm but she survived diving in.

She and the Sloan uncle and nephews splashed around for twenty minutes, but that was enough. Aidan got out first, huddling on the blanket under two towels. Tyler lasted another two minutes before he raced out of the water and joined his younger brother.

Adam eased close to Adrienne. She was crouched to keep her body in the water, but he stood up. The water was just waist-deep. He gave a small shudder. "Damn. Goose bumps. You all set?"

"I'm beelining for the towels."

"Assuming the boys didn't take them all."

Then what? Her suit wasn't as revealing as some she'd owned, but the conditions would put it to the test. "You first," she said.

He smiled mysteriously, as if he'd read her mind. "No problem."

"I'll be right behind you. I promise I won't get hypothermia."

She watched him get out of the water. He didn't waste any time, but he didn't run, either. Water streamed off him, accentuating his muscular body. Really, she thought, she should have stayed at Carriage Hill and made pesto. One last dunk underwater, and she surfaced and ran to the blanket. She shuddered with the shock of the cooler air against her skin.

Adam handed her a towel. "Brandon and Maggie are raising their boys right. They saved you a towel."

She wrapped it around her, shivering. "Well, this is…" What was the word she wanted? She smiled. "Exhilarating."

"I'll go with that."

Adrienne tried to read his tone but found she couldn't. He took Tyler and Aidan back to the guesthouse to get changed. She sat on the blanket, wrapped up in her towel. The lake sparkled in the late-afternoon sun, the water reflecting trees and sky. A year ago, she'd never have imagined the life she had now. But she'd moved around often enough that a big difference between one year to the next wasn't that unusual for her. It was this place, she thought. Echo Lake. Knights Bridge. Vic. She glanced up through the trees at the guesthouse. And Adam? Was she falling for him? She shifted back to the lake. It wasn't wise to think about her feelings about Adam when she'd just seen him in nothing but swim trunks.

She pulled on clothes over her suit. It wasn't ideal, but it was preferable to changing behind a tree or up at the guesthouse. In a few minutes, the Sloans rejoined her and gathered up the blanket and wet towels. A couple of dinosaurs had found their way to the lakefront, too. Adam set everything at the end of the stone walk that led to the guesthouse. Adrienne noticed Brandon walking down from the main house. He didn't linger. He thanked her for helping Maggie and said she'd recovered from her headache, and then he was off with Tyler and Aidan and their dinosaurs and backpacks.

"Violet will be mad I left her inside," Adam said, grabbing the blanket and towels.

"I don't blame her."

"It would have been bedlam. Come on. I'll get you a dry towel. I might even have a hair dryer."

Adrienne figured she could slip into her change of clothes at the same time. She grabbed her canvas tote and walked up to the guesthouse with him. Violet, indeed, was agitated, pacing at the door. She settled down quickly, though. "I'll pour wine while you put on dry clothes," Adam said. "I've got a bottle Vic gave me the other night as a belated housewarming present. That means you picked it out?"

"Probably."

She ducked into a full bathroom off the kitchen. There was another one in the master bedroom, presumably where Adam was staying. She dried off with a fresh towel, changed into her spare outfit and stuffed her wet clothes and suit back into the tote bag. She found a hair dryer in the cupboard and tackled her hair. She hadn't brought a brush or comb and didn't see any in the bathroom, but she used her fingers and did an okay job. She checked her face for smeared makeup. All good on that front. She took a deep breath, gave her reflection an encouraging smile and returned to the kitchen.

Adam and Violet had gone out to the deck. Adrienne joined them, and he handed her a glass of wine, a cabernet sauvignon Vic knew she particularly liked. "You'd think Vic planned for us to share it," she said.

"One never knows with Ambassador Scarlatti."

They exchanged cheers and a clink of glasses, and

she took one sip before she knew what was going to happen. Not that she'd planned it, or Adam had planned it. But she knew. And just like that, she was in his arms, his body as warm and taut as she'd anticipated, his mouth descending to hers as he whispered could he kiss her…

Yeah. Of course.

Had she said those words aloud?

Yes…she had. No question.

The taste of his mouth on hers, the feel of the strong muscles in his back as she held him and the surge of a thousand different sensations got her in their grip. She shut her eyes and let herself take in the kiss and all its possibilities.

Violet barked.

And Vic called hello from the back door.

Adam grinned. "Just like in the movies." He didn't look even slightly embarrassed. He touched a thumb to her lips. "To be continued."

Adrienne managed to nod as Adam called to let Vic know they were on the deck. Rohan bounded up the steps, Vic following him at a slower pace. The two golden retrievers charged from one end of the deck to the other. Vic grinned at them and then noticed the wineglasses on the table. "Starting early, I see."

"It's not that early," Adam said lightly. "Can I pour you a glass?"

"I'd love it."

Oblivious, Adrienne thought, amused—and relieved.

Adam got a third glass from inside and brought it out to the deck. "Here you go, Vic."

Vic winked at Adrienne. "See why I like having Adam here?"

She did, indeed. "How was Elly's?"

"We picked the last of the tomatoes. I suppose it's too late in the season for me to get a farmer's tan. She was preoccupied. Ruby is coming home from Hollywood after Christmas. She and Ava are cooking up plans again, none of which include raising goats and canning tomatoes. Elly can't keep up."

"The O'Dunns are never bored, are they?"

"Not a chance. Better too much on your plate than not knowing what to do with yourself because there's nothing to do." Vic studied Adrienne a moment. "Did you go swimming?"

She smiled. "I did."

"Dear heavens. Did you freeze?"

"Only a little. Adam and his nephews got in the water, too. He picked them up after school and brought them to the inn, and then…" Too much explaining. Vic would see right through it. "Swimming, kayaking, fishing, playing Scrabble, writing your memoirs. You have the life, Vic."

"What if I live another thirty years?"

"You can write a fresh set of memoirs."

He didn't seem convinced. He shifted the conversation to the wine and how much he enjoyed his new wine cellar, especially when he had company. He seldom drank alone. Then Rohan surged past him down the steps, and Vic set down his glass. "He's going to be in the lake until midnight if I don't stop him."

"Won't he come if you call him?" Adrienne asked.

"No."

"Rohan," Adam called. "Up here. Now."

Vic shrugged. "Worth a shot."

Adam had Violet sit next to him before she could chase after the puppy. "They got each other wired." He whistled. "Rohan, come!" He grinned at Adrienne and Vic. "Who knows, it might work. Why don't you call him, Vic?"

He made a face and walked to the top of the stairs. Just as he started to call the puppy, Rohan burst up the stairs past him onto the deck and raced straight to Violet. Vic laughed. "Figures. I'll get him back to the house."

"I'll go with you," Adrienne said, then turned to Adam. "Thanks for the wine. I'll see you tomorrow."

"Sure thing. I'll finish work on the wall."

Vic snapped a leash on Rohan's collar, and Adrienne followed them down the steps. "I have to remember it gets dark earlier," Vic said.

"Yeah."

"You okay?"

She nodded. "Sure. I'm glad Adam's at the guest-house. It's good you're not up here alone all the time. You have friends in town, and Elly's close by, but still." She took a breath. "I won't screw things up for you here, Vic. I promise."

"You don't have to promise. Just live your life."

"I'm not intruding by being here?"

"No."

He didn't hesitate and spoke with such decisiveness that Adrienne had nowhere to go with his response.

Her mother was more concerned about her screwing up Vic's life than Vic was. Was that why she'd never told him they had a daughter together? Or had she just not wanted to risk Vic screwing up *her* life? But the anger and resentment didn't feel right anymore, or even justified.

"Adrienne?"

She smiled. "It's easy to get lost in thought with this beautiful lake air."

He hooked his arm into hers. "It is," he said.

Rohan walked easily on Vic's opposite side, and when they reached the main house, Adrienne turned down his invitation to join him for dinner. "I've got some work to do tonight," she said.

"Be careful you don't let flexible hours become always hours."

"I will. Have a good night, Vic."

"You, too."

She got in the car, touched her lips and felt the lingering effects of Adam's kiss. She didn't regret it, but she meant what she'd said to Vic.

Best she get out of here. Go back to Carriage Hill and make her pesto.

Justin surprised Adam by clomping up the deck steps as dusk settled in. Adam could tell his older brother had something on his mind. Justin helped himself to a beer out of the refrigerator and sighed at the empty wineglasses. "You know what you're getting into at Carriage Hill, right?"

Adam shrugged. "A stonework job that's almost done. Briars. Grapevines."

"With Adrienne."

"Our accidental innkeeper."

"Vic Scarlatti's long-lost daughter who played games with that fact last winter. She was pretty messed up then. She doesn't stick anywhere. You're a steady guy, Adam. You want that kind of drama in your life?"

"She'd say you have a point."

"You?"

"I appreciate the concern. Where's your pirate expert tonight?"

Meaning adventurer Samantha Bennett hadn't been an obvious match for solid Justin Sloan, either.

Or he for her.

A muscle in Justin's jaw worked. "I'll mind my own business."

"Glad you're looking after me, big brother."

"Yeah, I bet you are." Justin grinned, but his expression quickly turned serious again. "Think Eric admitting he and Trish split helped?"

"He seemed okay at breakfast."

"Yeah, I guess. Takes time to get past a broken engagement, I imagine. He knows how to find us if he wants to talk."

A Sloan talk about his emotions? Ten to one Eric would finally get drunk, throw a few glasses at the wall and put his ex-fiancée and the life they weren't going to have together behind him. Maybe he'd done that already and was just focusing on his job.

Either way, he and Justin had said all they were going

to say about Sloan brother romantic lives. "Do you like pesto?" Adam asked.

"What? Have I had pesto?"

"It's that stuff with basil, Parmesan, pine nuts and olive oil."

"Yeah. I've had it. That's the stuff Maggie freezes in ice-cube trays and drops in soups and sauces when she comes to family dinners. You're not making pesto, are you?"

"Adrienne is. She mentioned it after our swim."

Justin gritted his teeth but stopped himself from blurting whatever had come to his mind. He drank some of his beer. "She knows wine. She probably can handle a batch of pesto. Just warn her the basil could have ants."

"She's getting used to New England wildlife."

"At least familiar with it. Where do you fit in with our New England wildlife?"

"Ha."

Justin didn't let it go. "Does she see you more as an annoying ant or a rabid bobcat?"

"Maybe a cute little rabbit."

"Ants and bobcats aren't on a dinner menu. Rabbits could be. Might keep that in mind."

"Enjoying yourself, aren't you, Justin?"

"Immensely," he said, finishing his beer. He set the bottle on the table. "See you around, brother. Adrienne's attractive, I'll say that, and she's off to a great start at Carriage Hill. She'll be busy through foliage season."

"Just as well?"

"You said it, not me."

Twelve

Adrienne dug out an index card with a pesto recipe Olivia had jotted herself, in purple ink in her artistic penmanship. The recipe called for mashing fresh basil with a mortar and pestle. Adrienne figured she was out of luck on that one and would have to use the food processor, but she noticed Olivia had written "lower cupboard" in parentheses.

"Worth a shot."

She placed the recipe faceup on the butcher-block island and started opening cupboards. Sure enough, she discovered an old-fashioned, well-used mortar and pestle in the back of the lower cupboard next to the refrigerator. Making pesto with a food processor would be quick and easy, but she loved the idea of using a traditional mortar and pestle. Olivia must have, too.

And it would be the perfect activity after kissing Adam Sloan out on Echo Lake.

Adrienne washed the mortar and pestle and got out the basil. She rinsed it and dried it, keeping an eye out for ants and tiny spiders. She didn't spot anything she wouldn't want in the pesto. It was dark outside now, cool enough that she shut the windows and had a hard time imagining she'd gone swimming earlier. Likely their near-nakedness had affected Adam. No question it had affected her.

If not for Vic and Rohan, would they have gone further?

No point going down that particular road.

The pesto was simple enough to make and filled the kitchen with the homey, delicious scent of fresh basil, pine nuts, olive oil and Parmesan cheese. Adrienne had enough ingredients to make three batches. She froze two of them in ice-cube trays, per the suggestion in the recipe. She let them firm up while she cleaned up her pesto-making mess and then popped the cubes out of the trays into freezer bags.

"Presto, pesto," she said cheerfully, shutting the freezer door.

Working with her hands and getting a tangible result—pesto, not letting the fresh basil go to waste—helped settle her down after her impulsive trip to the lake. Swimming, kissing the local stonemason. Almost getting caught by Vic and Rohan. Would that have mattered so much? But she knew it would have, at least to her. She didn't always think things through. For the most part, her seat-of-the-pants approach led to positive things in her life. Adventures, friends, even income. Being here, though...

"I can't screw it up."

That night, of course, she had luscious, erotic dreams involving water, damp skin, hard muscles and such.

When Adam appeared at the kitchen door the next morning, she almost melted. She'd already downed half a pot of coffee, two scrambled eggs with fresh herbs and two slices of toast with Maggie's impossibly delicious strawberry jam, and now, three hours later, it was almost lunchtime and she *still* hadn't shaken off her dreams.

Adam smiled at her. "Morning."

Adrienne peeled off her apron—one of Olivia's, emblazoned with chickens—and tossed it on the back of a chair. "Come in. Hello. Welcome." *Why* was she so awkward? But she knew why. "I just cleaned up the breakfast dishes. I wasn't in the mood to do them earlier. What can I do for you?"

He pushed open the door and stepped into the kitchen. He wore close-fitting jeans and a canvas shirt in a deep shade of blue that matched his eyes. He peered at the pesto on the counter that she hadn't frozen. "Any plans for this?"

"I thought I'd throw some into a bit of pasta for lunch."

"Sounds good."

"You're welcome to join me." The invitation was out before she could stop herself. "I picked up fresh pasta at the country store yesterday," she added quickly. "I'll make enough for dinner, too, but I'll still have more than I can or should eat. I can always put some into a container for you to take home."

"I'd like that," he said. "To join you, I mean."

She realized she'd kept talking after she'd invited him. She *wanted* his company at lunch, but she was all tingly and on edge again, being around him. It wasn't just the last echoes of her dreams, either. "But you're not here about pasta and pesto. Did you need to ask me something?"

"Justin mentioned we need to check the lights in the closet in the downstairs suite. I said I'd take a look."

"I know the light you mean. It's balky. Sometimes it works and sometimes it doesn't."

"That's the one."

Adrienne wiped her hands on a towel. "I'll go with you."

His gaze rested on her for a half beat longer than she felt was necessary. "I can wait if that's better for you."

"Now's fine. You're not intruding. I didn't leave a trail of slinky lingerie."

"That's good, I guess."

Adrienne bit down on her lower lip. "I really should curb my tendency to blurt out whatever I think."

His eyes sparked with humor. "Don't on my account."

"My mouth is as restless as the rest of me, I guess. Oh…well…" Why had she brought up lingerie and being restless? "Let's have a look at the balky light."

She spun out of the kitchen and led him to the suite. She moved through her morning routines quickly, but she tended to be tidy, making her bed, putting away clean clothes, tossing dirty clothes in a small hamper.

She pulled open the closet door. She noticed a single hiking sock on the floor. She could live with that. She stepped back. "I'll leave you to it. I'll see what else is in the garden for our pasta."

She returned to the kitchen and dashed out through the mudroom into the garden, welcoming the cool breeze. The next few days promised to be pleasant but not as warm. Maggie and Olivia had tucked vegetable plants here and there, and Adrienne managed to find a summer squash, carrots and spinach, all slowly succumbing to the end of southern New England's short growing season. She loaded the veggies into her arms, feeling more composed, less agitated about her dreams and having Adam here.

He was in the kitchen when she went back inside. She dumped the vegetables in the sink. "What's the verdict? Can you fix the light yourself, or do you need to wait for Justin?"

"Already fixed it," Adam said with an amused smile and his usual equanimity.

"Oh. Well, that was fast. Great, thanks."

"Would you like a hand with the vegetables?"

"Don't you have to work on the wall?"

He opened a drawer and withdrew a paring knife. "Wall's done. We can look at it later."

"Oh. Okay. I'll wash, you start chopping?"

He smiled. "Will do."

They got busy washing, chopping and then sautéing the fresh vegetables. Adrienne dug a pot out of a cupboard and filled it with water. She turned off the faucet, and Adam lifted the pot out of the sink and set it on the stove, turning on the gas burner. While water came to a boil, they went outside so he could get her approval on the wall.

"It looks great to me," she said. He'd tidied up, raked the disturbed ground and reseeded any bare patches. "It's amazing how seamless everything is here with the new addition, the yard and now the wall."

"Good planning on Maggie and Olivia's part."

"And execution on Sloan & Sons' part, too." She ran her fingertips along the top of the waist-high wall. "I have a hard time picturing whoever built this wall the first time. Do you think most of the stones are from nearby fields?"

He shook his head. "It's quarried stone. It matches stone used in several buildings in the village."

"Imagine following that trail," she said, fascinated by the idea. "I love the history here. Anyway, yes, the wall has my stamp of approval. If you need Maggie or Olivia to approve—"

"They're good with whatever you say."

Obviously approval wasn't a concern for him. He trusted himself and his work.

They went back inside and added the whole-wheat linguine to the boiling water. Since it was fresh, the pasta only needed a couple of minutes before it was ready. Adrienne placed a colander in the sink and Adam drained the pasta while she got out plates.

Pasta, veggies and a healthy dollop of the freshly-made pesto, and they were good to go.

It was cool but not too cool to have their lunch out on the terrace. "Take every opportunity while we can," Adam said.

"It was already winter when I started house-sitting for Vic last year."

"Must have been a shock after California."

"I'd been in New York, so not too bad."

"How'd you like New York?"

"It didn't stick."

"Leave behind an ex-boyfriend?"

"Mercifully, yes. I liked Knights Bridge, but I was—" She hesitated, aware of that stonemason focus of his, that penetrating, blue-eyed gaze, as if he could see straight to her soul. "I wasn't in a good place."

"Because of Vic or the ex-boyfriend?"

"Not the ex. We only saw each other for a short time, and it never worked. No, I wasn't in a good place because of me. Vic had no idea. I regret not being more forthcoming with him from the start, and with Heather, too. We worked closely with each other planning Vic's renovations."

"She had Brody to distract her," Adam said. "She understands where your head was then. How forthcoming were you with yourself?"

"Not very. The truth is, I didn't know if I'd tell Vic he was my father. I didn't know how I felt. I told myself I wanted to get to know him before I said anything. That I didn't want to mess up his life. That I needed to hold back in case I discovered something about him that made me *not* want to tell him. I didn't know how my parents would react, especially my mother. It felt more her secret than mine. But she told me not to consider that, and to do what I wanted to do."

Adam studied her a moment. "Did that make it tougher,

knowing you couldn't leave it to her and had to make the decision yourself?"

She frowned at him. "I hadn't thought of it that way, but yes—at first, at least. But I never had a firm plan. I just seized the moment to house-sit and went from there."

"You read the situation and decided on your next steps based on that information."

She nodded. "That sounds quite sensible when you say it."

"You had a lot of needles to thread," he said, his tone matter-of-fact.

"I'm not indecisive most days. I couldn't have become a successful wine blogger and consultant if I were, but I admit I was thrown when I found out about Vic. But I wasn't thirteen. I could have been more adult about my choices."

Adam steadied his gaze on her. She noticed warmth— empathy—in his Sloan blue eyes. "Vic got a great wine cellar out of the deal, and he got you."

She swallowed despite the tightness in her throat. "It didn't have to be so messy for him."

"He's an adult, too. Life can get messy. We're none of us perfect."

"The Sloans seem like a tight-knit family."

"We are, maybe to a fault. We have our disagreements."

"I suppose that's not unexpected with six siblings."

"That's what Gran says. When push comes to shove, we have each other's backs, and we know it."

"Two of you got married to Knights Bridge new-comers this past year. How are Samantha and Brody fitting in?"

"Brody doesn't give a damn if he fits in. He's all about Heather. As it should be."

"But you like having him as your brother-in-law?"

"Yeah." Adam didn't seem as if he'd given it much thought. "He wasn't in good graces with us big brothers when Heather got involved with him, but we worked it out."

"Vic says she's as hardheaded as the guys in your family."

Adam smiled. "More so."

"Are you competitive with each other?"

"Nah. We worked all that out as kids. Eric sometimes feels the need to be perfect but that's in his head. I have no problem if he proves to be human once in a while."

"He's a police officer, too. He was great when the boys took off. If we hadn't found them when we did, he'd have pounced. The whole town would have pounced," Adrienne added, knowing it was true. "What about you—do you let people see your vulnerabilities? Do you have secrets that even your brothers don't know about?"

"Like having lunch with you? Should that be a secret?"

Adrienne sighed. "I should have known you wouldn't be serious. There's a difference between a secret and something that's no one's business."

Adam grinned at her and pushed his empty plate aside. "That means you don't want the rest of Knights Bridge to know we've got something going on between us?"

"I don't think I was hired to get involved with Maggie's brother-in-law."

"Want me to get her permission?"

"No! I don't need her permission."

He got to his feet and walked around the table to her.

"Don't worry, Adrienne. I'm not going to mess things up for you here. Not without your okay, anyway," he added lightly. Before she could figure out how to respond, he leaned over and kissed her softly on her forehead. "I enjoyed having wine with you yesterday, and I enjoyed lunch. Thanks."

"You're welcome."

He smiled, as if he knew the effect he was having on her, and stood straight. "Great job on the pesto. Maggie and Olivia will be happy to know their basil isn't all going to seed. I need to get up to my folks' place to do some work at the office. Okay if I leave you with the dishes?"

"Of course. Adam…" She touched his wrist, noticed the smashed hand had healed well. "I'm trying to be patient and deliberate for once."

"Yeah. I get it."

He left abruptly, and as Adrienne collected the dishes onto a tray and took them into the kitchen, she felt her knees wobble from the shock of pure awareness. Adam hadn't left because he had things to do, although he probably did. He'd left because he'd wanted more than a quick kiss and then off to do the dishes. An image of him carrying her into her innkeeper's suite on the cool, breezy afternoon brought her up short.

She breathed, settling herself down, and then she got busy cleaning up the kitchen and readying the inn—and herself—for the eight friends arriving that weekend.

The next two days, Adrienne focused on her work, escaping to Echo Lake late on Thursday to visit Vic. He was wrestling with his voice-activated software again and muttering about his latest Scrabble loss. They walked Rohan together, enjoying the cooler weather and the hints of autumn. They didn't run into Adam. But he stopped by the inn the next morning with the promised fire supplies. He had Violet with him this time. She slipped into the mudroom to finish food left in Buster's dish.

"My kind of dog," Adrienne said as Violet returned to Adam's side in the living room.

He stood up from the small copper kettle he'd filled with kindling. "Violet's her own kind of bold. Good luck this weekend."

"My first big event."

"It'll be great. Want me to fill the wood box while I'm here? Your guests will want a fire tomorrow night for sure. It's going to get chilly."

Adrienne nodded. "Cold enough to do in the basil."

They collected wood together and got the wood box filled in just a few trips to the shed. She thanked him for his help, and he didn't linger. Work beckoned. He had to take the weather into account, too, even more than she did at the inn.

Lisa Zalewski and her cleaning crew arrived shortly after Adam left and finished their work just before the first two friends parked under the Farm at Carriage Hill sign. Adrienne greeted them warmly, confident she was ready for their weekend get-together. Felicity would stop by soon to check on everything. Maggie was in good shape to do the food, and Olivia would be around if needed.

And so it was.

The weekend flew by, and on Sunday night, Adrienne sank onto the floor in the living room in front of a toasty fire. The friends' get-together had earned rave reviews from all eight women as they'd loaded up their cars and departed. At the same time, it also revealed a few gaps in Carriage Hill's workings—not unexpected, Adrienne thought as she stretched out her legs, her stocking feet almost touching the hearth.

Maggie and Olivia burst into the house and made their way into the living room. "We're celebrating," Maggie said. "I brought wine. Olivia will have sparkling water. Felicity can't join us but said to tell you she's with us in spirit."

Adrienne started to get up. "I can grab glasses—"

Maggie shook her head. "Nope. You sit. We know how you feel after this weekend."

In minutes, she and Olivia returned with two glasses of a Kendrick Winery chardonnay and a glass of sparkling water with fresh mint from the garden. "Our first fire of the season," Olivia said, sinking into a chair by the fireplace. "We had a fire on Christmas Eve when Dylan and I had our wedding here."

"It was cold that day," Maggie said. "Borderline fire weather tonight, but I love the atmosphere." She held up her glass to Adrienne. "Cheers."

Adrienne responded in kind. "After this weekend, I see just how much you two have been doing. Even a cleaning service and Felicity—both of whom are amazing—it's a lot. You've been doing everything yourselves from food to sheets, windows and toilets."

"I've potty trained two boys," Maggie said. "Toilets are nothing to me."

Olivia grinned at her. "I don't want to think about potty training right now."

Maggie laughed. "Diapers. Think about lots and lots of diapers."

"That I can handle. I think." She sipped her sparkling water. "I never expected this place to make a real profit early on. I was always going to freelance as a graphic designer until I got things sorted out here."

Maggie sat cross-legged on the floor. "Then Dylan swooped into your life."

Olivia nodded, obviously pleased at that development. "Adventure travel, entrepreneurial boot camps, friends and family far and wide. Married. Baby on the way. New house, new barn camps. Now we have new business offices in the village. Well, not new. New to us. We're renovating a fantastic Victorian house off the town common. I don't know if I mentioned that to you, Adrienne."

"I heard."

"Felicity," Maggie said, no doubt in her tone. "Gabe's partnered with Noah and Dylan and a friend of theirs from California. She's working with them remotely. The house is on the other side of the library from us. The boys won't go near it. Someone told them it's haunted."

Adrienne drank some of her wine. "How's your head, Maggie? Sorry I didn't ask earlier."

"We were all too busy. I got the stitches out. I'll have a scar but it should fade some in time. I don't know what we'd have done about this weekend without you here. It wasn't too trial-by-fire?"

"Not at all," Adrienne said. "The women friends were terrific. They loved having the run of the place to do their own thing. I had to dig out the first-aid kit for a few minor scratches and stings, but nothing out of the ordinary."

"No close encounters with wildlife meandering out of the Quabbin wilderness," Maggie said. She drank her wine, no sign her injuries from her fall bothered her. "Brandon enjoyed leading the friends on a hike. He said you pulled together books on the history of Quabbin and various towns in the area. They loved that. I wouldn't have thought of it, maybe because I'm from here."

"So many possibilities," Olivia said. "History, nature, local food and lore."

"And a beautiful spot for a quiet evening by the fire," Adrienne added.

Olivia placed a palm on her expanding middle. "Maggie and I weren't kidding when we told you we didn't have everything all figured out."

Adrienne smiled. "That's half the fun."

"Great attitude," Maggie said.

Maggie and Olivia's diverse interest and skills coupled with their capacity for hard work had helped them get the inn up and running. They'd hired a temporary help as needed but now it was time for a more comprehensive, systematic approach.

Olivia flipped through the comment cards the women had filled out and left on a side table. "All positive reviews for your first weekend event."

"That's a good start," Maggie said.

Adrienne thanked them but Olivia wasn't done yet. "I'm glad it worked out, but we've been keeping our noses above water, so to speak. Our scattershot approach isn't sustainable. Having you here is a godsend, Adrienne, but it's not enough. It's not just about help. We need a vision for this place. So much has changed since I bought it."

"Before Dylan," Maggie supplied.

"Exactly," Olivia said. "But you and I have launched new ventures, too. We could do more with the goat's milk products. I want whatever we do at least to be self-sustaining. We can book more events here but that brings its own headaches."

"So much for your plan to build slowly, step by step," Maggie said.

"Sometimes you have to get started and make adjustments as you go along," Adrienne said. "I might do that too much but I like where I am right now. You'll figure out what you want this place to be for you."

"Autumn is a big season in New England," Maggie said.

Olivia nodded. "We turned down events we could have booked."

"We'll figure it out," Adrienne said. "We don't have to do it now."

"Even when I first moved to Boston, I knew I wanted to come home to Knights Bridge one day. I saved my money and snapped up this place when it came on the market." Olivia eased to her feet and placed a hand at the small of her back as she stretched. "Dylan...we

were a surprise for him. Knights Bridge, me. Grace."
She smiled. "Buster."

"Grace was a surprise for all of us," Maggie said.
"Have you met her, Adrienne?"

She shook her head. "Not yet."

"She got to meet Dylan's father before he died. He
and Dylan talked about going into adventure travel together, but it didn't happen. Grace is excited about the
baby. The knitters and crocheters at the assisted living
center are having fun. Blankets, booties, sweaters, hats."

"You need twins," Maggie said, a mischievous glint
in her turquoise eyes.

Olivia laughed and gave a mock shudder. "I can't
imagine."

"A wonder my mother survived Ava and Ruby."

"I almost forgot," Olivia said. "I asked Adam to stop
by to take a look at the chimney in my office. It kept
slipping my mind. I saw some cracks in it before you
got here, Adrienne. I have no idea if they're a problem,
a potential problem or nothing. I hope you don't mind."

"Not at all," Adrienne said, trying to ignore a twinge
of something she couldn't quite describe. Longing? For
what? She'd never had the kind of community Maggie
and Olivia did here in their hometown. Although she
lived in Knights Bridge now, she was an outsider.

Olivia was clearly tired. Maggie abandoned the last
of her wine. She'd picked up Olivia at her house and
insisted on dropping her off, ignoring her friend's in-
sistence she could walk. They thanked Adrienne and
congratulated her again on the successful weekend, and

in thirty seconds, they were out the front door, leaving her to deal with Adam and the chimney on her own.

The chimney in Olivia's former office was fine.

Adrienne wasn't surprised.

"That crack's probably been there for seventy-five years," Adam said, joining her in the side yard. It was nearing dusk but she'd needed air, exercise. "I can go into details if you want."

"You don't need to touch it?"

"Nope."

"All I need to know."

She'd grabbed a baseball and glove she'd discovered in the mudroom. She hadn't really thought about what she'd do with them. She figured Maggie had them there for her sons, or maybe for guests.

Aware of Adam watching her, Adrienne tossed the ball between hand and glove. She hadn't realized how keyed up she was until Maggie and Olivia left and he arrived. So much for a quiet, easygoing life as a New England innkeeper—but she did love it so far. She just needed to resist being impulsive and causing trouble. *Always remember the law of unintended consequences*, she thought.

Adam's tall frame was silhouetted against the darkening landscape. "Want me to throw to you?"

"Sure. Thanks. I'm just burning off some excess energy. Then I'll probably turn to jelly."

"But everything went well this weekend," he said.

It wasn't a question but Adrienne nodded. "Yes."

She lobbed him the ball. He didn't have a glove but

he caught the ball easily bare-handed. He turned to Violet, flopped in the grass. "The ball's not for you. Got it?" The golden retriever blinked up at him expectantly. Adam grinned at Adrienne. "I think she's too tired to chase balls."

"I'll try not to miss so she's not tempted. Just don't throw me a fastball."

"We'll just play catch."

She stuffed her hand into the glove. "I don't think I've ever actually played catch with a baseball and glove. In fact, I'm sure I haven't."

The glove fit okay. Dylan having been a professional hockey player, there were street and ice hockey sticks in the mudroom, too. Adrienne had never played hockey, either. She liked to walk and she'd taken a few yoga classes. Dylan's adventure travel programs would never be her first pick for a vacation. Vineyards, museums, quaint Parisian streets. Her idea of a break. Trekking up Mount Washington? No. But not all the "adventures" were physically demanding.

Well, she could figure out how to throw and catch a baseball. It was Adam she wasn't sure she could handle. Herself around him, to be more specific.

His second toss of the ball bounced off her glove. He walked over to her and showed her how to hold the glove. "Do you play baseball with your family?" she asked him.

"Softball. We missed Heather this summer. She's our best pitcher."

"We've stayed in touch," Adrienne said. "She loves London but she gets homesick."

"Helps to have Brody in her life," Adam said.

He stood close to Adrienne. It wasn't easy to wind down with him touching her, but he focused on the finer points of handling a baseball glove. "I can show you how to do a perfect downward dog," she said.

He laughed softly. "What makes you think I don't already know?"

"Oh, just a wild guess."

He headed across the grass to his spot next to Violet, near the window above the kitchen sink. Adrienne hoped she didn't have a wild throw, but that was more likely to happen if she let herself get distracted by his broad shoulders, muscular forearms and sexy, easy manner. He moved smoothly, comfortable in his own skin, with being out here in the near-darkness with the hoot of an owl in the woods, the rustling sounds of squirrels and who-knew-what, the faint scent of herbs and evergreens. His throws were on target and at a challenging speed—respectful of her abilities. He wasn't patronizing or showing off. She did better catching the ball than throwing it but improved even after a few minutes.

They tossed the ball back and forth for about fifteen minutes before it became too dark. "We'll have you pitching and hitting by spring," Adam said as they started back to the house. "Assuming you're still here then."

"I wouldn't miss another winter of snow, ice and subzero temperatures."

"Only occasional subzero temperatures."

"Subfreezing, then. Days and days of subfreezing

temperatures. Vic's house will be warmer than it was last winter."

"A proper heating system helps."

"Definitely." Adrienne tucked the glove under her arm. Adam carried the ball. "I look forward to cozy evenings in front of the fire here, on the nights we don't have guests."

"Any interest in snowshoeing or cross-country skiing?"

"Sure, why not? I've done both a few times. Something to do on a cold winter day." She started toward the terrace, not surprised Adam and Violet walked with her. "I think about ice-skating on the rink on the common. Do you do winter sports?"

"Snowshoeing and some backcountry skiing. No ice-skating."

"Ever?"

"I played hockey as a kid. Not my thing."

"I had a lot to sort out last winter," she said. "Maybe I still do."

Adam didn't respond at once. He handed the ball to her when they came to the terrace. "This job's a big change for you," he said finally. "I get that. And Vic…"

"He likes having you out at the lake." She angled a look at him, only dim light from the house on his face. His eyes were navy blue in the near-darkness, the shadows on his face somehow adding to his air of calm, patience and control. "Anything to sort out in your life?" she asked him.

He shrugged. "Where I'm going to live. Can't stay

in Vic's guesthouse forever. Beyond that…" He paused, his gaze settling on her. "Can't say there is."

"Your time in the military—were you in combat?"

"Yes."

Adrienne pictured him in a Marine uniform. "Are you the only one in your family with military experience?"

"Of my siblings." He stepped up onto the terrace. "What about your family?"

"My grandfather. My mother's dad. He was in the navy in the Pacific during World War II. He died when I was in high school."

She heard how stiff and awkward she sounded. For what felt like the millionth time she reminded herself she usually had no trouble talking to people. It wasn't that Adam was making her uncomfortable. She just wanted to get her words right. "It must have been good to get home," she added, hoping it was enough, not too much.

The slightest smile. "It was."

"You mentioned you apprenticed with a master stonemason during high school. Did you know you wanted to get back into that work?"

"I knew I liked the work and was good at it. He died suddenly of a massive heart attack, and we needed someone to build a chimney on a site. That was my first solo project."

Adrienne reached down and patted Violet. "Rohan was abandoned out at the lake as a young puppy, but he was healthy. Were you ever worried Violet wouldn't make it when you nursed her back to health?"

"It was touch and go at first but she got there."

"That's wonderful. Would I be correct in guessing a woman was involved in the reasons Eric let you know about Violet?" Adrienne regretted her question immediately. She'd been so careful and now an intrusive question had to pop out of her mouth, bypassing all her good intentions. "I'm sorry. I withdraw the question."

Adam pulled out a chair and sat in the near-darkness, the light from the house not reaching him now. "I was involved with a woman my last few months in the service. She decided to make a career in the military. I didn't. That was that."

"No way to resist Violet once you saw her?"

He smiled, rubbing his foot on Violet's back as she lay down. "I didn't stand a chance."

"You and Violet were good for each other, then."

"Yeah. You could say that."

Adrienne realized she'd remained standing. "Why did you tell me that story?"

He angled her a look. "You asked. You'd find out. Someone would tell you. Vic knows. My brothers know. Heather. I had too much to drink one night before Violet and spilled it at a Sloan family bonfire on Echo Lake."

"That's how Vic found out?"

"Uh-huh." Adam looked up at the sky, a quarter moon high above the endless woods that bordered the backyard. "My brothers and sister would have dragged it out of me if I hadn't told them on my own. I'd written from Afghanistan that I was coming home with someone."

"Ah," Adrienne said. "You jumped the gun."

"Big-time."

"I've had my share of failed relationships, most recently with the guy in New York I mentioned. Owns a wine shop. Total snob." She shuddered. "Bullet dodged. Sorry. I shouldn't use that kind of metaphor."

"But it's the first thing that comes to mind when you think about this guy?"

"Meaning we weren't a good match." She set the ball and glove on the terrace table. "I didn't have my head screwed on straight, either. I needed this past year-plus."

"To get over him?"

"To figure out myself. Finding out about Vic didn't help, and I was on the go a lot. I wasn't ready for a relationship. We broke it off."

Adam picked up the baseball glove and worked the soft leather with his strong fingers. "That's when you got in touch with Vic about house-sitting."

She nodded. "I'm glad I did, but I really do wish I'd been more up-front with him—with everyone."

"It wasn't an easy situation. You were sure Vic didn't know about you?"

"I was sure my mother hadn't told him."

"Not quite the same," Adam said.

"No. But he didn't know. He didn't have a clue. I wish I'd made things easier for him."

"You made a choice. It wasn't like there was a right choice and a wrong choice. You didn't do anything wrong."

"Everyone in town knows, right?"

"I'd make that an operating assumption."

"I have," she said.

He placed the glove back on the table. "There are

secrets in Knights Bridge, but it takes some effort to keep them."

"I hope my blurting out about a past relationship didn't open old wounds for you."

"Nope," he said, getting to his feet.

"Vic says your stonemason mentor was a loner."

"He was." Adam moved close to her, taking a few strands of her hair and tucking them behind her ear. "Good night, Adrienne. I'm glad this weekend went well. Any issues with the chimney, let me know. But there won't be any."

She expected him to walk through the mudroom and kitchen, but he walked through the side yard, around to the front, where he'd parked. She listened in the darkness until she heard his truck. Then she listened to an owl, saw the silhouette of something flapping around out by the shed—a bat, no doubt—and went inside to heat up leftover soup with pesto for a quick bite, and to pour more wine.

She returned to the fire. It was dying down, but she didn't revive it. Instead she got out her laptop and distracted herself from thinking about Adam by connecting with friends online, checking her wine blog archives and otherwise reminding herself she'd never intended or imagined becoming a small-town New England inn-keeper.

Thirteen

Adam got started early the next morning on another section of Vic's driveway stone wall, one that hadn't been hit by the delivery truck but still needed attention. It was a simple job that could easily turn into a big, time-consuming expensive job if not taken care of as soon as possible. He had company financial work to tackle later, and he was organizing his masonry projects for the next few months, a mix of ones he could complete on his own and others for which he'd need a crew. It was warm enough today he figured he'd take his laptop onto the deck at the guesthouse.

With a little luck, he'd stay away from Carriage Hill Road and let Adrienne work in peace, without having to deal with the sexual tension between them. It had become impossible to ignore.

He didn't want to ignore it. Last night, he'd wanted to pick her up and carry her into her suite with its nice new bed.

He'd thought maybe his attraction to her would ease once he'd kissed her, but it hadn't.

Hell of a dumb thought that had been.

Violet settled next to him in the dew-soaked grass by the driveway. Bright red and orange leaves on some of the trees along the stone wall and in the yard indicated fall foliage season was already upon them.

Vic walked down from the house. Adam assumed he was checking on the wall, but he had a tight look that suggested he had something else on his mind. "I need to go out of town again," he said abruptly. "It'll be at least a week but it could be longer. Can you keep an eye on the place?"

"Not a problem. That's part of the deal."

"I didn't know I'd be heading out again so soon. Adrienne has her hands full at Carriage Hill. I'll ask her to pick up the mail, not that I get much."

"I can look after your mail, Vic. What about Rohan?"

"Elly's taking him. She considers us having shared custody but allows he is my dog." Vic eyed Adam. "Aren't you curious where I'm going?"

"Sure, but I figure you'll tell me if you can and if you need me to know."

"Washington." He bit off the word as if it was a bad health diagnosis. "As in DC."

"They say diplomats never truly retire," Adam said, keeping his tone neutral.

"I didn't say the trip was for professional reasons."

"Visiting the Smithsonian? Lady friend in town?"

"Ha. Right." A spark of humor, anyway. "A car's picking me up in twenty minutes, so don't think I'm being kidnapped."

Adam smiled. "Okay, good to know."

"Not that Violet would go wild and chase the car," Vic added.

"She was never into chasing cars." Adam waited, but Vic didn't start back to the house, instead shifting from one foot to the other as if he was a twelve-year-old who hadn't turned in his homework and knew he had to fess up. "What else is on your mind, Vic?"

He made a pained face. "Adrienne's in Knights Bridge because of me."

Here it is. Adam chose a trowel from several he'd brought with him. "You're worried she'll feel rejected if you let yourself get lured out of retirement and take a new position."

"I didn't say that," Vic snapped, although it was clear Adam had hit the proverbial nail on the head. "Adrienne feels rejected and abandoned as it is. It doesn't matter that I didn't know she was my daughter. It's a gut thing. Deep emotion. I wasn't there when she was growing up. She comes here now to start a new career, and I take off just as she's settling in herself."

"She wants to spend time with you," Adam said.

"I know. And I want to spend time with her."

Violet rolled onto her back and yawned. Adam watched her a moment before shifting back to Vic. He knew he'd already said too much. "You two will work it out."

"Not stepping in that one, are you? I don't blame you. But we will work it out. I know we will." Vic bit his lower lip and glanced down at the lake. "Right now

I need to take the right next step for me, and that's getting in that car in a few minutes."

"Adrienne doesn't plan to stay in Knights Bridge, either."

Vic frowned, shifting back to Adam. "Either?"

"I'm reading between the lines," Adam said. "I have experience dealing with you career diplomat types. You're about to be called back into service, aren't you, Vic? I know you can't answer, but the signs are there. I imagine you know where a lot of bodies are buried and have a lot of contacts after forty years."

"More contacts than bodies, one would hope."

Adam didn't let Vic distract him. "Maybe being retired gives you a certain perspective. Who knows, maybe the US needs an ambassador to Mars, and you're it."

"I'm always open to new adventures and service—but it wouldn't be to Mars."

"Where, then?"

"Nice try, Adam. I can't say what's going on."

"We'll go with Mars, then."

But Vic couldn't quite roll with Adam's sense of humor. "It might not happen. I might say no. I have a good life here. I'm investing in Elly's goat's milk business and getting into wine now that I have a proper wine cellar, thanks to Adrienne."

"New hobbies are great, but I don't see you milking goats and mucking out stalls."

"That's correct. Elly's hired help. She wants to be free to travel. My interest is more in the goat's milk products themselves. She's working with Olivia and Maggie. I'm a sounding board for ideas."

"You could be a sounding board from Mars," Adam said.

"So I could."

"What do you know about goats and goat's milk?"

"I'm learning. I like to learn new things. I don't know why I sit around playing Scrabble on my iPad. I know quality bath and spa products."

Adam grinned at him. "You know spas?"

"A spa visit wouldn't hurt you, Adam. You've got enough scar tissue to keep a masseuse busy for hours." Vic stepped back onto the driveway, his shoes wet with the morning dew. "You have my cell phone number. Call or text if you need me for anything."

"Have you told Adrienne you'll be away?"

Vic cleared his throat. "I thought you could do that."

Adam grinned. "Chicken."

"I just…" Vic looked awkward, uncomfortable. "I've never had to consider anyone else in making my choices."

And he wasn't sure he liked it? Wasn't sure he liked having Adrienne in Knights Bridge? Adam wasn't going there. "Your call," he said.

"Yeah. Okay. I'll get a backbone and let her know."

"I'll look after the place," Adam said.

"But not my daughter, huh?"

"She's an adult, Vic."

"So she is." He waved vaguely toward his lake house. "I'll grab my bag and turn off my iPad before my car gets here."

* * *

Adrienne was taking the day off and lingering at the kitchen table in her leggings and an oversize shirt when a sleek black car eased to a stop in front of the inn. She glanced at the stove clock. Almost nine. She wasn't expecting guests. Maggie and Olivia had warned her she might get the occasional drop-in who didn't realize it was a destination inn, but what kind of drop-in would try to check in this early?

She felt a stab of panic. Had something happened to Vic? Her mother? Her dad? If it resulted in a car being sent for her, it had to be bad news.

But she knew she was leaping *way* ahead, and then she saw Vic get out of the back of the car. He held up a hand to the driver as if to say "one minute" and headed up the stone walk to the kitchen door.

Adrienne was on her feet and had the door open before he could knock. "Good morning, Vic. You didn't hire a car to drop by for coffee, did you?"

He glanced back at the car, as if it could tell him something, provide him some necessary insight. Finally he turned to her again. He was smartly dressed in a sport coat, lightweight sweater and dark trousers, not his typical attire out at the lake when he was playing Scrabble and pretending to write his memoirs.

"I'm heading out of town," he blurted. "I have meetings in Washington. I tried to get Adam to tell you because I didn't want it to be a thing. He balked. He was right. I needed to tell you myself."

"I see. Do you want to come in?"

"I can't stay."

"When did this come up?"

"Last night. I wasn't positive until 5:00 a.m. I didn't say anything to Adam until thirty minutes ago. He'll look after the place." Vic hesitated. "I didn't ask for this to happen, Adrienne, but I didn't feel I could say no."

"Was it an option?"

He nodded, straightforward. "Just not one I felt I could exercise."

"And live with yourself?"

"Something like that. I wish I could tell you more, and I wish the timing was better since you just got here."

"We're not sewn into each other's pockets, Vic," Adrienne said, meaning it. "I've got plenty here to keep me busy. I hope everything goes well for you. Be careful, okay?"

"Always. I could be back on my porch fighting with voice-activation software before you know it."

But she heard the doubt in his voice. She said nothing as he glanced around, as if seeing the country kitchen for the first time. "This really is quite a place. Do you like living here?"

"So far, yes. It'll take some getting used to being here at the same time as guests, but the innkeeper's suite is spacious and lovely."

"Yeah. That helps."

"Don't worry about me, okay? I have plenty to do. The inn's booked solid the next few weekends to take advantage of foliage season."

He looked marginally relieved. "Olivia's and Maggie's lives were different when they started with this place. Olivia didn't know Dylan existed. Maggie's marriage was on the rocks. The changes in town this past year are good, Adrienne. Knights Bridge is building on what's special about it."

"What attracted you twenty years ago," Adrienne said.

"I'll always be an outsider here."

His tone was matter-of-fact, without any hint of self-pity. She thought she understood. "Here and everywhere, Vic. You wouldn't have it any other way, and the people in town are fine with that. They take you as you are."

"And you, Adrienne?"

She smiled despite his sudden melancholy. "You're a better man than I thought you'd be this time last year."

That broke the downward turn in his mood. "You figured I'd be a cad."

"I thought you knew about me and didn't care. At first."

"Be who you are, Adrienne. Don't let what we didn't have get in your way. Don't stay here in this job because of me. I love the idea of having you in town, but I don't want it to hold you back."

"You love the idea but you're on your way out of town for who knows how long. I don't mind, honestly. I want you to do what's right for you, too."

"Thank you. I appreciate that. Knights Bridge is home for me now. There's nothing that will change that."

"Not even falling for some hot young thing in Paris?"

His eyes sparked with humor. "Not even that."

She kissed him on the cheek. "Go on now. Duty calls. Relish being needed and courted by your old crowd, whatever comes of it."

"You have free rein at the lake if you want a change of scenery. Stay at the house. Throw a party. Check out the wildlife. Throw sticks for Violet. Grab Rohan from Elly for a visit. Adam's there if you need anything."

"I appreciate that. Thanks, Vic."

Adrienne stood out on the kitchen steps and watched his car turn around in the driveway and then head up Carriage Hill Road, presumably on to Boston and the airport. She'd come here because of him and now he was leaving—and it was fine. She hadn't faked it. She felt no sense of irritation, loss, rejection or abandonment.

She went inside and made more tea. Maybe she hadn't come to Knights Bridge just to get to know Vic better and spend time with him. Maybe she'd come here for herself—for this job, these people, this life.

She'd just poured her tea when Buster burst into the mudroom ahead of Olivia. "Sorry, sorry," she said, shutting the mudroom door behind her. "He still doesn't get it that we don't live here anymore."

Adrienne laughed, putting aside her conflicted emotions about Vic's departure. "Tea?" she asked.

Olivia beamed, hand on her swelling abdomen. "That would be perfect."

Two hours later, with Olivia and Buster on their way back up the road, Adrienne grabbed her jacket and drove out to Echo Lake. She noticed a small front-end loader and a shallow trench by the wall just down from where the delivery truck had hit it. She parked behind Vic's fancier car and got out, welcoming the cool breeze off the lake, scented with evergreens. She walked around to the front of the house and mounted the steps to the front porch. She took a breath, looking out at the sparkling water, the blue sky and the first bright leaves of the fall season. Did she dare fall in love with this place? Let it feel like home? Did everyone in town believe she'd bolt after a few months? It was what she believed, wasn't it?

Adam walked out of the house, startling her. "Sorry," he said. "I was making sure Vic turned off the lights and locked the doors."

"Did he?"

"Missed the cellar light. He must have gone down for a bottle of wine."

"I saw your equipment by the stone wall. Disaster discovered or disaster averted?"

"A little of both."

Instead of his stonemason tools, he had his camera in hand—a good one, if not particularly new. He was dressed in khakis, a lightweight shirt and canvas shoes, not his usual sturdy work clothes. "Taking photos?" Adrienne asked.

"I'm on my way to take a few shots at a stone bridge on the other side of the lake. The light's not great right now, but it should improve by the time I get over there. We'll see. Join me if you'd like. I have work to do later this afternoon but I have some time now."

"I'd love to join you." Adrienne realized she hadn't hesitated, had gone with her gut. "I'm taking the day off. I didn't get to the other side of the lake when I was here over the winter. Too cold and snowy."

"The bridge is on a stream that feeds into the lake."

She zipped up her jacket. "It's the one in your photograph at Carriage Hill. Vic recognized it."

"It's unique," Adam said. "Olivia and Dylan asked me to take a few photographs to use on their websites for their various ventures. It's a favor. If the photos don't work, no harm done."

They headed down the porch steps and out to a one-track dirt road that led to the "quiet" side of the lake. "Where did you learn photography?" she asked as they walked.

"My grandfather got me started. My dad's dad. He was a great guy. No one expected him to hook up with Gran. She grew up in Amherst."

"It's just a stone's throw from here."

"It was a different world from Knights Bridge back then. Some would argue it still is. And in Gran's eyes— even she says she was a snob at first. She was in town to visit a friend whose parents owned Red Clover Inn. She met my grandfather. She looked down her nose at him and the rest of the people here. Thought they were all hicks. She was just a kid herself."

"But she changed her mind, obviously."

"She saw she was wrong about Gramps, and about Knights Bridge, and she's been here ever since. Her friend moved away but Gran stayed."

"It became her home. Your grandparents were happy together?"

"Very. No question."

The road ended at the lot where Brody Hancock's childhood home, razed years ago, had been. He and Heather planned to build their own house upon their return to

Knights Bridge from London. Adrienne followed Adam onto a path that hooked past a cove and then along the edge of the lake. The trail grew rougher and then disappeared altogether, but Adam didn't hesitate as he led her over tree roots and around boulders, through underbrush and saplings.

Just a few yards up from the lake, they came to a small stone bridge that arced over the clear, freely flowing water of a narrow stream. "When did you take the photo that's part of your series at the inn?"

"Last November."

"What's a bridge doing out here?"

"The original owners of Vic's house had it built. They planned to put up another house out here but decided against it. They sold off some of the land on this side of the lake, but this is still part of the original estate."

"Meaning Vic owns it," Adrienne said. "I didn't realize that. Why would they build a bridge before deciding on whether to build a house?"

"They were eccentric."

As if that explained it, and maybe it did. "I assume this wasn't all woods then."

"Correct. Most of this land was farmland a hundred years ago when Vic's house was built."

Adrienne squatted down for a closer look at the bridge. It looked so small. "It'll hold me?"

"Yes."

She glanced up at Adam and smiled. "I like that you didn't hesitate."

She sat on the bridge and kicked off her shoes, dipping her feet in the crystal clear water. She rested her toes on a submerged rock, slippery with moss, and leaned back, placing her hands next to her on the rough stone of the bridge. "A bit chilly but feels great. Probably you don't want me in your photos, though."

"You'd be a modern touch," Adam said.

She pulled her feet out of the stream and shook them off as best she could before slipping on her socks and shoes. He held out a hand, and she took it, standing up and jumping lightly from the small bridge. Her toe caught a stone and she plunged right into him. He slipped an arm around her waist, and she clutched his upper arm, just managing to avoid his camera.

"Phew." She laughed, steadying herself. "Skinned knee and sprained ankle averted, although I like to think I'd have landed in a bed of ferns if I hadn't found my footing."

"Your feet are probably numb from the water."

"Definitely numb."

"It can throw you off." He loosened his hold on her. "Steady?"

She wasn't really, but in another way from what he meant. "Sure. Go on and take your pictures."

"Light's still bad," he said. "Too harsh. I'll come back later. I want to get some shots with fall foliage, but most of the trees out here turn later."

"So this is a scouting mission."

"Yep."

"Sure you don't want to dip your feet in the stream?"

He looked at her as if he had no idea why he would want to do such a thing.

Adrienne laughed. "I know you Sloans are rugged, but your feet get hot, too."

"Let's walk down to the lake. The water will be warmer there."

If not as warm as the afternoon of their swim in the lake. The cooler nights in particular would have taken their toll.

In fact, she quickly discovered, this was true, although the water *was* warmer in the lake.

She and Adam sat on a sunny boulder, rolled up their pant legs and eased into the water, wading up to their knees. The lake bottom was sandy, with only a few rocks and slimy things. Adrienne found herself relaxing, noticing the nuances of her surroundings, and of the man next to her. His scarred hands, his blue eyes that seemed to soften and spark in the sunlight, his hard muscles—from his work, maybe still from his military training, just from being a Sloan.

"I must trust you if I'm out here in the boonies alone with you," she said lightly.

He turned to her. "You can trust me, Adrienne."

"I didn't think twice about it. We were alone a half-dozen times last winter. Did you ever think about kissing me in Vic's kitchen?"

"Nope."

"Kissing me at all?"

"Bold questions, Ms. Portale."

She squinted at him in the autumn sun and tried to assess whether he was shocked or offended. "I guess I'm not going to pretend what happened didn't happen."

"I was wondering about that."

"Were you?"

"Ah-huh." He eased to her, the water rippling off him at each step. With one hand, he tilted her chin up. "I thought about walking with you out here on a beautiful day and kissing you here."

"Not last winter—this morning."

"Yes, last winter, and yes, this morning."

"Good," she whispered, as his mouth found hers.

He lifted her up out of the water, their kiss deepening as she wrapped her arms around him. He was a strong, solid, sexy man. But that was her only thought once he held her tighter, her feet dipping back into the cool lake water. If he was standing on any slimy, slippery things, he didn't tilt or teeter off balance.

Then it was over. She was standing on a rock up to her knees in pretty Echo Lake, a thousand sensations going through her. She'd been thoroughly kissed and the rest of her body was reacting accordingly. She squinted up at Adam in the sunlight. "Regrets already?"

"No regrets."

Succinct. "Me, either." Not yet, anyway.

"I have to get to work."

He took her hand and they waded back to their boulder. They put on their shoes and socks and unrolled their pant legs.

"Your pants aren't as soaked as mine," she said.

"I'm taller."

"There's that."

He didn't smile. He scooped up his camera and slung it over one shoulder. Adrienne got to her feet and they made their way back to the path. "Does Vic ever walk out here?" she asked.

"I've seen him head this way a few times."

"Keeps the trails open, I guess."

"Yeah."

Was he feeling awkward or just his usual untalkative self? Adrienne stopped hard when they reached the dirt road. She put her hands on her hips and turned to him. "Are we going to talk?"

"About what?"

"About what just happened."

"We walked out to an old stone bridge, light wasn't good for photographs, we cooled off in the lake and you slipped and I caught you and one thing led to another."

"I didn't slip."

"You didn't?" He gave her one of his slight, impossibly sexy smiles. "My mistake."

"Ha. It's going to happen again, isn't it?"

"Slipping?"

"Very funny. One thing leading to another."

His eyes, deeper blue in the shade, settled her in that steady, focused way he had. "I expect it will."

Then he started up the road.

Adrienne touched a finger to her lips. She still could feel their kiss. Just what were they doing? She shook off the question. It was easier to get carried away out here in the middle of nowhere, wasn't it? Nothing and no one else to think about. Just themselves and their attraction to each other. But as they walked down the road and Vic's house came into view, and then the guesthouse, Adam's van and her car, the realities of their lives took hold.

"I need to take Violet for a walk before I head out," Adam said. "She's going to be annoyed we didn't take her with us."

"Next time," Adrienne said.

He turned to her, touched his knuckles softly to her cheek. "I'll tell her that."

Fourteen

The promise of that wild kiss in the lake didn't materialize through the next two weeks, and Vic didn't return. Adrienne concentrated on her work. With autumn taking hold in Knights Bridge's corner of New England, she had plenty to keep her busy. Carriage Hill was booked every weekend and several weekdays with adventure travelers and guides, a wedding, a family reunion, an entrepreneurial boot camp and lunches for local nonprofit organizations. Even with Felicity MacGregor as their event planner, Adrienne honestly didn't know how Maggie and Olivia would have managed without an innkeeper. But they'd realized they'd needed help when they'd started booking for fall, and they'd found someone.

"Me," Adrienne whispered to herself as she drove out to Echo Lake in Vic's old car. It was late afternoon on a beautiful, crisp day.

She'd done well with the first round of events, if not without a few small mistakes—fortunately none involving 911 calls or negative feedback from guests. Normal stuff, Maggie called them. The worst had been letting the wood box get emptied on a frosty evening. She'd trekked out to the shed in the dark, remembering, of course, encountering Adam that first time.

Adrienne doubted she'd have managed—or at least managed as well—without Felicity MacGregor. Felicity was thorough, experienced and unflappable, and Adrienne was fast becoming friends with her and her fiancé, Gabe Flanagan. Gabe and Felicity were comfortable with each other in the way two people who'd grown up together and had been friends forever often were.

Unlike Adam and me, Adrienne thought as she passed Elly O'Dunn's farm.

Not comfortable with each other in that known-each-other-since-nursery-school way. Attracted to each other, yes. Undeniably so. At the same time, unspoken between them was their mutual certainty that getting involved with each other would only lead to problems. For him, for her—for Vic. No one believed she'd stay in Knights Bridge. Adam was a member of a beloved family in town. He'd had his heart broken once and had ended up with a puppy he'd nursed back to health. Imagine if they started seeing each other for real and it didn't work out? Even if she hightailed it out of town, what about Vic?

Adam and Vic didn't need a romantic disaster on their hands, and neither did she.

She and Adam had run into each other a half-dozen times during the past two weeks but only in town, not at the lake. Just as well, with Vic off to parts unknown.

She'd had an innocuous exchange with Adam in the vegetable section at the country store. At least it'd seemed innocuous at first. By the time she returned to Carriage Hill, she'd realized his comment about getting things sorted out there the way she had at Kendrick Winery maybe hadn't been that offhand. She'd *left* the winery after getting things sorted out.

But how could she blame Adam for thinking she'd bolt after a few months when it was what she thought she'd do, too?

He wouldn't want to hem her in. He wasn't that type. From what she'd gathered, he'd let the woman he'd fallen for back in his military days go without a fight.

But that was different. She'd wanted to stay in the military. He'd wanted to come home.

Adrienne was relieved when she arrived at Vic's house. *Enough* thinking already.

She got out of the car, squinting at the bright sun, relishing the sight of the colorful foliage against evergreens, blue sky and sparkling lake. It was getting dark earlier and earlier. She was surprised when Violet wandered up to greet her. "Hey, Violet. You miss Rohan, don't you, girl?" The golden retriever wagged her tail as if she understood. "Where's Adam, hmm? I know he didn't leave you running around here on your own."

And he hadn't. He walked up the driveway toward her. She inhaled at the sight of him in an old barn jacket, jeans and work boots. Sweating. Damn, he was sexy when he was sweating.

"I thought I'd stop by and check on the place, get a change of scenery," she said.

"No problem. I hear you've been busy."

"Flat out. I hired a cleaning service. Apparently you went to school with the owner?"

"Lisa. She's a few years younger. Chris graduated with her."

Adrienne grinned at him. "I shouldn't be surprised you already know all about it."

"Justin and Samantha hired her to do some cleaning at Red Clover ahead of renovations. First thing she did was get them to rent a dumpster. It arrives next week. She mentioned she's taken on Carriage Hill, too."

"She's going to need to hire a bigger crew at the rate she's going."

With a sudden burst of energy, Violet streaked past them to a pine tree on the side of the driveway. Adam sighed. "She's about a half mile behind a red squirrel. She's not as quick as she used to be, but she's still got the fire." He turned back to Adrienne. "Vic emailed me this morning."

"Did he say where he is?"

"No. He told me he wants to build a proper firepit down by the water."

"Why on earth—"

"His guests often like to have fires."

"Meaning you and your brothers," Adrienne said.

"Brody and his DSS buddies, too. It's not a priority. He wants me to think about it and give him some options. I've got some big projects in the works but could fit it in at night, even if I'm not still at the guesthouse."

"Do you plan to move out?"

"Not at the moment but it was never going to be forever." He petted Violet as she returned to his side. "Justin and Samantha are coming up for a cookout tonight. Join us if you have time."

"Thank you." Adrienne debated a moment before she smiled. "I have time."

"Great. Come down to the guesthouse whenever you're ready."

He headed off with Violet trotting happily at his side.

Adrienne ignored the tug of longing in the pit of her stomach. She wanted to belong here, and she didn't. That was the truth of it. At least it was how she felt now, on a beautiful fall afternoon alone in Knights Bridge.

She took the back steps into Vic's kitchen. She wondered how many times he'd used it since he'd moved back into the house after renovations. He talked about taking cooking classes but never with much enthusiasm, and certainly never with a specific plan. Adrienne had no idea where he was. He'd mentioned in an email a few days ago he was on the way to the airport and would be in touch when he could but *don't worry if you don't hear from me for a while.*

Since he'd retired by the time she'd come to know him, she didn't know how to read between the lines of such messages, or even if she should bother to try.

She checked the refrigerator. Cheese, three kinds of mustard, pickles. That sort of thing. Nothing moldy or due to get moldy anytime soon. She found a nearly empty bottle of a rosé she had *not* picked out for him. She uncorked it and took a sniff. *Vinegar.* She poured the last bit into the sink, rinsed the bottle and set it in the recycling bin.

The mail took three seconds to sort.

She walked through the large front room with its wall-to-wall windows overlooking the porch and lake. She'd enjoyed the view in the winter, but now, in the midst of foliage season, it was breathtaking. She stepped onto the porch, shutting the door softly behind her as she breathed in the cool air, tinged with the scents of evergreens. She hadn't needed to check on anything. She knew that. Adam was here. She'd wanted to be here, she thought, and not just because of the views. Because of him, too, although she hadn't known for sure he would be around.

Was it risky to stay for dinner?

Maybe, but she spotted Justin and Samantha on the stone walk to the guesthouse and waved, skipping down the porch steps to join them. They greeted her warmly. They'd brought a Waldorf salad to contribute to dinner. Adrienne didn't have anything and offered to grab a bottle of wine from Vic's wine cellar, but the Sloans were fine with Adam's selection of beer and a pitcher of ice water.

It was warm enough to grill chicken outside on the deck. Adam added potato salad and rolls he'd picked up at the country store. With the evening turning cool, they ate dinner inside, using dishes and utensils that came with the guesthouse. Adrienne didn't detect any tension between Adam and his brother and sister-in-law. If they had issues with each other, they didn't crop up. As intensely aware of Adam as she was, she forced herself not to give herself away when he glanced in her direction, laughed or brushed past her.

Her seat at the table looked out at the lake. She couldn't help but relive their kiss on the opposite shore. How they hadn't fallen into the water was beyond her. But she knew why. Adam had kept it from happening. He'd had her up on his hips. In that position, there wasn't much she could have done to keep them from tumbling into the lake. She'd had to rely on his strength.

She put the image out of her mind and called upon her skill and considerable experience with small talk, honed during her time as a wine consultant. The conversation ranged from an update on the progress of Red Clover Inn renovations, leaf peepers wandering the back roads for the particularly brilliant foliage season and dogs—Violet, the Sloan family dogs, Rohan and, of course, Buster, who was becoming something of a legend in little Knights Bridge.

For dessert, they shared most of a box of Lake Champlain chocolate truffles. Adam had purchased them on a trip up to Vermont to pick up a particular kind of stone he needed for one of his upcoming jobs. Justin and Samantha offered to help with dishes, but Adam sent them on their way—with a truffle each.

Adrienne slipped out to the deck to collect the throw she'd brought out when they'd finished the grilling and opened the first beers of the evening. Before she could go back inside, Adam pushed open the glass door and joined her. "We'll be turning the clocks back soon," he said, standing at the rail looking out at the lake. "It'll get dark even earlier."

"Next you'll be warning me about snow."

"A hard frost tomorrow night."

She'd seen the forecast. "Maggie and Olivia put the gardens to bed for the winter. That's how they describe it. They love that sort of work—Olivia in particular doesn't want to give up her gardening."

"Parts of my job I wouldn't want to give up," he said. "Other parts—someone else is welcome to them."

"Any examples?"

He didn't hesitate. "Bidding on a job. Once I'm into the work, I'm fine. Doesn't matter if I'm working solo or with a crew. We've talked about creating a separate masonry business, but so far we haven't." He turned so that he was facing her. "What about you? Any sense yet of what you like and don't like to do as an innkeeper?"

"Well, there's that cordwood all the way across the backyard."

He smiled. "We'll have to work on that."

"I don't mind filling the wood box, though. I'm not sure about staying on the premises when guests are there. It feels weird."

"Think you'll get used to it?"

"I think so. I don't mind being there by myself, but I do hear every creak and groan in the house. And if an owl hoots, I'm wide awake. Vic's house is different."

"It's bigger and newer—"

"A hundred years old instead of two hundred."

"A sprawling Arts and Crafts lake house versus a center-chimney farmhouse. Makes a difference. He's not right up on the Quabbin woods, either. He has the lake, a guesthouse, a long driveway and extensive landscaping."

"I guess all that does make a difference. Lots of wildlife out here but it doesn't feel like it's about to crawl in bed with you." *Damn.* She realized her mistake instantly. At least it was dark, not much light coming from the living room. She held the throw close to her chest. "I should go. I have a few things I need to do tonight. I'm trying to set a schedule for myself, but fall's busy. I was warned, at least."

"I can take that," he said, touching the throw. "Vic left it when he moved back into the house. I try to keep Violet off it. He has expensive tastes. It's probably cashmere or something."

Adrienne smiled, relaxing slightly since Adam hadn't seized on her mention of crawling into bed. Never mind she was talking about bears and bobcats and owls and whatnot, it had fixed the thought in her mind…

"How's Olivia?" he asked.

Adrienne breathed again. "She says she feels great."

"That's good. I ran into Dylan in town this morning. He's counting the days if not the hours until the baby comes. Grace can't wait. She never got to hold his dad after he was born."

"I can't imagine," Adrienne said. Suddenly she could see Adam as a father, but she pushed the thought out of her mind before he could sense it. "I can help with the dishes."

"Nah. You've got work to do."

She really did. "Thank you for dinner."

"No problem. Do you need a flashlight?"

"I can use my phone."

She was at the steps when he spoke again. "I enjoyed this evening, Adrienne. Thanks for joining us. Let me know if there's anything I can do to help with your up-coming events. Besides moving the cordwood, that is."

She nodded. "I will."

She got out of there. She did end up using her phone as a flashlight on the walk to her car. She moved fast and was out of breath when she climbed behind the wheel and started the engine. But it wasn't hustling up from the guesthouse that had her breathing rapidly.

"It's Adam."

Again with that effect on her.

He didn't have to touch her to light up her senses. Did he know that? Was he playing to it? *Deliberately* torturing her?

Maybe. Maybe not.

Of course, if he'd touched her...

Don't go there.

But she did. Just taking the throw from her had sent a rush of heat and awareness through her. By the time she arrived at Carriage Hill, she imagined him sneak-ing into her suite, crawling into bed with her. He could pass as Knights Bridge wildlife.

She regretted she hadn't insisted on staying to help with the dishes. Why was she being so cautious? But she knew why. She didn't trust herself. She didn't want to screw this up. In New York, no one had cared about her breakup with the wine-shop boyfriend. His circle of friends and her circle of friends barely intersected and encompassed multiple cities and even continents. Knights Bridge was different, and it was Adam's turf, not hers.

And there was Vic.

Mercifully no one was at the inn. Maggie had stopped by earlier with the boys, who had done their homework on the kitchen table before Brandon picked them up to take them to soccer practice. Dylan had waved a hello as he'd walked Buster down the road. Olivia had spent the day at the barn updating the inn's website.

A comfortable, quiet, *normal* day.

Adrienne made herself a mug of hot chocolate and took it into the living room just as her mother called to check in. "Vic's still out of town?" she asked in surprise after Adrienne had filled her in on the highlights since their last conversation. "I thought he was only going to be away for a few days. What do you think he's up to?"

"He hasn't said."

"It must be something to do with a past assignment, perhaps people he dealt with before he retired."

"He's not used to sharing details with anyone even when he can." Adrienne sat cross-legged on the floor in front of the unlit fireplace. She could use a fire tonight but she'd have to fetch wood, not her favorite chore in the dark with no one else around. "I hope having a secret daughter doesn't mess things up for him, in case he's up for a sensitive position."

"Does he want to come out of retirement?" her mother asked sharply.

"I don't know."

"Well, he wasn't the one who kept you a secret. I was. I thought I was doing the right thing for everyone involved."

"I know you did, Mom." It was well-plowed ground between them. Adrienne didn't have to put herself in her mother's shoes or understand her decision thirty years ago to accept it. "Vic and I are both fine. You are, too, aren't you?"

"Yes—yes, I am."

She *sounded* fine. Adrienne sipped some of her hot chocolate and set the mug on the hearth. "I hope you don't think I've abandoned you by taking this job and moving east."

"What? No, of course not." Her mother gave a short laugh. "Please. Don't think twice about *that*. You know, maybe this move has freed me up to do my own thing. I don't have to stay in California for your sake."

Adrienne frowned at the phone. "Is that what you've been doing?"

"No, but there are certain opportunities I've ruled out because of the distance from you."

"Like what?"

Her mother laughed. "I do have a life, you know."

"I know. Sorry."

"Oh, I was the same at your age," she said without any hint of criticism. She wasn't one who took offense easily. "I've often thought I might like to spend a few months in Europe. Live in Paris, maybe. I didn't have the chance to study abroad when I was in college. I didn't have the money—I had to work. Well. One never knows."

"I've been an adult for a while, Mom."

"I know. I didn't like the idea of being too far from you. I still don't."

They were tight in their own way, a single mother

and her only daughter. "I'd visit you in Paris," Adrienne said lightly.

"You've always loved to travel. A six-hour time difference is easier to manage than a nine-hour one. But I've thought about New Zealand, too."

New Zealand? She was on a roll. Adrienne smiled. "There are some great wineries in New Zealand."

"It'd be a jaunt for you to visit from New England."

"I'd manage."

"I bet you would. You're making friends in Knights Bridge—building on the friendships you established last winter?"

"Absolutely."

But she didn't go into details, particularly about a certain Knights Bridge stonemason. They shifted to other topics, and when they disconnected, Adrienne felt settled in her own skin, happy, filled with possibilities. She didn't know how long it would last, but she liked it.

After two intense days of back-to-back lunches for twenty and then thirty guests, Adrienne treated herself to a visit to the library. She wanted to investigate books on the area that she might want to buy for the inn, and get something to read for herself. She hadn't had a chance to stop at the library since she'd returned to Knights Bridge. She'd spent many quiet hours here last winter. She loved its late-nineteenth-century atmosphere, complete with a marble fireplace, a small stage, ornately carved dark wood and a dour oil portrait of its founder and benefactor, a local manufacturer.

Adam approached her with two dinosaur books under

his arm. "I'm returning them for Tyler and Aidan," he said, easing next to Adrienne at the circulation desk.

"I figured they weren't your bedtime reading."

"Despite their best efforts, no. I walked over with my grandmother. It's her book club day. Eric will get her home. She insists she doesn't need our help, but we tell her we use it as an excuse to visit."

"Does she believe you?"

"She snorts and tells us not to patronize her. Right now her book club's reading a World War II novel. Gran says she remembers the end of the war."

"Never mind Vic, she should write her memoirs."

"She'd make up half of it and hold back on the good stuff."

From what Adrienne had seen of Evelyn Sloan, Adam wasn't exaggerating.

"Are you here for anything in particular?" he asked her.

"Taking a break. I'm looking into books for the inn, and I'll pick out one or two for myself. It's quiet when we don't have guests. I don't want to spend every dark, chilly evening working or watching television."

"Not diving into Knights Bridge's nightlife?"

"Such as?"

There was the slightest pause before he answered. "You lived here last winter. You must have a pretty good idea. The library and historical society hold events. There are a variety of groups—book clubs, hiking, snowshoeing, knitting. My mother teaches a quilting class."

"I've never even thought about quilting," Adrienne said.

He grinned. "Now, why doesn't that surprise me? Maybe you could teach a wine class."

"That could be interesting."

There were college towns nearby and day trips to Boston were easily managed. "I know there are things to do in the area. I guess I'm feeling my way as I get into some routines. I'm trying to pace myself and rest up between bookings."

"Need time to regroup? I get that. I read, too. Vic brought a box of photographs down to the guesthouse for me to digitize for him. He'll pick out a few for his memoirs."

Adrienne checked a cart of novels by the circulation desk. "Think he'll ever really write his memoirs?"

"Write, yes. Finish? Not for decades." Adam nodded vaguely toward the main reading room. "Gran keeps shooting me looks. She's going to guess there's something between us."

Adrienne noticed he said *guess* not *think* but realized he probably hadn't given his word choice much thought. "Grandmothers," she said, figuring that was enough.

Clare Morgan Farrell emerged from a back room. Widowed with a young son, Tyler and Aidan Sloan's friend Owen, she'd fallen in love with the Boston ER doctor grandson of two beloved locals last Christmas, during her first months in Knights Bridge. She'd taken Owen's moose adventure in stride, smiling and chatting briefly as she took the dinosaur books from Adam and set them to one side. He headed out, and Clare, fair-haired and in her early thirties, pointed Adrienne in the direction of the local history section.

She'd jotted down a list of local books and settled on the World War II novel Evelyn Sloan's book club was reading when Eric Sloan arrived to meet his grandmother. He was in a sweatshirt and jeans, sporting at least a three-day growth of beard. "I hear things are going well at the inn," he said.

"Just diving in and figuring it out as I go."

"That makes sense. I sometimes have to do that in my work, too. Adam's the planner in the family." Eric grinned. "You work with rocks, you have to plan." He pointed vaguely toward the library entrance. "I just ran into him."

"Ah. I wondered why you brought him up."

"Heard you had dinner with him and Justin and Samantha out at the lake."

"It wasn't— I just happened to be there—"

Eric's grin broadened. "Yeah. That's what I heard."

Using her cane, Evelyn edged toward them. She eyed her eldest grandson with a healthy dose of skepticism. "I'm hearing rumors about you."

He shifted his grin to her. "That I've won the lottery? Not true."

"Not funny, either," she said with a scowl. "People are worried about you. They think the stress of the job is getting to you."

"It's Knights Bridge, Gran."

She tucked her cane under one arm and smiled at Adrienne. "I don't really need it." Her refrain, apparently. She turned to her eldest grandson. "A friend of mine wandered away from home last week. She was going to visit a friend. She was so happy. She forgot to tell her daughter what she was up to, and she called the police. The daughter. Not my friend."

"Right, Gran. Come on."

"You picked her up and brought her home. The minute she got there she remembered her friend died fifteen years ago. I suppose you couldn't have let her keep walking so her fantasy could go on a while longer?"

"If I had, who knows where she'd have ended up."

She sighed. "Good point. I forget things more than I used to, but I've never forgotten your grandfather is gone."

"Your friend's hanging in there, Gran," Eric said.

"She could have frozen to death."

"Not that night. More likely she'd have keeled over from dehydration."

"Eric!"

"Sorry." He turned to Adrienne. "Gran and I tease each other but sometimes I go over the line."

"It's the stress of the job," Evelyn said. "When are you getting married?"

"Let's go, Gran." Eric, clearly brushing off his grandmother's question, smiled at Adrienne. "See you around."

Evelyn sighed and took his arm. "Lovely to see you again, Adrienne."

"You, too."

After they left, Adrienne checked out her books and headed out herself. She decided to drive to Echo Lake and have dinner on Vic's porch overlooking the lake. Maybe he'd sense she was there and email her. She hadn't heard from him in days. She walked across the common, enjoying the bright foliage and warm, beautiful afternoon. The country store was bustling, and she found herself greeting people she now recognized and who recognized her—Gabe Flanagan, Lisa Zalewski and Olivia's mother, Louise Frost. Adrienne bought take-out pulled pork and a salad and walked back across the common to her car, still parked at the library.

If Adam was at the lake, she'd invite him to join her for dinner. She'd bought enough food for two.

Adam returned to the lake just before dark and was outside on the deck with Violet when he spotted Adrienne on the sand, close to the water. "Amend that," he said. She was *in* the water. A hard frost tonight and she was going for a swim? "Come on, Violet. Let's see how this turns out."

They walked down to the lake. He noticed three towels stacked atop a folded blanket. At least Adrienne was prepared to freeze her ass off. She was up to her waist in the water, her back to him. She had a swim shirt on over her bathing suit. He could hear her counting out loud. When she got to five, she dived, going under.

She popped up. "Yikes, that water's *cold*."

He wasn't sure she'd spotted him. She streaked out of the lake, straight for her towels. She wrapped one around her shoulders and another around her waist, shivering as she muttered *cold, cold, cold* and turned purple.

"Water's colder than you expected, I take it."

She went still and spun around at him. "I didn't know you were here."

"Just got here. I'm glad I didn't need to send Violet in after you."

"You wouldn't have gone in yourself?"

"Too damn cold."

She grinned and grabbed another towel, wrapping it around her wet hair. "I thought one last dip in the lake for the season would be fun. It was, in its own way. It's as close to a polar-bear swim as I'll ever get. I only stayed in…oh, all of—what, ten seconds?"

"More like three seconds. Warm up. You don't want hypothermia."

Her teeth were chattering. As she adjusted her towels, he noticed how her wet swimsuit hugged her curves, the water drops on her exposed skin. "Guess what? The water's not getting any warmer. Big surprise, huh?" She let the towels around her waist and shoulders drop into the sand and reached for the blanket, pulling it around her. Violet barked. Adrienne laughed. "You think I'm nuts, don't you, Violet?"

"She probably wants you to jump into the lake with her."

"She's welcome to jump in by herself."

Adam pointed up toward the guesthouse. "Why don't you come inside? I just lit a fire in the woodstove. You can warm up. Take a look at Vic's photos."

She nodded, tightening the blanket around her. "That'd be great. Thanks."

"Did you bring clothes down with you?"

There was the slightest pause before she shook her head.

"No problem," he said.

She'd brought shoes and socks with her and slipped them on. Violet balked at leaving without chasing a stick into the water, but Adam finally persuaded her. When they reached the guesthouse, the fire had taken hold. He put on another log and fetched one of his T-shirts out of his downstairs bedroom. She had her swim shirt off when he returned and handed her his shirt. She seemed oblivious to her sparsely-clad state, intent only on getting warm. She pulled off her hair towel, and he took it and set it on the brick hearth by the woodstove to dry.

She flipped her wet hair out from inside his shirt and smiled. "Much better. I didn't get a chance to swim when I was here last winter, obviously. I went snowshoeing a few times, which I enjoyed, but I often wondered what it would be like to swim in the lake. Definitely better when it's summer." She gestured toward the table in the adjoining dining area. "Are those Vic's photos?"

Adam nodded. He had a few of the photos arranged faceup but there were scores more in a wooden box Vic had brought down from the house. "They're all prints from negatives. He's saving his digital photos for another time."

Adrienne pulled her blanket around her and walked over to the table, glancing at a few of the face-up photos. "That's Paris." She pointed at one of Vic as a much younger man standing on a bridge. "The Seine by Notre Dame. I wonder who took it."

"It was thirty-two years ago. He never put the photos into albums but he marked the date and location on the backs."

"Before he had the fling with my mother, then."

She peered at more photos. Apparently she was warm enough that when the blanket edged lower, she didn't immediately yank it up or break into uncontrollable shivering. Her lips were less purple. Adam figured if he hadn't come upon her, she'd have been fine with her blanket and towels. She'd have made a mad dash back up to the house, put on dry clothes and poured wine or made herself hot tea. Her swim might have been colder than she'd anticipated, but she'd been reasonably prepared.

"I'm going through all the photos before I start scanning," he said.

"You're a stonemason. You're thorough and patient. You don't rush."

"Depends." Water had collected at the ends of her hair and was about to drip onto the shirt he'd given her. He caught a few drops with his fingers. "I can move fast when the situation calls for it."

"Good to move fast when a rock's about to fall on your hand."

"No argument there."

"Have you avoided more scars than you've incurred?"

"Ah-huh."

She looked at him, her dark eyes standing out against her chilled skin. A tiny stream of water ran from a thick, wet strand of her hair down her forehead and onto her nose. "That's good," she said finally.

He brushed his thumb on her jaw and lower lip. "I am patient. I don't rush." He paused. "To a point."

"Right." She licked her lips as he lowered his hand. "I'm not patient. I have a tendency to rush. Sometimes it works out and sometimes it doesn't. I want this to work out. Everything here in Knights Bridge. I don't want to mess up Vic's relationship with the town by rushing things with a Sloan. You all *are* Knights Bridge."

"You have your own relationship with Knights Bridge."

He watched her swallow, watched the water slide off her nose onto her cheek. "This is Vic's home," she said. "I showed up last winter and turned his life upside down."

"Hear me, Adrienne. What's going on here right now isn't between you and the town or you and my family or you and Vic. I respect your relationship with him." He leaned closer to her. "But what's going on now is between us. You and me."

"And what do you think that is?"

"A lot."

She smiled. "I'd say so, too. It's taken me by surprise."

"But no complaints?"

"No complaints."

"Except you're cold," he said, skimming his palm down her back, the shirt he'd loaned her damp from her swimsuit. He settled his hand on her hip. "Do you want a long-sleeved shirt to throw on over this one?"

"It's okay. I'll jump into dry clothes at the house. I won't run into a bear, will I?"

"Probably not."

"*Probably* not?"

He grinned and stood back. "I'll walk with you just in case. Leave the wet towels. I'll let them dry by the fire and bring them up to the house tomorrow."

She nodded. "Okay, thanks. I have food if you haven't had dinner."

"Food sounds good."

They walked up to the main house together and had dinner on the porch. Adrienne had changed into dry clothes and wrapped one of Vic's porch blankets around her as she sat on an old rocker, one Vic never touched. He'd told Adam. No rocking chairs.

He and Adrienne talked about everything except the simmering attraction between them. Carriage Hill events, progress on Red Clover Inn renovations, rumors about ghosts at the old Victorian Dylan was converting into offices, the difference between sugar pumpkins and regular pumpkins and local apple orchards. A few other things that didn't have anything to do with him carrying her down to the guesthouse and into his bedroom. *If* they got that far and didn't just tear off each other's clothes by the fire.

But deep down, despite his attraction to her, he realized Adrienne wasn't ready to end up in bed with him. Her mind was on Vic and his life in Knights Bridge, not her life here.

When Adam got up to leave, she unfurled her blankets and got up, slipping her hand into his. "Thank you," she whispered. "Have a good night."

He kissed her lightly, his fingers at the back of her neck, her hair almost dry now. "You know how to reach me if you need anything."

"Yes. Right." She took an audible breath. "I do."

As he descended the steps onto the dark walkway to the guesthouse, Adam realized she'd expected more than a quick kiss—a lot more, he thought.

He smiled to himself. *Good.*

He glanced back at the big lake house. Adrienne had turned off the porch lights. She must have gone inside. Did she plan to spend the night here? He hadn't asked, but when he got back to the guesthouse, he heard her car start up in the driveway. He could have invited her to stay with him. Maybe wished he had. But then where would he be? Maybe what she needed now was some time. She'd gone from believing she was Sophia and Richard Portale's daughter to discovering she was Sophia Portale and Vic Scarlatti's daughter, and she was feeling her way into her new job—her new life here.

Adam put another log on the fire. He had self-restraint but he wanted to make love to her.

A lot.

He looked out at the lake, stars and a quarter moon sparkling in the clear evening sky. It would be chilly tonight. He'd be crawling into a cold bed alone. His own doing, he thought. But he felt in his gut that when the time was right, he wouldn't be alone. One night soon,

Adrienne would join him in bed, and it wouldn't stay cold for long. He knew it was the case. He felt it with a certainty that probably should have taken him by surprise but didn't.

He grabbed a beer out of the refrigerator and went through more of Vic's old pictures.

Fifteen

After the madness of swimming in cold Echo Lake and falling into Adam's warm arms—at least sort of—Adrienne looked into resurrecting her wine blog. She curled up in her bed with her laptop. She could work on the blog in her free time, but it wouldn't be easy to rekindle her past success without traveling. Glancing through the archives, she didn't feel the same passion she'd once had for the work. If she left Knights Bridge, though, for whatever reason, she'd need an income.

Why all of a sudden was she thinking about leaving? She hadn't thought about it in weeks.

Because of tonight.

How would Maggie and Olivia react if they knew what was going on between her and Adam? She wasn't exactly involved with him. That was too strong. Intrigued by him. Susceptible to his physical appeal. She loved being with him, but she didn't want to screw things up for him, for Vic or for herself by being impulsive, not thinking things through. But what did that look like when it came to a matter of the heart? It wasn't as if she was taking on a house mortgage. She wasn't dealing with numbers, calculations, projections.

"You're dealing with a sexy man who wants to go to bed with you."

Of *that* much she was fairly certain.

She shut her laptop and placed it on the bedside table. It was a quiet night. She couldn't hear so much as an owl through the shut windows. She flopped against her pillows. "I need a white-noise playlist."

What would she have done if Adam hadn't pulled back earlier? If one thing had led to another...

She knew herself. She'd have slept with him. She'd probably have made love to him right there on Vic's porch. They'd have managed it. They were both fit. He was strong. He could have lifted her, carried her down to the guesthouse...

Did he know she wouldn't have turned him away, and that was why he hadn't gone any further with her? He'd wanted to. She felt that in him, in the tightness of his muscles, the sexy edginess in the way he'd looked at her. But he lived in Vic's guesthouse. They were on Vic's porch. He and Vic were friends. For that matter, Adam knew Vic better than she did.

She switched off her bedside lamp. She wouldn't resurrect her wine blog anytime soon, if ever. She had too much to do with fall events. Right now she needed to hunker down and make things work here at Carriage Hill. She would quit overthinking and let whatever was going on between her and Adam happen naturally. He had a busy fall ahead of him, too.

Adrienne pulled the covers up over herself. She was warm and cozy and felt more in control of herself—her spinning mind, her jumble of emotions, her frustrated body. She shut her eyes, and for a moment, she swore she heard an owl, even as she felt Adam Sloan's arms around her, as if they had come back here to her inn-keeper's suite after all.

A week later, Adrienne decided she hadn't heard from Vic in too long for her taste. She grabbed her laptop and sat in Carriage Hill's kitchen with a pot of tea and one—that was her limit—of Maggie's incredible brownies and typed him an email.

Dear Vic,
I'm winding down after a nonstop couple of weeks. We had two weekday lunches for local groups and a bunch of adventure travelers met here ahead of a trip to the White Mountains. They're up there now. Brandon Sloan is leading it. No snow in the forecast at least! A two-day entrepreneurial boot camp next week. It'll be great when Red Clover Inn opens and can take overnight guests. We fill up fast here. There are some Airbnb properties around, at least. I'm hiring more help. Gotta.
Everything's great at the lake. I helped Adam after a wild storm took out a few branches and half a pine tree landed on the driveway. Mr. Unflappable. I was up there checking things out when the storm hit. I want you to know that I did not hide in your wine cellar. Maybe I should have. It's Sloan-built. It's not going anywhere!

The lake's gorgeous in autumn. Breathtaking, really. I'm
sorry you're not here to see it but I hope you're doing
well wherever you are.

Okay, those are a few highlights of my goings-on.
I think of you often. No problem if you can't respond.
I understand.
Love,
Adrienne

She reviewed her email before hitting Send. Would
Vic read between the lines about her and Adam? Did
it matter if he did? But it did, she realized. She wanted
to see how their relationship developed before she let
anyone find out.

And it is a relationship.

No commitments, and they'd been right to step back
from jumping into bed with each other. It would have
been the proverbial cart before the horse. It wasn't that
she didn't want to. She *ached* to. She felt certain he was
of a like mind. No, it was because her life in Knights
Bridge was new, and she wanted to get it right. She'd
been impulsive for as far back as she could remember,
and she didn't want to trigger that lurking urge to leap
up and move on to the next thing.

More than that, she didn't want to mess up Adam's
life. Knights Bridge was his home. He'd come back here
after his military service—with his heart broken. It was
his refuge, where he could be himself. He wouldn't stay
at Vic's guesthouse forever, but she didn't want to leave
him with sour memories.

"Only good memories," she whispered as she stared at her blank laptop screen.

Jumping in bed with him risked stirring up emotions that could overwhelm them both.

Not only was Adam unflappable, he was patient.

She saw she had an email and smiled when she saw it was from Vic.

Dear Adrienne,
You caught me at the right moment. I only have thirty seconds but it's so good to hear from you. I think of you often, too. I'm not really surprised innkeeping suits you. I know you still worry you'll get things sorted out and then be off again. One day at a time, okay?

I've been at the lake for a few storms but on my own, no unflappable Sloan.

Gotta run.
Love,
Vic

Adrienne shut her laptop. She did feel a bit like Mary Poppins. Did anyone in Knights Bridge expect her to stay through spring? What if she wanted to stay? But Maggie and Olivia hadn't said anything about making the job temporary.

She had a meeting with Felicity MacGregor in an hour. Best focus on that.

Adam stopped at Red Clover Inn and found Eric tearing out wallboard in a small upstairs bedroom. "I didn't realize you still knew how to wield a crowbar."

"Muscle memory but it's not that hard." Eric whacked at the last of a section of wall. He was in a baseball shirt and cargo pants and had worked up a sweat. "Feels good."

Adam stood back as bits of sawdust and plaster flew into the air. "Burning off some steam?"

"You could say that."

"Rough day on the job?"

"Job's good." He leaned the crowbar against the wall and stood back as he pulled a folded bandanna from his pocket and wiped his face. "Heard from Trish. Stirred things up. I finally told Gran we called off the wedding."

"How'd she take it?"

He tucked the bandanna back in his pocket. "Asked me if I got the ring back."

"Gran's practical."

"There was no ring to give back. I didn't give Trish one. We were just…" He took another whack at the wall. "Engaged, I guess. We never set a wedding date. Probably should have been a clue."

"You said she got in touch."

"Yeah. No big deal. She's fine. Wanted to know how I was doing."

"And you said—"

"I'm fine, too. It's the truth."

"You're tearing out a wall, Eric."

"It needs tearing out. It's in the schedule, isn't it?"

"Yeah, it's in the schedule."

Adam glanced around the room. Peeling, yellowed wallpaper clung to the remaining wallboard. The hardwood floors had deep scratches, and there were chunks missing from the woodwork. It was in the toughest shape of any of the guest rooms.

Eric tore at more wallboard.

"Hope it feels good to bash in a couple of walls," Adam said.

"Always does. I told the folks about Trish, too. It's not a secret. It was time to quit— I don't know. Pretending, I guess." He flicked plaster dust off his forehead. "I should have worn a mask. This needed doing and I needed to do it. It wasn't breaking off the engagement that got to me. It was having to tell family and friends. I didn't want to disappoint Gran and the folks especially."

"Were they disappointed?"

"They'd already guessed. They'd figured I'd tell them when I was ready. Trish is settling into Atlanta. It's the right thing for her. As if I had any doubt. I didn't. Don't feel sorry for me." He raised the crowbar again. "That's the worst."

"No pity. I get it. You didn't have to go through this alone, you know."

"I didn't. My little brothers have been around." Eric grinned, his dark hair matted with sweat. "I didn't need to bare my soul to appreciate the company."

"That makes sense in a weird way," Adam said.

"Of course it does." His brother stood back, admiring his handiwork. "Justin wants to convert this room into a storage room. Samantha wants to combine it with the adjoining room to create a suite."

"What does Heather say?"

"She hasn't weighed in yet."

"She's got all the plans in London," Adam said. "She's

always had a good sense of space, but her interior design coursework gives her real expertise—she has some good ideas."

"Just have to keep us all from going overboard with the budget?"

Adam shrugged. "Always."

"Samantha admits she doesn't know much about construction or interior design, but she's stayed in a lot of inns and hotels around the world. She knows what people like. Justin knows what can be done." Eric grinned at Adam. "You know what it all costs."

"This place could turn into a classic money pit." Adam hesitated. "Eric…"

"I'm fine, Adam. Never better, in fact. It wasn't just procrastination that stopped Trish and me from setting a date for the wedding. Atlanta helped us stop fooling ourselves that we were meant to stay together. She grew up in the city. Small-town New England never appealed to her. She loved the idea of a fresh start."

"So tearing apart this room isn't related to Trish?"

"It's related to liking to wield a crowbar once in a while. Keep my hand in with the family business. But if anyone irritates me, it's not a bad way to let off steam. There are more rooms I can tear apart. You've got rocks if you need to let off steam, but you never do."

Eric whacked at another section of wall. Adam left him to it. Eric seemed as fine as he said he was but it could be hard to tell with him. With any of his siblings. His eldest brother and Trish both deserved happiness, and it was best they'd split up instead of pretending, going through with the wedding. With Gran now in the loop, Adam figured the whole town would know by nightfall. Only Eric's experience as a closemouthed police officer and Trish's not living in town had prevented word from getting out by now. If there'd been rumors and rumblings, Adam hadn't heard them.

There had been rumors and rumblings about him and Adrienne, though.

When he drove out to the lake, she was sitting on the porch rail at the main house. She'd heard about Eric. "Maggie knew a few weeks ago. Brandon told her, I guess after you all dragged it out of him. Once she knew he'd told your parents and grandmother, she told Olivia and me."

"We knew something was up but it took some work to pry it out of him. Chris heard Trish wanted more action as a paramedic, but he didn't work with her. Different town. He didn't know she'd left for Atlanta."

Adrienne leaned back against a support post and stretched out her legs on the rail, crossing her ankles. "Would you rather be the one chucked or the one who does the chucking?"

"I'd rather not look at it that way."

"But sometimes it is that way," she said pragmatically. "Sometimes a breakup isn't a mutual decision."

Adam sat on a chair and put his feet up on the rail next to her. He noticed neither of them had taken Vic's usual chair. The lake was still, glass-like under the late-afternoon sky. He had on a canvas shirt over a T-shirt but Adrienne wore a fleece jacket. Black, of course. He supposed it was easy to pack if everything was black. It looked good on her, but she'd mentioned wanting to get some warmer colors into her wardrobe for when she dealt directly with guests. He suddenly envisioned her in red. She'd look great in red.

She glanced at him. "You're thinking about your ex-girlfriend?"

"Nope. But she did the chucking, if you're wondering. I was the chuckee. Is that even a word?"

He thought she'd smile but she didn't. "It must have been particularly bad timing."

"Tell me a good time. I couldn't wait to get back here and pound rock after I got out. She didn't have any interest in that."

"The grass was greener where she was?"

"Probably."

She touched the scars on his hand and wrist. "Wounds heal. We learn."

"We can make fresh mistakes despite our best efforts. I'm in a line of work where nicks and the occasional smashed finger aren't unusual."

"But you take appropriate precautions to protect yourself from debilitating injuries."

"I do what I can."

"I'm torturing this metaphor, huh?"

"It's a metaphor? I thought we were talking about stonework."

She laughed and kicked his foot playfully, not dislodging it from the rail. "It can be easy to overcompensate."

"Get gun-shy, you mean. In stonework, that can lead to more injuries. You've got to work your plan. Be patient. Know when you have to make your move and then do it."

"Without hesitation," she said.

"Hesitation causes injuries."

Adrienne frowned at him. "Are you making that up?"

"Torturing the analogy. What about you and this wine guy?"

"I did the chucking. Absolutely. But he didn't care. We seemed perfect on paper but we never—" She broke off. "It just didn't work."

"He wasn't so perfect in real life?"

"Entitled, self-absorbed, condescending. Also smart, witty, charming. If I'd stayed with him..." She placed her feet on the porch floor. "Well, I wouldn't be here in Knights Bridge with you, would I?"

"This guy tempted you to be part of a life you realized you didn't want."

"We didn't bring out the best in each other."

"He read your wine blog?"

"He pretended to."

Adam grinned. "That when you chucked him? When you found out he was faking it?"

"It was the straw that broke the camel's back, so to speak. It wasn't a requirement that he read my blog. I just didn't want him to lie to me about it."

"I've read your blog," Adam said.

Her eyes brightened. "Really?"

"I don't lie to you, Adrienne. I won't lie to you."

"I lied last year—I lied to everyone close to me. I can understand why Eric kept his news to himself. Sometimes you just need to adjust to it, figure out your next moves on your own. It's your pain, your responsibility, your confusion."

"We're not talking about the wine guy now. We're talking about you and Vic."

"I guess. I wish I'd told him who I was on day one, but I didn't."

"Your mother didn't tell either of you for years. I'm not criticizing her, or you."

She studied him a moment, a smile playing at the corners of her mouth. "Have you always been an honest and straightforward type?"

"With five siblings and my grandmother?"

Adrienne laughed, her dark eyes sparkling. "Yeah, why bother to lie and pretend with that crew? Did your parents always know what was going on with all you kids?"

"Hell, I hope not." Adam lowered his feet from the porch rail. "Dinner?"

"What do you have?"

"Frozen burritos."

"Vic has some of Maggie's lasagna in his freezer."

"Sold."

"I'm not sure I want to tell him you and I had dinner together on a chilly October evening while he was away. He's a savvy diplomat. He'll figure out…" She stopped herself. "Never mind."

"You're worried he'll figure out we like each other's company."

"It's Maggie's lasagna. Vic loves Maggie's lasagna." Adrienne grinned as she got to her feet. "He'll figure out I was the one who mentioned he had some in the freezer."

"She's my sister-in-law. I'll get her to replace it."

"Perfect."

"And it's okay if he finds out we enjoy each other's company?"

"He's going to find out anyway. It's all over town, isn't it?"

Adam shrugged. "Gran mentioned us to Eric."

"Did she figure it out on her own?"

"Heard it at her book club."

"I do love this town," Adrienne said lightly, leading him into the house and straight to the freezer for the lasagna.

Sixteen

❧❧❧

The lasagna was perfect reheated out of the freezer. Adrienne chose a Chianti from Vic's wine cellar—she'd replace it, too—and they set the table in the dining room, complete with candles. "I'd have offered to fetch salad fixings at the guesthouse, but I don't have any," Adam said. "I meant to stop for a few groceries on my way back here, but I ran into Eric with his crowbar and it slipped my mind."

Adrienne smiled at him across the table. "Is this a white lie?"

"Nope. Truth. I was going to pick up some kombucha, too." He smiled. "Now, that's a white lie. I hate the stuff."

"It's an acquired taste."

"Meaning you drink it?"

"Certain brands and not every day. The country store carries it."

"I know. Town's going to hell in a handbasket."

She glanced around the softly lit dining room. It retained some of its original Arts and Crafts features—its leaded windows, beamed ceiling and built-in glass-front cabinet—and Vic had decided to have the original table refinished and the chairs reupholstered. The kitchen had been remodeled with creamy white cabinets and granite counters that worked with the house's style. Adrienne had stayed out of the decision-making on renovations, offering her opinion only when asked. It was Vic's house. He was the one who needed to be comfortable here.

"I need to run up to New Hampshire tomorrow," Adam said. "I'm checking on stone from a demolished town hall in a little town near Peterborough. It's from the same quarry as the stone in a job I'm doing in town. It should match."

"Is that important?" Adrienne asked.

"It's an aesthetic consideration rather than a structural one. It's nice if the visible stone in the new work matches the existing stone." He picked up his wineglass. "Are you due for a day off? You're welcome to join me."

"I am, as a matter of fact. I've never been to New Hampshire. I'd love to join you."

"I'll pick you up first thing, then."

They cleaned up the dishes together and kissed each other good-night. Somehow anything more after eating Vic's food and drinking his wine seemed wrong, and if he suddenly walked in—which was entirely possible...

Adrienne squeezed Adam's hand. "See you in the morning."

When she reached Carriage Hill, she realized she hadn't left on so much as a night-light. She used her phone to make her way up the walk, unlock the door and find the light switch for the overhead in the kitchen.

She almost screamed when Buster lumbered out to her. She'd forgotten he was here. He'd arrived before she'd left for Echo Lake. He'd escaped from Olivia and she hadn't had the oomph to chase after him. She'd called Adrienne just as the big dog had burst onto the terrace of his old home. "He's protesting," Olivia had said. "I've been distracted with the baby coming. I'm not taking him on long walks the way I used to. Dylan does, but Buster senses he's in for more changes around here."

Or he knew Adrienne had dog biscuits.

She'd offered to let him stay and promised to bring him back in the morning. Now, though, that meant she had to walk him. She grabbed a proper flashlight and headed out with him, snapping a leash on his collar.

It turned out that he walked her. He led her up to Dylan and Olivia's house, not, thankfully, down the dark road toward the Quabbin wilderness. She'd have argued with him if he'd tried that one. It wasn't late, just very dark. Dylan greeted her at the front door. "Buster wants to come home," she said.

Dylan insisted on driving her back down to the inn. She'd left the kitchen light on, but the house still felt very dark, even lonely. She had a fresh perspective on what guests would experience on these shortened late-fall and winter days. The long summer days allowed for walks into the evening, but who would want to venture out in the pitch dark? The lack of light pollution did allow for spectacular starry skies. Why not add that to the list of possible activities? Torchlight snowshoeing excursions. She'd need guides, people with expertise.

"It could work," she said aloud, heading to her suite.

She couldn't believe she was taking tomorrow off so she could join Adam for a drive to New Hampshire to examine rocks.

Life could be worse. A lot worse.

The weather forecast looked good. Sunny, in the low fifties. It would be a fun day.

She sat on the edge of her bed. What if she'd invited Adam to spend the night with her? Dylan and Olivia would know. Felicity. Maggie.

Do I care?

Adrienne shut her eyes, feeling the muscles in Adam's back under her palms, tasting his mouth against hers. They'd come so close to stopping their would-they/wouldn't-they dance. She could have invited herself down to the guesthouse, too, but she hadn't. He wasn't pushing her, he'd told her more than once. He was getting to know her, letting her get to know him. There'd been some spectacularly speedy relationships in Knights Bridge lately, and maybe he'd want to be more certain about what was going on between them after his brother's experience with his fiancée.

Or maybe he just wanted her as a friend.

"That's the Chianti," she said. "You're overthinking again."

She pulled on warm pajamas and climbed into bed, pulling up the covers. She checked her email one last time. She had emails from friends in Australia, Kenya and San Francisco.

And a text from Vic.

I heard about Eric and Trish. They never were the right match. Glad he's okay.

Adrienne smiled and typed her response. You see? You're a part of this town now.

He texted her back almost instantly. It didn't tell her much. Just that wherever he was, he was awake. Elly keeps me posted on local gossip. You're okay?

I'm taking tomorrow off.

Putting your feet up?

Helping Adam pick up rocks in New Hampshire.

This time, Vic's reply wasn't instantaneous, but a few seconds later, she saw his text: I heard about that, too. He told Brandon, who told Maggie, who told Elly.

Who told you.

Have fun with the rocks.

She smiled and texted good-night. She *would* have fun with the rocks, and with Adam.

The quarried stone in New Hampshire matched. Adam had known it would, obviously.

On their way back, they stopped for apple pie and cof-fee at a well-known diner and arrived in Knights Bridge just after dark. Maggie and Olivia were at Carriage Hill. "I should see what they're up to," Adrienne said.

"Sure thing."

"Adam…" She started to push open the passenger door to his van. "Today was fun, and I learned a lot."

"About rocks."

She grinned. "I love soaking up new information. Now you have to go home and explain to Violet why you took me with you instead of her."

"Let's hope she didn't chew up Vic's cashmere throw in revenge."

She found Maggie and Olivia in the kitchen, with their line of goat's milk products set out on the table. "Olivia needed a distraction," Maggie said.

"I've been obsessing about the baby." She left it at that, as if she didn't want to trigger a fresh round of anxious thoughts. "How was New Hampshire?"

"Beautiful scenery," Adrienne said. "We found rocks and we had pie. I was glad to see more of the country-side."

They didn't question her explanation for the day. They heated soup Maggie had brought and filled bowls at the table, turning the conversation back to goat's milk products and all the possibilities that went with them. After using the products in the rooms, many of the inn's guests had asked if they could purchase full-size versions, and the small amenity sizes often went home with them.

As they left, Maggie and Olivia invited Adrienne to join them Friday night for one of their periodic "movie

nights" with friends. "We've always had them here, but
we can have it up at the barn," Olivia said.

"Here's fine. I can get everything together—"

"Oh, we've got it down to a science," Maggie said.
"You're not in your innkeeping role."

"We want you there as a friend," Olivia added.

Adrienne thanked them. "It sounds like great fun."

For the next two days, she busied herself with some
of the things she'd put off during the intense weeks of
peak foliage—such as figuring out where to relocate the
cordwood. It looked as if it'd involve building a lean-to
or some other type of structure. Having the wood out
in the open through cold weather would only deliver
her a fresh set of problems. Cordwood and snow, sleet,
freezing rain and just plain rain weren't a good combi-
nation. A tarp would help, but then she'd have to pry it
off every time she needed to get wood.

"No wonder the wood's in the shed," she said to
herself.

She drove into town for more books at the library
and stops at the country store, post office and bank.
She saw Adam and his crew working on the building
with the stone from New Hampshire. They looked as
if they had their hands full, but he spotted her car and
waved to her.

By movie night, she was ready for a distraction.

Clare Farrell, Jess Flanagan and Samantha Sloan
were free for the evening and showed up with food and
drinks. It was an informal, "come if you can" sporadic
get-together. Adrienne had lit a fire and set out nap-

kins, utensils and small plates but otherwise stepped back from an organizing role.

Samantha pulled her aside in the kitchen shortly after she arrived. "I felt as if I'd never fit in around here at first. Movie night? I'd never done anything remotely like it. Then I realized it's not about fitting in. It's about being myself and enjoying being around other women who were being themselves." She screwed up her face. "Does that make sense?"

Samantha Bennett Sloan wasn't particularly introspective, something Adrienne appreciated since she'd been overthinking everything lately. She smiled. "It makes perfect sense. Thank you."

Maggie burst into the kitchen with hors d'oeuvres hot out of her oven at home. Adrienne didn't need to know what they were to know they were delicious. Everyone gathered in front of the fire and decided to watch *Vera*, a beloved British detective series. They put on the first episode of the first season and enjoyed simple snacks, Kendrick Winery reds and sparkling water with slices of lemon and lime for Jess and Olivia, both pregnant. Jess announced that to help her get through morning sickness, she'd binge-watched *Shetland*, another detective series based on books by Ann Cleeves, the same author who'd created Vera. "I had morning sickness bad," she said.

Maggie shuddered. "My mother was sick as a dog with the twins. She says if they'd been first, there'd have been no Phoebe and me. I sailed through with Tyler and Aidan. A good thing, because they're putting me through my paces now." She pointed cheerfully to the spot where she'd hit her head. "I have the scars to prove it." She grinned. "Don't worry. I love them to bits and won't guilt-trip them. It's my own damn fault I stumbled. I still haven't seen the moose. Have you, Adrienne?"

"Early on," she said. "Not recently. I don't think he's around anymore. It's been busier here with events and more hikers on the road."

Samantha, who'd chosen to sit on the floor, stretched out her legs toward the fire. "Tyler and Aidan suggested we choose *Walking with Dinosaurs* for our movie tonight. They said Adam watched it with them and insisted he loved it."

"He probably did," Maggie said. "He was a dinosaur nut at their age. It's a fun movie but I'm good with *Vera.*"

They all loved DCI Vera Stanhope, a woman comfortable in her own skin, witty, occasionally caustic and always dedicated to her work. "She has cute detective sergeants," Olivia offered as she helped herself to a handful of popcorn.

"That's an understatement," Jess said.

It occurred to Adrienne that however by happenstance, she was the only single woman at tonight's gathering. If any of the other women guessed what was going on between her and Adam, nothing was said or even hinted at. Which probably meant they didn't know. Clare was discreet by nature and might not have said anything, but Maggie, Olivia, Jess, Samantha—they'd want details. Adrienne smiled, not as threatened or uncomfortable at that prospect as she would have been even a couple of weeks ago.

"Eric's unattached and has been for a while now," Maggie said. "We just didn't know."

Jess nodded. "He seems fine. I bet he won't have any trouble getting back into the saddle, so to speak. He's good-looking."

"All the Sloans are," Olivia said. "He's rougher-looking than Vera's detectives."

"I like Kenny," Clare said, referring to an older detective constable in the series, as opposed to his good-looking younger colleagues.

"My talented, ambitious little sister Ruby broke Christopher's heart, I think," Maggie said. "I don't know how happy she is in Hollywood. She says she's learning a lot, taking it all in. I doubt she'll stay out there."

Jess helped herself to more water. "Adam had his heart broken when he left the military. That's when he got Violet. I remember how sick she was."

"They helped each other heal," Olivia said.

Clare smiled. "Knights Bridge itself has a way of helping people heal."

"Yeah, being back home definitely helped him," Maggie said. "We worried about Adam night and day when he was deployed, even Brandon, who's not a worrier. It never would have worked between Adam and the woman he was involved with—I just realized I've never known her name. See? He's a hometown guy to his core. No way would she have wanted to be here."

"It's a welcoming town," Clare said. "More so than I expected when I moved here. It's only been a year but

Owen and I are very much at home. I certainly never expected to have a man in my life by now, but here I am. No cute British detective sergeant."

"A cute ER doctor, though," Samantha said.

Maggie nibbled on a few cashews. "It's best to move on when a relationship isn't right, but you need to know it's not right, especially once you've made a commitment to each other. You work at it before you walk away for good." She was pensive, staring at the television as a new episode of *Vera* loaded. "Brandon and I almost called it quits. I'm glad we worked through our issues."

"Trish never wanted to be a part of Eric's life here," Olivia said. "She's solid, a good person, dedicated to her job—I hope she loves Atlanta and does well there."

Maggie glanced around the room. "I just realized that except for Jess, we've all lived somewhere besides Knights Bridge. I never thought I'd come back. Olivia always wanted to come back. Samantha wandered into town looking for pirate treasure. Clare moved here for work. Adrienne—well, you're here because of work and Vic, right?"

"That's the short answer," she said.

Maggie's turquoise eyes settled on her knowingly, but she smiled and settled in to watch the next episode of their British DCI at work.

Once the dishes were cleaned up and the leftovers stored in the refrigerator and everyone had gone home, Adrienne poured herself a small glass of wine and stood out on the terrace in the dark. She could hear animals in the woods and smiled, not the least bit concerned.

When she went inside, she saw she had an email from Vic. I haven't abandoned you.

I know you haven't.

Then, later, a text from Adam. Full moon tonight, did you notice?

I noticed.

It was a while before she dropped off to sleep.

In the morning—Saturday—Adam and Brandon arrived at the inn to build a lean-to for the cordwood. "If this isn't a good time, we can come back," Brandon said.

"No, it's fine," Adrienne said. "Thank you."

They took her out back and explained what they thought would work. They'd run it past Olivia, who'd long known the shed wasn't a permanent solution, but she wanted Adrienne's opinion. *Not* her wheelhouse, but their choice of size and location—just off the terrace, toward the addition—were in line with what she'd imagined. She gave her approval. "It'll take us the morning," Adam said. "We're making cider this afternoon."

"You'll have to join us," Brandon added, seemingly oblivious to the sparks between her and his younger brother.

She glanced at Adam. "Cider?"

"Apple cider," he said. "It's a family tradition."

How could she resist?

The two brothers made short work of the lean-to and

even transferred the wood from the shed. Adrienne admired their handiwork—the lean-to, the neatly stacked wood—and thanked them profusely. Brandon took off in his truck, and she rode with Adam out to the Sloan place. The old farmhouse had white clapboards and black shutters, set atop a hill with a red barn, shade trees and views of the fields and hills and a sliver of the reservoir in the distance.

Except for Heather, all the Sloans were present for the family tradition of making cider, using their own hand-cranked press and their own apples. Adam took Adrienne to one of the gnarly trees in the backyard, and they picked the last of the Baldwin apples—an old-fashioned variety—and placed them in a bushel basket. Tyler and Aidan joined them. Of course they had to get up into the tree. Adam laughed and helped them.

Adrienne loved learning about cider making, a New England tradition that went back generations. "Hence Cider Brook and Justin's old cider mill," Adam explained. "Hard cider was a staple back in the day. Chris likes to make a batch. I prefer beer and fresh cider."

He handed her a glass of the first pour from the press. "This is wonderful," she said after taking a sip.

The atmosphere helped, she thought. She watched him with his family. He was quiet but he had a firm place with them. His brothers relied on him to rein in expenses and keep them from overextending. He was solid, intelligent, strong and hardworking, and she doubted she was doing a good job hiding her attraction to him.

In a few minutes, Evelyn Sloan confirmed Adrienne's suspicion by easing next to her. "Cider's good this year," she said. "I remember when my husband and I got the cider press. It was just the five boys then. Heather wasn't born yet. Adam always loved making cider."

"What wonderful memories you must have," Adrienne said.

Evelyn finished her cider and returned her glass to the table set up next to the press. "Don't let Adam's military service fool you. He's never wanted to live anywhere but Knights Bridge. Brandon did. Couldn't wait to get out of here." She was silent for a moment. "It's good he and Adam are both home to stay."

Christopher joined them, taking his grandmother by the arm and edging her toward her great-grandsons. Adrienne smiled to herself. "He's a firefighter," Adam said, easing next to her. "He likes to rescue people."

"Your grandmother loves you guys."

"It's hard to believe but she's even more outspoken in her old age."

She looked out across the fields toward Quabbin in the distance. "I wonder where Vic is right now."

Maggie and Brandon set up food on the porch. Evelyn Sloan settled into a comfortable chair and pointed her cane at her walking shoes. "I need to buy new shoes for England and make sure I give myself enough time to break them in."

Samantha and Maggie both volunteered to take her shopping.

"She could have planned D-Day," Eric told Adrienne. "She ran a nursery school for decades. She helped potty train most people in town. Gives you a certain perspective on life."

She helped herself to food and, especially, cider doughnuts.

"Come on," Adam said finally. "I'll get you out of here."

"It's been fun."

"Cider and Sloans." He threw a jug of cider into the back of his truck and drove Adrienne back to Carriage Hill. "A solid family doesn't mean we're without conflicts and problems."

"No rose-colored glasses for me, then."

He grinned. "Good idea. Want me to fill the wood box for you?"

"I already did."

"My brothers and a few other guys are coming out to the lake. We'll make sure Eric has his head screwed on straight."

"This will involve a bonfire, beer and pizza?"

"Who said anything about pizza?"

"You all have a good life here. I saw that last winter. Your grandmother says you never wanted to live anywhere else."

"I didn't, and I don't," he said. "I've always known Knights Bridge is home. I didn't think about it that much until I wasn't here."

"You took it for granted," Adrienne said, reaching for the jug of cider in back.

"I guess you could say that."

She set the jug in her lap. "Now you're making sure nothing disturbs your tranquility."

"I have a big family. My tranquility gets disturbed on a daily basis."

"Mostly in good ways," she said.

He studied her a moment and then nodded. "Yeah. You all set here?"

"All set. Thanks." She pushed open the door.

"Enjoy the cider."

"Enjoy the beer and bonfire."

He winked. "We'll have cider, too."

Seventeen

A few minutes after Adam arrived back at the lake, a man he didn't recognize walked down from Vic's house. He was thin, fair-skinned, in his early fifties at a guess. He held up a hand. "It's okay. I'm one of Vic's former colleagues. Sorry if I startled you." He pointed up through the trees behind him. "I parked up there. I've been wandering around the area. I wasn't prepared for rain. I thought I might see a deer."

"There are a lot of deer out here," Adam said, keeping his tone neutral. Violet raced to him with a stick he'd thrown for her. He got it from her and threw it again. "What can I do for you?"

"Nice place Vic has here. I'm not a lake-and-woods sort but I wanted to have a look around." He tilted his head back slightly. "You're staying in his guesthouse, aren't you?"

"Are you and Vic friends?"

The man shrugged. "Not really. I heard he retired out here. His daughter's living in town now. Adrienne…"

He paused, shook his head. "I can't come up with the last name. Porter or something. It's not Scarlatti."

Adam didn't supply it. Violet streaked to him with her stick. He took it and had her sit at his side. His brothers and whoever else they rounded up would be here soon. He wanted this guy on his way by then.

"I found out about her through small-town gossip," the man added. "People were talking at breakfast about the three boys who took off into the woods out here. I guess Adrienne found the mother of two of the boys injured? Glad it all worked out. I was at the local diner this morning. Smith's, I think it's called. I had the cornmeal pancakes. Delicious." He smiled, an obvious effort to appear nonthreatening. "Not that I should be eating pancakes."

"Smith's makes good pancakes," Adam said.

"No kidding. I cleaned my plate. Vic's daughter came up in conversation at the next table. I wasn't trying to eavesdrop." He didn't sound particularly defensive, just stating the facts. "I understand she's the new innkeeper in town."

"Vic's not here. If you give me your name, I can let him know you're in town."

"He won't remember me. I should get rolling. I don't need to take up any more of your time. Apologies for startling you. I won't be back." He glanced out at the lake, as if he were debating what to say next. Finally he turned back to Adam. "I know Brody Hancock and Greg Rawlings by reputation. They're the best. Apologies for any negative impression. Have a good night."

He nodded to the firepit. "Roast some marshmallows. I used to love that as a kid."

"A kid where?"

He grinned. "No place you've ever heard of."

He started up to the house. Nothing in his manner suggested he wasn't on the level, but "former colleague" was a vague description and his mention of Brody and Greg—two Diplomatic Security agents—was provocative. Was this guy DSS?

Adam walked up to the main house. A gray sedan was disappearing around a tree-lined curve. He didn't get the plates. Thought that might be going overboard, anyway.

He returned to the lakefront and lit the fire. He texted Adrienne: Any visitors since I left?

Four-legged or two-legged?

He smiled at her sense of humor. She'd relaxed so much in the weeks since she'd started at Carriage Hill. Two.

No one. I'm not counting birds. Why?

One of Vic's colleagues stopped by. Didn't give a name. Passing through.

You don't believe him.

Adam thought a moment before he responded. I believe him. I just think there's more to it.

Vic being Vic.

He smiled. Yeah.

How's the bonfire?

Just lighting it now. Join us?

It's a guy night. I'm having cider and in my new fuzzy slippers.

It was an image. Adam texted her a snooze emoji and then grimaced at it. So much for his Sloan testosterone. But Eric and Justin arrived, and he slid his phone into his pocket. They'd parked at the main house and walked down to the lake. Adam told them about the guy. They'd seen him passing Elly O'Dunn's farm. "It felt like he's checking out Vic's life here or something," Adam said. "He didn't say so, but I wouldn't be surprised if he's doing some kind of background check or just getting a feel for Vic's life here."

"Think Vic's up to something besides writing his memoirs?" Justin asked.

"If he is, this guy wasn't going to talk about it. I don't know where Vic is, who's with him, what he's doing."

It was enough to get Eric's attention. "What about Adrienne?"

"I don't think she knows, either."

"I'll check in with Brody."

"Maybe I should," Adam said. "It's a thing if you do it."

"Why?"

His oblivious eldest brother. "You're a cop, Eric."

"Oh, yeah, that's right." He grinned. "You're Vic's—what? Friend? Soon-to-be son-in-law? Ex-friend if you mess up with his long-lost daughter?"

"Nice try. I'm a guy having a couple of beers with his brothers."

"Don't forget Violet," Justin said.

"She doesn't drink beer."

Brandon and Christopher hopped onto the sand from the stone walk down from the main house. They'd driven together. They hadn't run into Adam's visitor. Whoever he was, he was a dead end for now. They moved on to other topics. "Gran interrogated me about Adrienne," Brandon said. "She pulled me aside while we were doing the cider. She figured I'd know more because of Maggie."

"What did she want to know?" Adam asked, keeping his tone neutral.

"It's Gran. She wanted to know everything."

Adam frowned. "Why?"

Brandon snorted. "Hell, Adam, like you don't know? You brought her to our annual cider-making get-together. Gran can put two and two together. We all can."

"She's protective of you," Eric added.

Justin nodded in agreement. "To her, you're not the tough combat vet and stonemason. You're the little boy who skinned his knee and left her here and went off to war."

"I wasn't a little tyke when I became a Marine."

Justin turned to Eric, Brandon and Christopher. "Is he dense or playing us?"

"Both," Brandon said with a grin. "Gran's not sure about Adrienne. That's the point."

Adam was amused. "Gran has room to talk."

"I have to agree with you there," Christopher said. "Her family didn't approve of her choice of a Knights Bridge carpenter for a husband."

Eric held up his beer to Adam. "Not that you're marrying Adrienne. Right, brother?"

Adam wasn't going there. Not. A. Chance. "More beer?"

But the eldest Sloan wasn't giving up. "You're like our dear departed paternal grandfather. You want advice, you'll ask for it."

"There's that," Adam said.

"You and Adrienne…" Eric paused, sipped his beer as he looked out at the dark lake. "There's such a thing as being too patient."

"Are we talking about you now?"

"Sort of. No, not really. Hell, I don't know. Gran asked me a while back why Trish and I didn't set a wedding date. I dismissed her as being old-fashioned. Looking back—we didn't set a date because we sensed something was wrong." He turned to Adam. "Why are you waiting with Adrienne?"

"Who says I'm waiting?"

"Tell her how you feel," Christopher said. "Put yourself out there. She could tell you to take a hike, or you could scare her into bolting."

"It's a risk worth taking," Eric said.

Brandon gave an exaggerated shudder. "Listen to us. Maggie would be choking on her teeth hearing us talk emotional stuff."

"I'm about to choke on mine," Adam said with a grin. "I'll just say you all shouldn't be so sure you know what's going on with Adrienne and me. She's new in town. She's here to do a job and spend time with Vic."

Brandon held up his beer. "Falling for you wasn't in the plan, huh?"

"She doesn't want to screw things up."

"She doesn't strike me as the cautious type," Justin said. "Don't write a script for her."

Adam stared at him. "A script?"

"Yeah. Decide what she's thinking and planning without asking her." He took a sip of his beer and winked. "I got that from Samantha. I didn't come up with it on my own."

Adam sighed, shaking his head. "You guys are getting way, way ahead of yourselves."

His brothers, however, clearly didn't doubt themselves even slightly.

"I jumped in too soon with Ruby but it wouldn't have mattered," Christopher said. "I wasn't going to get between her and what she wants. She's got a good job in Hollywood. I'm not moving out there and she's not moving back here. But even if I did or she did, it wouldn't have worked. Just as well—one O'Dunn in the family is plenty."

Brandon clapped a hand on his youngest brother's shoulder. "You got that right."

"Maggie's the best, Brandon," Christopher said. "You're a lucky man."

"Yeah. Most days. The days she tries new mushroom recipes on me, not so much."

By the time his brothers left, it was too late for Adam to call Brody without it being a thing, and he was hesitant to send an email or a text for the same reason. Vic had a forty-year career behind him. He knew a lot of people. Adam debated getting in touch with him about the "former colleague," but Vic hadn't been in communication much. He didn't want to turn nothing into something with him, either.

He'd wait.

Having decided, he thought about his brothers and their comments about his relationship with Adrienne. They'd only been half teasing. Was he writing a script for her, as Justin had said, never mind he'd quoted Samantha? Avoiding risk with her? Patience was one thing. But was he lying to himself? Telling himself he was holding back because she wasn't ready when he was the one who wasn't ready? Not because he didn't want to make love to her. He did. Anytime, anywhere. He convinced himself he was biding his time, not rushing her. New job, new town, new father, new life. She needed a chance to get her feet under her before adding a relationship to the mix. She didn't want to mess up his life, but he didn't want to mess up hers, either.

Yet…as he and Violet put out the last of the fire and walked up to the guesthouse, he felt a wave of emotion that was so strong it nearly knocked him over. He wasn't an emotional guy. He looked at life the way he looked at a masonry project. He'd figure out what he needed to do, what he needed to fit together, to complete the project so that it was sturdy and lasting, and he'd get on with it.

He let Violet into the house and stood at the windows, looking out at the stars sparkling on the lake. "Adrienne isn't a rock wall," he said, half joking, half serious.

And he realized he'd never felt so certain, so confident about her—about what they could have together, be together. No way did he want to screw that up. At the same time, he didn't want to jump in too late, either. He wasn't going to let his past dictate his actions now.

He rubbed Violet's belly. Because of his past, he'd nursed a sick golden retriever puppy back to health and he'd had her at his side as he'd transitioned from military life back to his hometown. It was a positive that had been made possible by a crushing setback.

He knew to his core that he and Adrienne were right for each other.

She had a role in what happened next, too.

He heated a mug of cider and stretched out on the couch by the woodstove. He ended up falling asleep there. When he woke up to the early-morning sun in his eyes, he made coffee and called Brody Hancock in London, on the DSS agent's cell phone.

"No one's hurt or died," Adam said when Brody answered.

"Well, that's good. What's up?"

Adam told him about his visitor. Brody listened without interruption. He and Heather would be back in their hometown for the Thanksgiving weekend nuptials of Greg Rawlings and Charlotte Bennett. They wanted their wedding to take place at Red Clover Inn. They didn't care if it'd been stripped down to the studs by then, but Adam knew there was zero chance the renovations would be that far along—even if Eric kept up with his crowbar.

"I know this guy," Brody said once Adam finished.

"Is it news to you that he was here?"

"Yeah. It's news. He's legit, though. He's not a threat." Even so, Brody didn't sound happy about him showing up in Knights Bridge. "Thanks for letting me know."

It was as far as he was willing to go. Adam didn't object. He knew it wouldn't do any good to press Brody for more information. But what the hell was Vic up to? He had to be scoping out—or getting scoped out himself—for a new assignment. That made more sense than any other explanation Adam could think up. "You'll tell me if I need to watch out for things here?" he asked his brother-in-law.

Brody promised he would. "How's your grandmother doing?" he asked, changing the subject. "Will she be okay to fly back to London with us after Thanksgiving?"

"She says she's up to the trip. She told Eric if she's going to die on the plane, she wants it to be on her way home not on her way to London."

"That sounds like her. I went to her nursery school, you know."

"We all did," Adam said dryly. "Will this guy—Vic's 'colleague'—want to talk to anyone else in town?"

"You mean like Evelyn? No. Trust me on that, Adam. No. I bet he left town after talking to you."

Bet or knew? Adam didn't ask. No point since Brody wasn't going to tell him.

"See you soon, Adam. Thanks for getting in touch. Heather's out for a walk or I'd put her on with you."

"No problem."

After they disconnected, Adam got Violet up for her morning walk. He'd worked with enough diplomatic security types during his time in the military to recognize Brody's brush-off for what it was, but he wasn't offended. Brody had a job to do.

And Vic?

Well, that could get interesting, couldn't it?

Adam finished work early and stopped at Carriage Hill with his camera and assorted lenses. Adrienne was raking leaves in the front yard. She asked him about his visitor last night. He told her about his call with Brody but left out his suspicions. He motioned back toward his truck. "I'm taking more photos for Olivia for her website. She wants shots of the old stone bridge out by my folks' place, and a few shot here."

"I think I know the one you mean."

"You can join me, but I don't want to interrupt your raking."

"Interrupt it. Please." She leaned the rake against the handrail to the steps. "I have discovered I actually like to rake leaves—for five minutes. One second longer and I start to get blisters and get bored."

"Gloves and earbuds help."

She grinned at him. "So practical. I'll buy gloves. I like to hear what's rustling in the woods. I don't want to be listening to Beethoven and look up and I'm face-to-face with our bull moose."

Who hadn't been sighted in weeks. "Beethoven?"

"Probably not the best to rake leaves to. Do I need boots or anything for the bridge?"

He picked an orange-colored leaf from her hair. "You're fine just as you are."

She climbed into the passenger seat with an ease and comfort she hadn't had at first, with his truck or his work van. The bridge was a short drive out Carriage Hill Road, on a narrow stretch of road below the Sloan farmhouse. He parked under an oak tree, with deep burgundy-colored leaves still on its branches.

They took a dirt trail down a steep, short hill to one side of the arched stone bridge that spanned rock-strewn brook Cider Brook. On its winding route to the reservoir, it passed the old, abandoned cider mill where Justin and Samantha had met when it caught fire in a fierce thunderstorm. She'd slipped into town to follow the brook in her search for pirate treasure.

"Never a dull moment for you Sloans, is there?" Adrienne asked, kicking through fallen leaves to a flat stone on the edge of the brook.

Adam smiled. "This from a Scarlatti."

She looked sideways at him, her dark eyes shining in the dappled light. She returned his smile. "Good point. What do Sam and Justin plan to do with the cider mill?"

"They're talking about converting it into a house. They toyed with the idea of living at Red Clover Inn after it's renovated. Samantha fantasized about being a live-in innkeeper. Justin was never keen on the idea."

"Not a surprise," Adrienne said.

"Imagine guests wandering down for breakfast and finding him in the kitchen. He wouldn't be comfortable there. He and Samantha both know that. Ava and Ruby O'Dunn have talked about starting a children's theater in town and considered the cider mill. Then Ruby went off to California. Ava is interested in rural development through the arts. Maybe she'll figure out something in Knights Bridge."

"This town's filled with possibilities, isn't it?" She looked up at the stone bridge. "I like the mix of old and new. It's easy to think nothing happens here, but these days I'm starting to think everything happens here. Babies, weddings, new ventures—a retired diplomat with secrets." She shifted back to Adam. "Red Clover Inn will be a fantastic addition to the town."

"If you have any suggestions for it, speak up."

"I'm hardly an expert."

"You've gained valuable experience since you started at Carriage Hill," Adam said, easing his camera off his shoulder. "Why didn't you last at the winery?"

She shrugged, watching him as he checked the light. It was decent. Not great, but it'd work. "I loved my time at the winery and appreciated the opportunity. It helped me in my work here. It always felt temporary. I didn't leave anyone in the lurch, and I didn't get fired—I just seized the moment to be here."

"To spend time with Vic. But there was no incident that triggered your departure from the winery?"

"Like what?"

He snapped a test shot of the old stonework. "A failed love affair, personality conflicts, stung by bees?"

Adrienne shook her head. "There was a man on the staff who was better suited to my job. Noah and Phoebe needed me to get in there and sort things out. I love wine. I love learning about it, sharing what I know. That doesn't mean, I've discovered, that I love the wine business."

"Innkeeping is different?"

"Innkeeping in Knights Bridge is different. Vic's here, yes, but he hasn't been around much since I started at Carriage Hill. Vic doesn't have deep roots here the way the Sloans and the O'Dunns and the Frosts and—well, a lot of families do. My mother couldn't wait to get away from her roots. My dad hasn't been a big part of my life since he and my mother divorced. I was seven. We get along okay, though."

"And Vic?"

She scooped up two freshly-fallen maple leaves. "I wanted to hate Vic for abandoning my mother, not being a part of my life, but that's not what happened. We're feeling our way but we do well together. It's as if he's been there all along and I just needed to tear through the gauze between us. Maybe that's my mother's doing in her own cryptic way." She tossed the leaves into the brook and watched as the current took them. "I wanted to come back here, Adam. Vic or no Vic."

As she turned, he snapped a picture of her, capturing, he was sure, her look of love, hope and confusion.

A heady mix it was, he thought. He lowered his camera. "What's on your mind, Adrienne?"

She glanced at the brook, one leaf hung up on a rock, the other still on its way to Quabbin. "I can't fall for you as a way to belong here, be a part of this town."

"Is that what you're doing?"

"No. It's not. It's what I worry I'm doing."

He stepped close to her. "You don't strike me as the worrying type."

She grinned suddenly, catching him by surprise. "You see? You know me well."

"And you like that?"

"I like it a lot." She nodded to the bridge. "How old is it?"

"Mid-nineteenth century."

"So it was built after Olivia's place."

"About the same time as the house that's now just the cellar hole where Tyler, Aidan and Owen hid. Turns out a stonemason lived there. He built this bridge and the wall I repaired at Carriage Hill. It wasn't original to the property. It was added later." Adam looked up at the bridge with its carefully constructed, enduring stone arches. "Thomas Eaton was his name. He did a lot of the old stonework around town."

"What happened to him?" Adrienne asked.

He heard the note of dread in her voice, and smiled. "He died at eighty-seven at home."

"For real?"

"I got curious and looked up his obituary at the library the other day."

"That means he died in the house that used to stand

where the boys hid from a moose they thought was a dinosaur."

Adam shook his head. "They never thought that moose was a dinosaur."

She laughed, and he snapped that photo, too.

The "golden hour" to grab decent photos had passed by the time they returned to Carriage Hill, and Olivia, Dylan and Buster had arrived. Adam left Adrienne with them and headed back to Echo Lake. He grabbed Violet and took her for a long walk. It was fully dark by the time they got back. He let her sleep by the fire while he walked up to the main house to check on a problem Vic had mentioned with the wine cellar. But it was fine.

When he made his way upstairs to the kitchen, he found Adrienne opening a cupboard. She jumped, let out a yelp of surprise.

"Sorry," he said. "I didn't know you were here."

"I'm trying out new breakfast menus for the inn. I figured it wouldn't hurt to turn on the stove and faucet here. Get a change of scenery."

"Restless?"

"I got to thinking about Vic. Do you think he could be in trouble?"

"In danger, you mean?"

She nodded and pulled a saucepan out of the cupboard.

"If he is, he has good people looking after him."

"Like Brody and Greg," she said.

Adam watched as she placed the pan on the stove. He

wasn't convinced she had a real plan for her breakfast items. "You thought it'd help you to be here."

"Cooking's a nice switch from getting templates and workflows in place. It's Maggie's territory, but she doesn't mind—I'm the one who sets up breakfasts and we both like to experiment."

He leaned against the counter. "We're not talking avocado toast, are we?"

She grinned at him. "Homemade apple butter and oatmeal bread. Warm plum compote with local yogurt. Traditional quiche lorraine made with local ham and cheese."

"Now my mouth's watering."

She laughed. "Mine, too."

Adam watched her dump a basket of small plums into the sink and turn on the faucet to rinse them. "Anything I can do to help?"

"Maybe when I get to the apples." Her eyes on the plums, she took a breath. "Vic asked me once what's my heart's desire. I didn't know what he was talking about."

"I wouldn't have, either."

"It got me thinking. I've just gone from one thing to the next, one place to the next since college—but I've made great friends. I wasn't running from anything. I was running *to* things. New adventures, I guess. Working on my blog and my consulting. Figuring out my life."

"Living your life," Adam said.

"Yeah." She beamed a smile at him. "Thanks for that. What's *your* heart's desire, Adam? A place here at the lake with golden retrievers, bonfires with your brothers, get-togethers at the family homestead?"

"Right now it's kissing you."

His words took her by surprise. "Is it?"

"Yes."

"Then…" She placed her hand on the back of his neck. "Far be it from me to keep you from your heart's desire."

He smiled, lowering his mouth to hers. Their kiss was deep, lending itself to more—her palms easing down his back to his waistband, his palms on her hips, lifting her onto him. He pressed himself into her, and she responded by tightening her hold, so her breasts were pushed against his chest.

It took supreme self-control on his part to set her on the floor and stand back, but damned if he was going to make love to her in Vic's kitchen. But that wasn't the only thing on his mind. "You can't let the town and Vic get between us—fall for me because of them, don't fall for me because of them. What's going on here is between us."

"I know." She touched her fingertips to her lips, still feeling the effects of their kiss. "Just let my pulse return to normal first, okay?"

He grinned at her and kissed her on the forehead. "Okay." He stepped back and pulled open the back door. "See you tomorrow."

"Right. Yes." She blew out a breath and smiled at him. "See you tomorrow."

Eighteen

Adrienne cut up damson plums into the saucepan, added sugar and water and put them on to simmer. She washed the cutting board and paring knife. Apple butter would take longer. She could at least get it started. She grabbed her bag of Cortland apples.

This town, she thought. Adam Sloan. They went together. Belonged together. She wasn't sure she did, but she loved Knights Bridge—and she was falling in love with him.

And she knew what he was doing. Why he'd left the way he had. It wasn't about patience or holding back this time. It was about intention and choice, and maybe a little foreplay, too.

Maybe a lot of foreplay.

The plums came to a boil and she turned them off. They could sit a while. The apples weren't going anywhere, and it wouldn't hurt to leave them on the counter. She could make apple butter later, or tomorrow—or never. She could buy locally-made apple butter at the country store. Then again, maybe Maggie would be making some.

Adrienne tore open the back door and ran down the steps, kicking through fallen leaves as she made her way down to the guesthouse. She stopped hard by the lake. Pluck Adam out of Knights Bridge and plop him in California? Would he be the same man he was now? Would she be attracted to him in the same way? But it was a stupid hypothetical. He was here and he wasn't going anywhere. *She* was the wild card on that score.

He was on the deck with Violet. Adrienne ran up the stairs and stood in front of him. She was breathless, but she wasn't changing her mind. She knew what she wanted, and when he settled those blue eyes of his on her, she knew she wanted it now.

"I don't want to see you tomorrow," she told him.

He smiled slightly, knowingly. "No, huh?"

"No. I want to be with you now. Tonight."

"That's good." He moved closer to her. "Because I was wondering what my next move would be if you didn't come down here."

"Make love on Vic's porch?"

"Don't think it hasn't crossed my mind."

He slipped his arms around her and drew her to him, kissing her slowly, deeply, even as he lifted her. She wrapped her arms around his neck and pressed herself into his chest. In a few swift steps, he carried her inside, into his bedroom. He laid her on the bed and smiled, still on his feet. "Let me tell Violet she's not invited." That amounted to shutting the door with his foot before returning to her. "Adrienne…"

She heard the urgency in his voice. "I know. I can't wait any longer, either."

But wait they did, because there was the matter of clothes. *Layers* of clothes, this being late fall in New England. She inhaled at the sexy warmth of his T-shirt under his canvas shirt, the tautness of his chest and shoulders, and then the feel of his bare skin. Her body filled with a thousand sensations that all cried out for him. He helped her with her practical thermal shirt. "I was freezing one morning and picked it up at the country store…"

"It does the trick." He skimmed his fingers across her breasts and smiled. "Definitely."

In the next instant, the shirt was on the floor, followed by her bra and then her pants—and his pants. He came to her, kissing her as she lay on her back. She stroked him from his hips to his shoulders, discovering a couple of scars she hadn't known he had. She'd ask him about them sometime…not now. She could hardly catch her breath, never mind utter a coherent word. Then he lowered his mouth to her breasts, took a nipple in his lips and she moaned with a longing that further took her breath away. She felt the heat of his tongue, writhed under him even as he positioned himself between her legs. He was hard, ready. And she couldn't wait.

He rose up from her and locked eyes with her. She grabbed his hips, and he thrust into her, no hesitation, driving deep as she managed to cry out his name. He was making love to her. Finally. At last. She gave herself up to the feel of him inside her, let her longing take over and guide her, until her entire body exploded with a million sensations. She dug her fingers into him, but he didn't stop, didn't slacken his pace.

They came together, in a shimmering, exquisite release that left them spent, sheets tangled, the cool night breeze rippling across their overheated bodies. She hadn't realized he'd had a window cracked open. She smiled, brushing her fingertips across his chest. Only a Sloan would have a window open on a night like tonight.

He caught her hand in his. "Cold?"

She shook her head. "Not yet."

"I'll keep you warm."

"I know you will." She did, too. She rolled on top of him. "We'll keep each other warm."

Adam left early to work on his big project in the village. Adrienne lingered in bed. He'd drawn the blankets over her before slipping out to have breakfast at Smith's in the village, but he hadn't shut the window. She could feel the clear, crisp early-morning air, and she could hear birds. A million birds, she thought, sitting up with the covers still around her. A flock of Canada geese had gathered on the lake, glistening in the sunlight. She smiled, taking in the perfection of this moment. She had no desire to be anywhere else.

She eventually gathered up her clothes off the floor and got dressed. She'd take a shower and put on fresh clothes when she got back to the inn. Nothing about last night felt impulsive. She had no regrets. She was positive none would pop up later, when she'd had a chance to rouse herself from the glow of a night of incredible sex.

It was quiet at Vic's house. She missed seeing him

on the porch or in front of the fire with his iPad. But that day would come.

She made coffee and warmed up the plums and had them with yogurt. She'd told Maggie and Olivia she'd be up here to cook. It wasn't a stretch to think she'd decided to spend the night. They'd know apple butter needed time to simmer.

Adrienne walked out onto the porch. With the leaves off the trees, she could see even more of the lake. She didn't have to be anywhere right away, but she did have to get back to Carriage Hill to meet with Felicity Mac-Gregor about events through the holidays.

It was hard to believe Thanksgiving, Christmas and New Year's Eve were upon them.

She didn't linger at the lake and instead returned to Carriage Hill. She waved to Adam and his crew at work in the village, but no one was at the inn. She took a quick shower and put on fresh clothes.

She and Felicity had agreed to meet for lunch in town. As Adrienne grabbed her keys in the kitchen, she checked her phone and saw she had an email from her mother. In Sophia Portale's usual direct manner, she informed Adrienne that the corporate executive she'd been seeing for a few years had exited. I'm not upset. He's not upset. Onward to...well, somewhere in Europe for starters.

Wasn't that typical of her mother? She was nothing if not resilient. Adrienne typed her response. Call me if you want to talk. I'm making apple butter. She grinned as she hit Send. Maybe her mother would surprise her and applaud the idea of her only daughter making apple butter in her quaint New England inn.

As she headed out to her borrowed car, Adrienne realized she'd had a perfectly fine childhood, if nothing like a Sloan childhood. She was relieved her enterprising mother had her own business to absorb some of her achievement-oriented energy and not just a daughter. Her mother hadn't planned on having a baby so soon. That was obvious now, but it would undoubtedly remain forever unspoken between them. And that was okay, Adrienne thought. It wasn't really any of her business. Her mother had no regrets, and Adrienne, now that the shock had long worn off, had no complaints.

Felicity was on a tear when Adrienne slid into a booth opposite her at Smith's. "I am prying the Rawlings-Bennett wedding out of Samantha's hands," Felicity said. "I'm not really a wedding planner, but it's going to be an unconventional wedding—and she's not the person to be at the helm. It's not a secret. I told her as much, and she said she'd pay me in pirate's gold if I took it on." Felicity dumped cream in her mug of coffee. "I wouldn't put it past her to have pirate's gold."

Adrienne wouldn't, either. She ordered a turkey club with chips and planned on having pie.

Felicity settled on the turkey vegetable soup. "Hungry, aren't you?" But she didn't wait for Adrienne to answer. "By the way, I stopped at Carriage Hill first thing this morning. You weren't there."

"I spent the night at the lake."

"Uh-huh. Adam Sloan lives in Vic's guesthouse, doesn't he?"

"Mm."

"You two…" Felicity sighed. "Never mind. I just dealt with town gossip when Gabe and I got together. It was all we could do to keep people from spying on us skinny-dipping at our old swimming hole on the river."

"Did you—"

She grinned. "We did not skinny-dip. Everything else, though. And no spies. But it felt like it. I heard you and Adam waved to each other when you passed him this morning. People assume you were on the way back from the lake."

"People?"

"Adam's grandmother. Elly O'Dunn. Clare Farrell at the library."

"And you found this out how?"

"People tell me things," she said, matter-of-fact.

"Well, it's true. Adam and I are seeing each other."

Felicity beamed a smile across the table. "No way. Really?"

Adrienne sighed at her teasing tone. "Everyone knows?"

"Everyone. We've all just been waiting for one or both of you to admit it."

"There are no secrets in this town."

"There are, just not that one."

"Is it a problem?"

Felicity frowned. "Problem for…?"

"I don't know. Anyone."

"It doesn't matter, does it? I haven't heard a single snarky word, but…" Felicity narrowed her gaze on Adrienne. "Did I blunder into a sensitive subject? It's not the first time. I'll shut up now."

Felicity was another one in town who didn't mince words, something Adrienne appreciated. She smiled past her awkwardness. "No—no, you didn't."

"You're a private person. Adam's a private person. I get it. Then there's Ambassador Scarlatti." Felicity paused as if debating what to say. "Never mind. Let's go through your events and then order pie and talk about Greg Rawlings and Charlotte Bennett's wedding at Red Clover Inn. You try planning something with those two." She was obviously not the least put out. "We're going to need Carriage Hill. Do you have plans yet for Thanksgiving?"

"You mean like family coming in?" Adrienne shook her head. "No, nothing. I hope Vic will be back by then, but I don't know."

"Well, you're welcome to join Gabe and me. We're having his grandfather and Mark and Jess to our place on the river. But maybe you'll end up doing Thanksgiving with the Sloans." She held up a hand and grinned. "You do not need to respond. The wedding is Friday morning—I want to have everything ready so we can enjoy Thanksgiving."

"We can talk about the wedding now and do Carriage Hill over pie."

Felicity sighed. "I'd rather plan ten entrepreneurial boot camp weekends than one wedding. Greg and Charlotte are laid-back, at least about their wedding, and we've had plenty of time to plan. But they swore most of their family members wouldn't attend. They invited everyone. And guess what?"

"They're all coming."

Felicity smiled. "Every last one of them."

Nineteen

Adam stopped at Carriage Hill that evening and helped Adrienne finish the apple butter, easy enough since it mostly involved simmering with occasional stirring. That meant they could slip into her suite. She thought they might take their time, but they tore off each other's clothes with the same urgency and abandon as last night. But she had to get the apple butter out of the oven and into jars, and that meant slipping out of her warm bed. She put on pajama pants and a tank top and went into the kitchen.

Adam joined her a few minutes later, fully dressed. "Change of plans. I need to get back to the lake." He kissed the top of her head. "Check your messages. Vic texted us. He's coming home."

She grabbed her phone and saw Vic's text: Home early tomorrow. See you soon!

"He sent this text while we…"

"Yeah," Adam said.

"That doesn't bother you, does it?"

"Nope."

"Of course not. Me, either." She smiled and texted Great! to Vic. She placed her phone back on the counter. "You know what I think?"

"You're glad we didn't spend the night together at his place and wake up with him in the driveway?"

"There's that."

"Spending the night here…"

"Yeah. Best at least let him unpack before he finds out about us." Adrienne opened the oven. Using thick pot holders, she lifted out the pan of apple butter and set it on a rack on the butcher-block island. "This stuff smells heavenly. I've become an apple butter fan since moving east. But no, I wasn't thinking about how we tell Vic about us. Or not just thinking that. I have a feeling he wants to take on another assignment but he's afraid it'll upset me. I move across the country to spend time with him and he's plotting to spend the next year in who-knows-where."

"Would that upset you?"

"I don't want him to feel hemmed in by me. Knights Bridge has been his home base for two decades. That's not going to change." She set her pot holders on the island next to the bubbling apple butter. "I might have felt differently in September."

"But you don't feel so alone now," Adam said. He dipped a finger into the apple butter and licked it. "Good but hotter than I expected."

"It's just out of the oven, Adam."

He winked at her. "Best time I've ever had making apple butter."

"Then you've done it before?"

"With my grandmother when I was ten." He tucked a finger under her chin. "See you soon. Maybe whatever Vic's been up to on these trips will help him finally settle into retirement and he'll get back to his memoirs."

But Adrienne knew Adam didn't think so, and neither did she. After he left, she put the apple butter in jars and let it cool while she cleaned up the kitchen. Then she put the jars in the refrigerator. She didn't need to do anything else. It'd get used before it had a chance to go bad.

She had apple butter with her toast for breakfast and was making apple crisp with Maggie when Adam texted her that Vic had arrived at Echo Lake with an entourage of DSS agents. They dropped him off, checked the house and grounds and departed. Something's definitely up.

She showed Maggie the text. "Wow. I don't think Vic's ever arrived with a security entourage. Then again, most of us in town never paid much attention."

She popped the apple crisp in the oven. Adrienne had helped with peeling and slicing the apples and measuring ingredients according to Maggie's instructions. They were baking not for inn guests but for Thanksgiving. Apple crisp, pumpkin pie and sweet potatoes with apple cider. Family favorites, Maggie said.

Then came a text from Vic: I'm home!

"Go, go," Maggie said. "I'll take care of things here."

Adrienne pulled off her apron. She was wearing the one with the chickens. Maggie had brought her own, with a big green dinosaur on the front. A present from her sons. "I won't be long."

"Take your time."

Adrienne jumped into Vic's old car. In the time he'd been away, foliage season had come and gone. A few spent oak leaves and such hung on, but most of the trees between Carriage Hill and Echo Lake had bare branches. The landscape had opened up, and she'd noticed fewer and fewer hikers and "leaf peepers."

It was a raw, rainy autumn morning, but when she arrived at the lake, she found Vic in his favorite chair on the porch, with Rohan asleep next to him. Vic—her father—looked an intriguing mix of exhausted and excited. "Are you in trouble, Vic?" she asked him.

"Not the kind you mean. I've been offered a job."

"A job. So much for retiring."

"It's a temporary assignment at NATO Headquarters in Brussels. A year at most. It would be a new chapter in my life but also a continuation of what I've done the past forty years."

"You say 'would be.' Does that mean you haven't said yes?"

"That's right."

"Why are you hesitating? Did you want to get back here and see if you could stand to leave your spot here on Echo Lake with your iPad, Rohan, your memoirs?"

"I would miss Rohan and the lake. He likes the lake better than me. Elly can take him, but he's bonded with Violet. I thought I'd ask Adam. But I'm getting ahead of myself. I honestly haven't made a decision. I'm used to coming here for a few days at a time, or on vacation for a couple of weeks. That wouldn't change. It's been my routine for twenty years. I've only been retired a year. Not even that." He got to his feet. "No, it's you, Adrienne. I won't take the job if it upsets you. You gave up California to head east to spend time with me."

"Would I be able to visit you in Brussels?"

"Yes. I'll be traveling frequently but I'll be based there."

"It sounds like an opportunity too good to pass up. It's what you want to do, Vic. There's an energy about you that wasn't there a few weeks ago. How long do you have to make a final decision?"

"Twenty-four hours." He shifted, biting his lower lip as he looked out at the lake. "I don't want to get this wrong, Adrienne. I want to do right by you. I didn't when you were a child."

"I've been to Brussels, Vic. I love it."

"It *is* an exciting opportunity, a chance to serve—to make a difference at least in a small way. Everyone in Knights Bridge thinks I retired too soon?"

Adrienne smiled. "We have a tendency to think Knights Bridge is even smaller than it is, but the people we know—yes, that's my impression."

"Adam's invited us both to Thanksgiving with the Sloan clan at Red Clover Inn. Heather and Brody will be there from London, and Greg will be up from Washington—he has his wedding the next morning. I'll say yes on behalf of both of us if you want to do it."

That was so Adam, she thought. He'd speak to Vic first out of courtesy, in case he had plans. "It sounds like fun."

"What about your…?" He faltered.

"Mom texted me this morning. She's decided to pop in. She gets here tomorrow night but she's only staying the one night. Dad is in New York on business and figured he'd drop by, too. It's last minute or serendipity, or both."

"That's wonderful. It'll be good to see them. It never would have worked between your mother and me."

"You don't owe me an explanation, Vic."

"These past few weeks especially, I thought about what might have been. I faced the loss of not having known you were my daughter. The regret over the life I could have lived but didn't. It wasn't just Sophia's doing. I never inquired when I heard she was expecting. I didn't know her well. We had a mad fling, but I knew her well enough that I should have realized you could have been mine."

"Because she never would have had a baby so soon after marriage if it'd been up to her."

"That doesn't mean she didn't want you."

"No, but it doesn't mean it was part of her planning, either. She's a great planner, my mother."

"When she was getting ready to leave Paris, I made it clear—as she did to me—that our week together was just that. I didn't want to ruin her marriage by asking about you. I saw her as a narcissistic barracuda. That was a bit sexist of me, I think. Sophia's driven and hardworking. There's a difference. She's not perfect but I'm not, either. She was going places those days back in Paris. Blazing her own trail. That's part of what attracted me to her."

She took his hand. "Take the Brussels job if it's what you want, Vic. I have friends who own a vineyard in

Provence. I'd love for you to meet them sometime when you can get away."

"Does that mean you're firing up your wine blog again?"

"No. I'll have to find time to get away, too."

"Keeping the innkeeping job?"

"It's changing, I think."

He narrowed his eyes. "And?"

"And I think I've fallen for the local stonemason."

"Yeah. I kind of got that impression. If you're worried about what I think—about what anyone around here thinks—" He stopped, put his arm around her and gave her a quick squeeze. "Don't."

Rohan woke up and bolted between them. They all walked down to the lake together. Adrienne could see Adam on the guesthouse deck. He was giving her time with Vic, she realized. Violet rose up. Of course she'd be there with Adam.

Adrienne watched Vic throw a stick into the water, Rohan leaping after it. She realized she was happy here. Making a place for herself as an innkeeper. Content, she thought. And she realized how much she'd come to care about Vic in the relatively short time she'd known him. He was a good man. She was proud to have him as her father. What would he think of her relationship with Adam? She wanted Vic to approve, to like Adam. But in the end it didn't matter. What she and Adam had together was theirs.

Adrienne had lunch with Vic and returned to Carriage Hill after he went upstairs to take a nap. By late afternoon, she was sitting on the terrace in a fleece jacket, loving the chilly November weather. She'd filled up the wood box, appreciating the shorter trek from the new lean-to. Aidan and Tyler Sloan and their friend Owen were playing dinosaurs out on the stone wall Adam had rebuilt while Brandon and Maggie mulched the garden. Olivia was "excused," as Brandon had put it. Adrienne felt positive about what she'd accomplished at Carriage Hill in such a short time.

"You're a natural innkeeper," Olivia said, joining her from the kitchen. "Maggie and I had a feeling you would be. Does it surprise you that you're so good at it?"

"It's hard work but I love it. I guess I wasn't sure if I'd fit in."

"You've made a place for yourself. That's what Dylan did here, too—and Russ, Kylie, Clare, Samantha and even Noah. It's home again for Brody and Gabe. It's not home for Greg and Charlotte, but they have family here, and they know the welcome mat's always out. And Vic," Olivia added. "Knights Bridge is home for him, wherever he might be."

"I love it here," Adrienne said. "I never thought I would, and even if I did come to love it, I thought I'd get restless. I've been a wanderer for so long."

"Well, we're glad you wandered here."

Maggie joined them. "Brandon and I want you to consider taking on Red Clover Inn, too. Samantha is never going to be an innkeeper. She has her pirates. Justin— he's got his hands full with his construction work. It'll be a while before the inn's open to guests. You've got time to get things sorted there properly."

"And we'd like you to become our partner here at Carriage Hill," Olivia said.

Adrienne swallowed past the tightness in her throat. "I'm overcome. Thank you."

"Take some time to think," Maggie said.

"Talk to Adam," Olivia said quietly.

Adrienne knew she wouldn't take on Red Clover Inn, a Sloan venture, if Adam had any reservations. Maggie and Olivia obviously understood that without spelling it out. The Farm at Carriage Hill and Red Clover Inn had so much potential, and countless options.

"I knew from the start that Justin and Samantha would never be innkeepers," Maggie said, amused. "No one else in the family is suited, either. Can you see Eric greeting guests on the front porch? They'd run. Christopher? Adam? Not a chance. But you, Adrienne." She smiled broadly. "You've got the gift. You'll make it work."

Adrienne put aside thoughts about her future in Knights Bridge to enjoy Thanksgiving Day at Red Clover Inn with the Sloans and Charlotte Bennett and Greg Rawlings, tomorrow's bride and groom. The eccentric Bennetts and rough-and-tumble Rawlingses were an odd mix but Greg and Charlotte were clearly deeply in love. And everyone was thrilled to have Heather and Brody home from London for a few days.

Vic helped Tyler and Aidan set up an epic dinosaur battle in the library. Adrienne hadn't seen him look so happy. The prospect of his new assignment agreed with him. She did notice the two DSS agents eyeing Vic knowingly. Whatever Vic's new job was, Greg Rawlings and Brody Hancock knew all about it.

Maggie got a text from Dylan letting her know Olivia had gone into labor early that morning. "He's taking her to the hospital now."

By early afternoon, as Thanksgiving dinner was being served, Dylan texted Maggie. She showed her phone around the table: Mary Grace McCaffrey, 7 lbs. 5 oz., healthy.

Adrienne filled glasses with sparkling wine, and Justin led the toast. "To Mary Grace McCaffrey, and to friends and family. Happy Thanksgiving."

Adam, his four brothers, Greg and Brody headed up to the lake after they cleaned up the dishes from Thanksgiving dinner. They got a fire going down on the sand. "It's not as cold as it was last time I was up here," Greg said. "Cold enough, though."

"I love it," Brody said.

Greg shuddered. "Figures. Didn't you propose to Heather on a cold winter night?"

Brody grinned. "The best time."

Justin handed Adam a beer. "Are you going to tell Adrienne you had a hand in asking her to take on Red Clover Inn?"

Adam opened the bottle. "Do I interfere in your relationship with Samantha?"

"Yes, but I'm not interfering. I'm asking. Brother to brother. And you're telling me it's none of my business."

Adam raised his beer to Justin. "Brother to brother."

Greg eased next to Adam with a beer of his own.

"Red Clover's set up for a wedding. You all will be tearing out walls, wiring and plumbing soon. We could do a double wedding. Why not?"

"Eric broke up with his fiancée," Adam said.

"Don't be dense. I'm talking about you and our dark-eyed innkeeper from California. Vic's daughter." Greg paused. "Adrienne Portale. I met her last winter. You two are good together."

Adam wasn't sure he wanted to get into his relationship with Adrienne with a senior DSS agent. "I wouldn't argue with that."

"Bet you wouldn't." Greg held his beer up to the firelight. "Four sips. Just what I thought. I'm stone-cold sober. Thinking straight and still marrying Charlotte Bennett tomorrow."

Adam grinned. It was a frosty evening, the flames of their fire outlined against the darkening landscape. "You're a lucky man," he said finally.

"Yeah. She and Samantha are probably off talking sunken pirate treasure." Greg took another sip of his beer. "Hold on. I didn't lose my train of thought. Why wait, Adam? Go for it."

Adam made no comment and drank more of his beer.

Brody nodded in agreement with his DSS friend and colleague. "Greg's got a point. No time like the present."

Justin, too, eased forward, as if he had a firm grasp on exactly what was going on here. "Vic's in town. Adrienne's folks are here or on the way. Seize the moment."

Adam hadn't mentioned to his brothers and friends that Adrienne's parents would be in town tomorrow—

but it was no surprise they knew. News traveled fast in Knights Bridge.

Heather arrived, bundled up in a warm jacket. She helped herself to a beer and dived into the conversation. "I married Brody in a whirlwind. Justin married Samantha in a whirlwind. You, Christopher and Eric had to deal with relationships that didn't work so you'd know the right woman when she turned up. Trust me, Adam. Waiting isn't going to change anything."

He sighed. "Are you all done now?"

"Done," Justin said. "Just let me know if I need to postpone tearing out the kitchen at Red Clover."

Adam didn't tell them he'd already made up his mind. Let his siblings and DSS friends think they'd talked sense into him. Meanwhile, he'd find Adrienne Portale, the woman he loved.

First, though, he had to talk to Vic.

"I'll be in touch," Adam said, then handed his beer to Justin.

He walked up to Vic Scarlatti's longtime house on Echo Lake. Had Vic ever imagined his life would come to this? A stonemason in love with the daughter he hadn't known he had when he'd first bought this place…

The not-so-retired ambassador was on his front porch, under a blanket with a bottle of fine port from his wine cellar on a small side table. He offered Adam a glass. "No, thanks," Adam said.

"You've got something on your mind, Adam."

He decided to get straight to the point. "I want to marry your daughter tomorrow. Unless you object—"

"Object? Why would I object?"

"You're her father, Vic."

He picked up his port glass. "Yes, I am. I really am." He bit back a sniffle. "Damn."

"I know tomorrow's short notice."

"Yes, but it works. Greg and Charlotte are on board, I assume? They would be. Married…" Vic sipped his port, set the glass back on the side table and threw off his blanket as he got to his feet. He put out his hand. "Congratulations, Adam. You have my blessing. I can't imagine a better son-in-law, or a better man for Adrienne."

They shook hands. Adam felt his own emotions surging. He looked out at the lake, and he could smell the last of the bonfire in the chilly late-November air. Violet and Rohan were racing around in the yard, a whirl of golden fur as they played and provoked each other.

Finally he turned to Vic. "Thank you, Vic. I love Adrienne with all my heart."

Vic cleared his throat. "That's enough for me."

Adam found Maggie in the kitchen at Carriage Hill. She had a pencil in hand and a checklist on the butcher-block island. "Adrienne's gone for a walk." Maggie barely looked up from her list. "I'm going through everything for tonight and tomorrow. It's family, I know, but Adrienne's mother arrives tonight and we have a full house of wedding guests."

"You're in your element," Adam said.

"I am." She raised her gaze to him. "So is Adrienne. She's not out walking because of her work here, or because of her mother."

"Uh-huh."

"That's all I have to say." Maggie checked off something far down on her list and smiled. "Adrienne's thought of everything. I always leave out three or four things."

Adam winked at her. "I love how you're pretending you're minding your own business."

She grinned. "Don't you, though?" She pointed her pencil toward the mudroom. "She went that way."

He went out to the terrace, welcoming the brisk air. He walked on a mulched path and ducked behind the shed, then continued along the stone wall between woods and field.

Adrienne was sitting on the edge of the old cellar hole, in a black fleece jacket, jeans and ankle boots. She had her hair down, blowing slightly in the gentle breeze. "The happy innkeeper at work," he said, approaching her.

She squinted at him and grinned. "I'm thinking about showing my mother this spot."

He sat next to her. "Did I startle you?"

"No. I heard you. It's hard to be stealthy with all these fallen leaves. Not that you were trying to be stealthy. Were you looking for me?"

"I knew I'd find you here."

"Not 'had a feeling,'" she said. "'Knew.'"

He brushed a few strands of hair from her face and tucked them behind her ear. "This is the spot where I realized you might do okay here. You handled yourself well when we searched for the boys. I didn't expect that."

"What did you expect?"

"You'd get lost or something."

"Add to the drama," she said, matter-of-fact. "City girl, new in town and last winter with Vic. He's the one who tore up his house and ran off in the ice and snow, but I'm the one who prompted it."

"He gets it, Adrienne. You both had to wrap your heads around finding out you were father and daughter." Adam paused. "Everyone gets it."

"Did you hate me then?"

"No." He didn't hesitate. "I thought you were attractive. But I wasn't optimistic when you took on the innkeeping job."

"Thought I'd run back to California?"

"Run somewhere."

"It's my pattern." She lifted her dark eyes to him. "It *was* my pattern."

He took her in his arms and lifted her from the wall into the fallen leaves. "I love you, Adrienne," he whispered. "Damn. I love you so much."

"Adam…"

"I was attracted to you last winter but I thought— hell, she's not the one. She can't be the one. I'll break her heart. She'll break my heart. But that was old wounds talking. Yours and mine."

"It wasn't the right time for us."

"Yes, but you know you started to fall for me when you had me build Vic's wine cellar."

"I thought you were very rugged."

"I am very rugged."

"A Marine, a stonemason, a Sloan."

"I'm all that, yes, but right now—I'm just a man who loves you, who will always love you."

Her eyes shone with tears, and she sniffled, laughed a little. "I can't tell you how much I love hearing those words. I love you, Adam Sloan. It's taken me time to trust myself enough to say that out loud, but I have no doubts. I'll stand on what's left of this rock wall and shout it to the world."

He tightened his arms around her. "You've been thinking about everyone else, and about your mistakes. I have, too. I trust you, Adrienne. I trust myself. What we have is special and it's forever."

"It is," she said. "I know it is."

"Meanwhile…" He settled his hands on her lower back. "There's a plan afoot to have a double wedding at Red Clover Inn."

"A double wedding?" She straightened, instantly in innkeeper mode. "Who's the second couple? Eric didn't get back together with his ex-fiancée, did he? Trish, isn't it? She's not on Vic's cheat sheet."

"No, Eric and Trish didn't get back together."

Adam noticed the late-afternoon November light on Adrienne's face. He listened to the bare trees clicking in the breeze. He wasn't nervous, he realized. He wasn't hesitating or second-guessing himself. He was…savoring the moment.

"Us," he said finally. "We're the second couple."

She angled him a look. "You and me?"

"That's right. Charlotte's all in because she's a Bennett and that's how she thinks. Greg says it's fine with him because he saved Vic's life a few years back. It's Rawlings's logic, but it works."

"You and me," Adrienne repeated.

It wasn't doubt, he knew. It was surprise. Taking in the idea, envisioning it—realizing he was the one who'd thought of it. Steady Adam Sloan. He kissed her softly, not taking it further. "If you get restless, we'll figure it out. We'll go somewhere on your someday/maybe list, we'll hike into the woods and find hidden stone bridges and cellar holes, we'll learn new things together—"

"We could sign up for an adventure travel excursion."

"So long as Brandon doesn't lead it," Adam said with a grin.

"Ah, the Sloan brothers and your healthy rivalry."

"You'll get used to it."

"I love everything about being here, and I love you, Adam. I swear you're the reason I knew I had to come back to Knights Bridge. It wasn't just Vic. It was you."

"It'll be one hell of a short engagement but I do have a ring. It was Gran's. She gave it to me when I left for basic training, as a reminder that I had a future. I knew one day…" He dug the simple ring out of his jacket pocket and held it between his forefinger and thumb. "Marry me, Adrienne. I love you and I want us to be together forever."

"The ring…it's perfect. A double wedding…marry you…" Her smile was as bright as he'd yet seen, and it reached all the way to her eyes. She was breathing rapidly. "Yes, yes, yes. Oh—yes, Adam, I will marry you. Yes, I want us to be together forever…"

"Slow your breathing," he said.

"I will, but if I hyperventilate and pass out, you'll keep me from splitting my head open on a rock. I know you will, because… Adam…" She gulped in another breath, touched his hand. "I love you and I love this ring, even if we'll only be engaged for less than a day."

"I do know my rocks," he said, and slipped the ring on her finger.

Twenty

Maggie knew, of course. "I'm a caterer," she told Adrienne in the Carriage Hill kitchen, after Adam left to tell his family. "I know everything. Actually, Brandon said this could happen. I've been bursting at the seams. I have a selection of dresses picked out for you. I don't know if you own a dress, but if you do, I bet it's black. I know that can work for a wedding, but we'd never hear the end of it from Evelyn."

Adrienne laughed, touched a fingertip to her engagement ring. "I have an all-purpose black dress. Show me what you have."

Maggie took her into the living room, where she'd laid out three dresses sewn forty years ago by a Knights Bridge teenager who'd secreted herself in the library attic and practiced her craft. Daphne Stewart, aka Debbie Henderson, granddaughter of the library's founder, finally took off for Hollywood and a successful career as a costume designer.

"I think these will fit," Maggie said. "We can always do some quick alterations. My mother is good with a needle and thread, and I've got safety pins and duct tape."

Adrienne realized Maggie was serious about the pins and duct tape. Well, why not?

She slipped into the innkeeper's suite to try on the dresses. One in particular—a dark coral silk floor-length gown that was one of Daphne's early designs, not one she'd copied from a movie—caught her eye. It fit well, and it suited her and a Thanksgiving weekend wedding.

She returned to the living room and showed it off to Maggie. "What do you think?"

"It's perfect. I love it."

Adrienne reminded herself to steady her breathing. She didn't have Adam here if she passed out. "I've never been so excited. I'm not the giddy type but I'm giddy right now."

Maggie hugged her. "We're going to be sisters-in-law. I couldn't be happier, Adrienne."

She lifted the hem of the gown and slipped back into the suite. She put her regular clothes back on and hung the dress in the closet.

She drove up to see Vic. "I took a nap and went out like a light," he said. "You look like you're about to burst at the seams. What's up?"

And she saw he knew. "Adam—he asked you for my hand?"

"In his Adam way."

"That's so fantastic! I assume you said yes…" She showed him her ring. "Isn't it great?"

"He's a romantic guy under all that sinew." Vic's dark

eyes misted. "If I'd known I had a daughter, I might have saved some of my mother's stuff. She had a spectacular hat collection. I suppose that wouldn't help with your wedding, though."

"My mother didn't save any family heirlooms. She's not sentimental."

"Well, one thing she and I have in common, then. Besides you."

"I'm all set with a dress. Turns out I'm a good fit for one of the dresses Daphne Stewart left behind in the library attic when she ran off to Hollywood."

"It's not black, I hope."

"Coral silk. It has a couple of moth holes that no one will see."

"That's terrific. We'll have Greg Rawlings and Adam Sloan in suits on the same day." Vic grinned. "I can't wait."

Sophia Portale burst into Knights Bridge just after dark. She'd celebrated Thanksgiving with friends in New York. Adrienne had texted her—before Adam had proposed—that she wouldn't be alone at Carriage Hill and got an immediate text back: Wonderful! The more the merrier. I'll help.

Help how? But after multiple events at the inn, Adrienne wasn't worried about tonight. The guests were all Bennetts and they were always game for an adventure. If a moose plunged through the back garden, they'd be fine.

Adrienne sent her mother Vic's Knights Bridge cheat sheet. Best to be thorough. It was a good thing Vic had included Loretta Wrentham and Julius Hartley on his cheat sheet, because Maggie had announced the couple was arriving in Knights Bridge from La Jolla next week to see Dylan and Olivia's baby. Noah and Phoebe would be back in town soon, too. Little Mary Grace wouldn't lack for people who loved her.

Sophia arrived in a rental car and carried her bag into the kitchen herself. Adrienne showed her to the inn-keeper's suite, but she refused to take it. She plopped her bag in Olivia's former office, where Adrienne had set up a cot for herself. "It reminds me of my bedroom as a kid," she said cheerfully. "When do your guests arrive?"

"Around eight."

"Excellent. We have time for wine. I brought a bottle. Don't tell me it's bad. Just let's enjoy it."

Adrienne grinned at her mother. "I thought you were helping."

She smiled back. "This is helping."

Adrienne fetched two glasses. Her mother insisted on sitting on the terrace and grabbed throws from the living room. "How romantic," she said. "Bundling up to the smell of fallen leaves. It is chilly, though, isn't it?"

"Forty-two degrees."

"At least the wine won't freeze." She held up her glass. "Cheers, sweetheart."

"Cheers, Mom."

"There's something I need to tell you. It's good news. I sold my business. I'm visiting Tuscany and then spending the winter in Portugal. After that, who knows what I'll do. Wherever I am, come visit me."

"Wow, this is big news. What made you decide on such a big change?"

"I had an offer. That helped. It came out of the blue, and I said no—immediately, reflexively. But I kept thinking about it. About what it would mean to let go of this business I'd created. To let it grow, change, be part of something new and exciting. I liked all that, and it would be great for my existing clients."

"And you? Did you think about what it would mean for you?"

"Eventually, yes. It didn't happen right away. Then I was walking in Sausalito after lunch with a friend and I did—I thought about myself and what it would mean to throttle back some. I'm fine financially. I'm not super-rich like your friends Dylan and Noah by any stretch, but selling the business sets me up nicely for whatever I want to do next. And I want a year off."

"Do you think you'll retire?"

"Maybe."

"Maybe you'll have another mad affair," Adrienne said lightly.

Her mother looked appalled, even embarrassed.

"Mom. It could happen. You're not *that* old."

She laughed. "Yes, it could happen. I'm trying to leave room for the unexpected in my life. Serendipity. Adrienne…"

Adrienne wasn't surprised when her mother hesitated. She had something to say, obviously, but heart-to-heart talks had never been her strong suit. She was a doer. Outcome-oriented, she'd say. Feelings, emotions, struggles—she was better at helping people solve problems than just listening to them, and that included herself.

"I never wanted you to be a clone of me," she finally blurted.

"I know that. I appreciate it."

"I wasn't a helicopter mother."

"The opposite, Mom," Adrienne said with a laugh. "I had the freedom to find my own way."

"That's a positive spin on it. You've always been independent. I'd have told you about Vic if I had to do it again. Sooner, at least. I remember holding you as a newborn, and all I wanted to do was to protect you. I wanted to protect Vic, too. What I did felt right at the time but I didn't have any easy choices, except to take care of you."

"I'm happy, Mom. Very happy."

She looked around at the inn's yard as if seeing it for the first time. The wet stone wall glistened in the light from the house. "The man who lives in Vic's guesthouse did this work, didn't he?"

"Adam Sloan."

"He did the photographs upstairs, too. I noticed them when you showed me around. He's both a brilliant artist and craftsman." She paused. "I'm glad you've found someone, Adrienne."

"How—"

"I'm your mother. I know these things." She laughed and winked. "Vic told me. He thought I knew. I'm not offended he found out before I did. He lives here, and it's a small town. People talk."

"Adam and I…" Adrienne was the one who hesitated

this time. She wasn't that great at heart-to-hearts, either. "Adam and I are getting married tomorrow."

"Well, well." Her mother smiled. "Congratulations."

"It's sudden, I know."

"Is it right for you, Adrienne?"

"It's perfect."

Although he and her mother had split when she was only seven, Adrienne had always had a good if not ultra-close relationship with her dad, Richard Portale. He arrived at Carriage Hill just in time to be at the double wedding. Adrienne showed him around the antique house and gardens.

"I'm only in town for the day," he said as they returned to the inn's country kitchen. "I'll come for a proper visit another time."

"I'm glad you're here, Dad."

He smiled. "You and Vic are two peas in a pod, Adrienne. I'm glad you've found each other." He kissed her on the cheek. "You'll always be my little girl."

"And you'll always be my dad."

He was a good-looking man in his fifties, successful, decent. That he and her mother had clicked for almost a decade was something of a miracle, especially now that Adrienne knew the secret her mother had carried.

All behind them now.

"What do you think of Knights Bridge?" she asked.

"There's more going on here than meets the eye at first. Come on. Let's get you married to the man of your dreams. Tall, solid, good-looking and knows how to use tools. You always wanted a guy who's handy."

She laughed. "You remember that?"

"You were twelve and we were on the way to Lake Tahoe for vacation."

"I remember. We stayed with friends of yours who had an incredible wine cellar."

"You were fascinated by wine at an early age."

"I still am."

He kissed her on the cheek. "I can tell by the inn's wine selection and Vic's wine cellar."

"You two—"

"Friends, Adrienne. Instant friends."

"Thanks, Dad."

"I have you because of Vic Scarlatti."

Twenty-One

"No, no, no," Felicity said when Adrienne attempted to get into the kitchen at Red Clover Inn to help with the weddings. "You are *not* working today. I hired a crew. We're self-contained. They're bringing a van. They'll be here in a few minutes."

"But you're sure you don't need me to do anything?"

"Not you, not Maggie, not anyone else. You all are to relax and enjoy yourselves. Consider it my wedding present. Everything is under control, except the Bennett and the Rawlings clans. Boisterous is an understatement. Go. You'll see what I mean."

The sprawling inn was filled with family and friends. Various Bennett and Rawlings teens were engaged in a rousing game of *Clue* in front of a fire in the library. Whoever had committed the murder, Adrienne knew it wasn't Colonel Mustard from the racket she heard as she passed the library into the living room, where Sloan, Bennett and Rawlings adults had gathered. They were helping themselves to shortbread Charlotte's father had managed to smuggle from Scotland. Or maybe it had been a colleague at the Edinburgh offices of marine archaeology where Charlotte worked. Or one of Greg's DSS friends. No, Adrienne thought, probably not one of them. The eccentric Bennetts and rough-and-tumble Rawlingses seemed very different on the surface, but together—they were having a great time, Adrienne saw. They were boisterous, fun and thrilled that Charlotte and Greg had found each other.

Adrienne changed in an upstairs guest room. Her dress was gorgeous but it did have a few more holes than she'd realized.

"No matter," her mother said, tears in her eyes for maybe the first time in her life. "You look beautiful, Adrienne. And happy. Very happy."

"I am happy, Mom. Sometimes I think I'm going to burst with happiness."

"Just be careful," her mother said, hugging her. "This dress might not hold together."

They laughed, and almost cried, but they managed to pull themselves together when Felicity rapped on the door and announced they were ready downstairs.

Two lovely, simultaneous weddings.

What could be more wonderful?

Charlotte wore a simple, traditional wedding dress. "I'm so glad we're sharing this day," she said. "Greg and I hoped we would the moment we saw you and Adam together."

The simple double wedding service in the rambling old New England inn, among family and friends, was everything Adrienne could ever have asked for, anything she could ever have dreamed of. Her focus, though, was on the man next to her. This, she thought, was love. And she could tell Greg and Charlotte felt the same about each other.

Felicity, of course, hadn't exaggerated. She had everything well in hand for the day. "I don't really do weddings, you know," she said afterward, grinning as she retrieved Adrienne's simple bouquet.

After the ceremony, Adam ditched his suit for jeans and a decent-looking shirt. Greg did the same. Not only did Adrienne and Charlotte not object, they'd obviously figured as much. Adam smiled at his reflection in the mirror of his room at Red Clover Inn, down the hall from where Adrienne had changed into her slightly moth-eaten and totally beautiful gown. But it was hearing the words *husband and wife* that had him choking up, and then smiling with pure joy.

Now and forever, he thought.

He headed downstairs to the living and adjoining dining room, set up for lunch and then dancing. It was warm enough people could spill out onto the porch and into the yard. Samantha and Justin had yet to take down the hammock. Ever the optimists.

"Adrienne's all right, Gran," Eric was saying when Adam joined the pair of them.

"I know. I had misgivings. I bit my tongue."

Eric snorted. "That was biting your tongue?"

"I wasn't rude to her, was I?"

"Transparent. There's a difference."

"What happened to that fiancée of yours?"

"You know she moved to Atlanta in July, Gran."

Her aged eyes narrowed. "That's a good place for her," she said finally.

Eric burst into laughter. Whatever hadn't worked with that relationship, he'd put it behind him. Adam was relieved. Their grandmother greeted Brody and Greg as the two DSS agents joined them with hors d'oeuvres. "You must have some exciting times with the FBI," she said.

"Assuming we can talk about it," Greg said, without correcting her.

"Since it's a wedding party, Gran," Eric said, "I'm not going to say a word."

"That's a first," she said.

Adam let his cop brother and DSS agent friends chat. He fetched his grandmother hors d'oeuvres from a tray and found her a spot to sit. He noticed a woman who seemed to be drinking too much, but Eric got to her first. "Drowning your sorrows?" he asked.

"No. Just getting pissed. I'm uncovering the mysteries of the Bennett brothers, Harry and Max, and their association with my grandfather. He was at Amherst College with Harry. I'm a— What am I? A historian, I suppose. Charlotte warned me there are mice here. Greg wouldn't warn me. He'd let me find out on my own. I've figured that out about him."

"There might be mice but at least there aren't any snakes."

"Well, then. Let's dance, shall we?"

Adam missed them exchanging names as he edged

toward the hall door, just in time to catch Adrienne walking down the stairs. She still had on her wedding dress, but she'd let down her hair and slipped into more comfortable shoes. He wasn't much of a dancer but he figured he could let that go for one day. As she came to him, he swept an arm around her and her moth-eaten dress and spun her onto the makeshift dance floor. Greg grabbed Charlotte, and the gathered friends and family laughed and applauded.

"Happy?" Adam asked his bride.

"Very happy."

Ten minutes later, Adam spotted Vic alone by the front door. "A car's picking me up in a little while," he said. "I'm off to Washington and then to Brussels."

Adam suspected Vic's new assignment involved other places besides Brussels. "Safe travels, Vic."

"Yeah. Thanks. I've got men and women like Brody and Greg breathing down my neck. It'll be fine." He glanced at his daughter, laughing with her mother. "Sophia's a force of nature, isn't she? Look, I want you and Adrienne to have the guesthouse. Tear it down, renovate—add a bunch of rock walls. Do your Sloan and innkeeper thing."

"Vic—"

"Don't say thanks. Just enjoy the place. Be there when I get back." Vic hesitated. "There's something else I need to tell you."

Now what?

"Mice and at least one red squirrel have taken up residence in the attic at the house. I think there might be a bat or two up there, too. I haven't dealt with them yet."

"Vic, I'm not worried about bats, mice and squirrels."

His new father-in-law grinned. "I should have known."

It was almost dusk and gray when Adrienne walked out to the old stone bridge on the stream on the other side of Echo Lake. Vic had left with a new entourage. Her dad had returned to his inn in Amherst. He'd been great through the wedding, at peace, she thought, with what they were to each other. He'd have lunch with her and Adam tomorrow before he went on his way. Her mother had left in time to catch her flight to Tuscany.

Adrienne wasn't surprised when Adam found her. "I'm a little overwhelmed, I think," she said as they sat on a boulder above the quiet lake. "I love this place, Adam. I love you. Vic could move and that wouldn't change. You could move and it wouldn't change. I'm home. I'm here. I'm not wandering anymore. With Vic taking this new position in Brussels…"

"Everyone around here loves you, Adrienne," Adam said. "Vic or no Vic. I love you."

She placed her hand on top of his. "I can see my future as never before, here in Knights Bridge with you." She nodded across the lake. "Look."

"I see him."

A bull moose stood in the marsh farther down the lake, his antlers casting a shadow on the still water.

Adam squeezed her hand. "Let's go home," he said softly.

That night, when he pulled the warm covers over

them, she slipped her arms around him. Her husband. The man she loved. "Heather and Brody have to go back to England early," she said.

"How early?"

"Tomorrow. Your grandmother doesn't want to change her flight."

He raised his head. "Gran can't fly to London alone."

"She insists she can."

"She can't," he said, adamant. "It's her first transatlantic flight. She's got a bad knee. She forgets things."

"Your brothers said much the same. She mentioned that you and I could fly to London with her and take a few days for a quick honeymoon."

Adam hooked an arm around her and lifted her onto him. "And you said?"

"I said it was an intriguing idea. She said she doesn't want to cramp our style. Eric was there. He said she would but we'd deal with it."

"One of those times I agree with my big brother."

"Then you're okay with this?"

"More than okay. I was thinking we'd honeymoon somewhere warm over the winter, maybe in the dead of January when Knights Bridge is quiet for both of us." He slid his hands over her hips. "But I like the idea of time with you now, too. Just the two of us."

"There are a lot of old stone walls and bridges to see in England."

"Then let's book our flights," he said, moving against her in such a way that talking became unnecessary, and then impossible.

* * *

Three days later, they were packed for London. Evelyn had packed before Thanksgiving. They'd drop her off with Heather and Brody, see where they lived and head out on their own. Adrienne had friends in the UK but she wouldn't see them this trip. "This is my honeymoon," she whispered to herself as she and Adam parked in front of Red Clover Inn to collect his plucky grandmother.

Evelyn was already on the front porch with her luggage. "I've been wanting to go to England since the end of World War II. I was a young girl, but I remember it."

"You took your time," Adam said.

"Yes, well, I did work, you know, and then along came six grandchildren. Then your grandfather died and I wasn't sure I wanted to go to England without him. I remember I wanted to see Winston Churchill and Big Ben."

"Churchill's dead, Gran," Eric said as he emerged from the house.

She sighed. "Yes, I know. I remember his funeral. It was before you were born. Heather said we can visit his war rooms. Aidan and Tyler were disappointed they didn't get to see royalty. Heather and I will have a cracking good time. That's a good English expression, isn't it?" She was too excited about her trip to wait for an answer. "You two don't need to fly back with me. I'll be just fine."

"We'll meet you at Heathrow in a week," Adam said.

Eric nodded. "We don't want you wandering around

Heathrow on your own. I don't need a call from Scotland Yard."

She rolled her eyes. "I promised my great-grandsons I'd bring them back something exciting. There are so many possibilities."

"Keep in mind you have to get through security," Adam said.

"You mean you all won't help me smuggle the Loch Ness monster onto the plane? It's in Scotland, anyway." She sighed. "Next trip."

Adrienne laughed. "You'll have a great time, Evelyn."

"I know I will. And you, too." She took Adam's hand. "Both of you."

Twenty-Two

London, England

Dear Vic,
I don't know how often you can get email. Evelyn tolerated the trip to London well. She's staying with Heather and Brody while Adam and I go exploring. Everyone says hi. Adam and I are on our way to visit Lincoln Cathedral to look at rocks. Turns out he's wanted to see it. Life is good.
Love,
Adrienne

Dear Adrienne,
We wandering Scarlattis have found a home in Knights Bridge. Life is good, indeed. I've amended our Knights Bridge cheat sheet:

Adam Sloan, married to Adrienne Portale, innkeeper
I added Olivia and Dylan's baby, and I changed Greg and Charlotte to married. I'm guessing you'll have to amend it again soon, though. I have good vibes about

the two unattached Sloan brothers. Elly tells me Eric is seeing the woman he met at the wedding, and Christopher is seeing the owner of the cleaning service. She's a dynamo, just what he needs.

And have you heard? Samantha and Justin are expecting. Aidan and Tyler are already thinking about what dinosaurs to give them.

Always something going on in Knights Bridge!
Love,
Vic

Dear Vic,
That's all wonderful news! I'll see you again soon on the shores of Echo Lake.
Love,
Adrienne

Dear Adrienne,
I'll be home for Christmas. I think.
Now...shut off your phone. You're on your honeymoon!
Love to you, and to Adam,
Vic

Dear Vic,
No wonder we get along. I'm on Adrienne's phone. She's shutting it off now.
Later,
Adam

When Adam handed her phone back to her, Adrienne switched it off. They climbed into their small rental car. "All set for today's adventures?" he asked her.

She smiled. "All set. I've been reading up on the Lincoln Cathedral. It sounds fantastic. See? You did have a someday/maybe list."

"I read about it on the plane."

They both laughed as he started the car. Four more days of touring England together, and then home to Knights Bridge, their small New England town filled with adventures, secrets, surprises, family and friends.

Adrienne snapped on her seat belt and touched her wedding ring.

Life was good, indeed.

* * * * *

Author Note

Every time I return to little Knights Bridge, I can't wait to see what this small town has in store. It's a creation of my imagination, but I grew up in a similar town on the western edge of the Quabbin reservoir. My mother and oldest brother still live on our family homestead with its fields, woods, streams and old stone walls. And, now, moose! My brother runs into one from time to time, but they don't bother each other. My six siblings and I love to take long walks in the woods on our family get-togethers. My daughter and two of my nephews got lost when they were kids, but they turned up safe and sound before we had to call a search party. Now my young grandchildren join us on walks in "the forest."

As a kid, I'd climb a tree with paper and pen and spin stories on my favorite branch. I don't climb trees anymore (despite temptation!), but I still love to spin stories as much as ever. A huge "thank you" to everyone at Harlequin for their support, insights, boundless creativity and tireless dedication to authors and readers.

As both an author and a reader, I'm forever grateful. Special thanks to Nicole Brebner, my amazing and brilliant editor for five years. I'm a very fortunate writer.

Thanks for your time, and I hope you enjoyed *Stone Bridges*! To stay up to date with my goings-on, please visit my website at CarlaNeggers.com and sign up for my newsletter. I look forward to being in touch.

Turn the page for six brand-new Knights Bridge recipes. You can find printable versions on my website. You'll also find recipes inspired by my Sharpe and Donovan series (scones, anyone?). Watch for *Rival's Break*, FBI agents Emma Sharpe and Colin Donovan's next high-stakes adventure. Enjoy, and happy reading!

Until next time,
Carla
CarlaNeggers.com

APPLE CRISP

4 cups sliced, pared apples
¼ cup orange juice or lemon juice
½ cup butter, preferably unsalted
¾ cup all-purpose flour or mixture of regular oats
and flour
½ teaspoon ground cinnamon
¼ teaspoon ground nutmeg
½ to 1 cup sugar, to taste

Preheat oven to 375° F. Butter a 9-inch pie plate. Place sliced apples in the pie plate and drizzle with orange or lemon juice. In a separate bowl, combine sugar, flour and spices. Cut in butter until mixture is crumbly and sprinkle on top of the apples.

Bake in preheated 375-degree oven for 45 minutes, or until apples are fork-soft and topping is browned. Serve warm or cold with whipped cream or vanilla ice cream.

PESTO

1½ cups fresh basil leaves
2 cloves garlic, split
¼ cup pine nuts
¾ cup finely grated Parmesan cheese
¾ cup extra-virgin olive oil

Using a mortar and pestle, pound the basil leaves. Pound the garlic and pine nuts together with the basil. Add the Parmesan and blend to create a thick mixture. Slowly add the olive oil and, using a spoon, mix together. May substitute a food processor for the mortar and pestle; just don't overbeat.

Drizzle olive oil over the top of the pesto, cover and refrigerate. May also freeze. Use in a variety of ways, e.g., with soup, baked potatoes, pasta and chicken.

HOT MULLED APPLE CIDER

2 quarts fresh apple cider
2–3 cinnamon sticks
1 teaspoon whole cloves
½ teaspoon whole allspice
¼ small orange
Dash nutmeg (optional)
Optional: ¼ cup brown sugar

Combine all ingredients in a saucepan and bring to a boil. Simmer for 20–30 minutes. Strain spices and serve. May combine spices into a cheesecloth to create a bag and simmer with the cider. May also heat the mulled cider in a slow cooker.

SWEET POTATOES WITH PECAN TOPPING

3 cups sweet potatoes, cooked and mashed
½ cup whole milk
¾ cup sugar
1 teaspoon vanilla
4 oz. butter, melted
¼ teaspoon salt
2 eggs, beaten

Butter a 9" x 9" baking dish. (May also use a 7" x 11" dish.)

Using an electric mixer, beat the ingredients in a large bowl just until combined. Pour into the prepared baking dish.

Topping:

3 tablespoons butter
½ cup chopped pecans
½ cup brown sugar (light)
⅓ cup all-purpose flour

In a small bowl mix the butter, brown sugar and flour with a pastry cutter or fork until it is crumbly (the size of small peas). Stir in pecans and sprinkle on top of the sweet potato mixture.

Bake casserole at 325° F for 30 minutes, or until the filling is hot and the topping is browned but not burnt.

CORNMEAL PANCAKES

1 cup cornmeal, preferably stone-ground
¼ teaspoon salt
1 tablespoon honey
1 large egg
½ cup whole milk
2 tablespoons butter, melted
1 cup boiling water
½ cup all-purpose flour
2 teaspoons baking powder

Stir boiling water slowly into the cornmeal. Beat together honey, egg, milk and melted butter; combine with cornmeal and water. Cover and let stand for 10 minutes. Sift together flour or use a fork to combine flour and baking powder; stir quickly into the batter. Don't overbeat. Cook on a hot buttered griddle and serve with honey or pure maple syrup.

EASY PUMPKIN ROLL

Cake:

3 large eggs
1 cup sugar
⅔ cup canned pumpkin
1 teaspoon lemon juice
1 teaspoon baking powder
¾ cup all-purpose flour
2 teaspoons cinnamon
½ teaspoon ground ginger
½ teaspoon nutmeg
¾ cup chopped walnuts (optional)

Preheat oven to 375° F.

Using an electric mixer, beat eggs on high speed for about five minutes. Add the sugar to the eggs slowly, by hand or on a lower setting. Using a wooden spoon or spatula, stir in the pumpkin and lemon juice. In a separate bowl, combine the dry ingredients; stir into the pumpkin mixture just until combined, without over-beating.

Spread the mixture on a jelly-roll pan lined with waxed paper or parchment. Top with walnuts, if desired. Bake for 15 minutes. Remove from oven and turn the cake onto a linen towel lightly dusted with confectioner's sugar. Roll towel and cake together and let cool. Un-

roll and remove towel. Spread the cake with the filling
(below), roll up and chill.

Filling:

> 1 cup confectioner's sugar
> 8 oz. whole-milk cream cheese, softened
> 4 tablespoons butter
> ½ teaspoon vanilla
> 1 cup heavy cream or Cool Whip
> 1 to 2 tablespoons sugar if using cream (optional)

Using an electric mixer, blend all the filling ingredients
in a medium bowl until smooth and a spreadable con-
sistency (add more or less cream as needed).